# Order of the Undying

*SPARX Incarnation Trilogy*

*Book I: Mark of the Green Dragon*
*Book II: Order of the Undying*
*Book III: Dark Waters*

*A roll of the dice…*

*To life's gambles*

# Order of the Undying

SPARX INCARNATION BOOK 2

2ND Edition

## K.B. SPRAGUE

GaleWind BOOKS    AN IMPRINT OF WHISPERWOOD PUBLISHING | CANADA

SECOND EDITION, 2020

ORDER OF THE UNDYING, SPARX Incarnation Book II by
K.B. Sprague

© 2016 by Kevin Sprague. All rights reserved

ISBN: 978-1-988363-20-2 (paperback)
ISBN: 978-1-988363-21-9 (epub)
ISBN: 978-1-988363-22-6 (mobi)

Cover designed by Damonza

Published in Canada by GaleWind Books,
an imprint of Whisperwood Publishing, Ottawa.



www.galewindbooks.com

PRAISE FOR WILLA DREW

Willa Drew's writing style blew me away.

Highly recommend this author and book without a doubt!

My first book by Willa and it won't be my last!

I look forward to reading other books by this author in the future. Because I went into this one with hope and promise, and it absolutely delivered! Now it's your turn!

This is a great story written by two clearly talented authors. The characters have been put front and centre of this book, with their story and development being what it is all about.

This is the first time I have a read a book by these authors and I enjoyed the collaboration. The book flowed well, seamlessly moving through the story.

I am glad I stumbled on this book and these authors, and I will definitely be adding them to my list of authors to keep my eye out for.

The authors did a wonderful job of writing the characters in a way that I felt connected to them right away.

## THE AND US SERIES

What starts out as a lie, turns into a passionate and heartfelt
romance story about finding oneself and love.
Told in dual POV, this series spans a year of their lives told with
the backdrop of major holidays across five parts and ends with
a guaranteed HEA.

Kisses, Lies, & Us
Passions, Hopes, & Us
Distance, Love, & Us
If you like secret identity, movies, soulmates, friends-to-lovers,
and a right person wrong time new adult romance, the And Us
Series is for you.

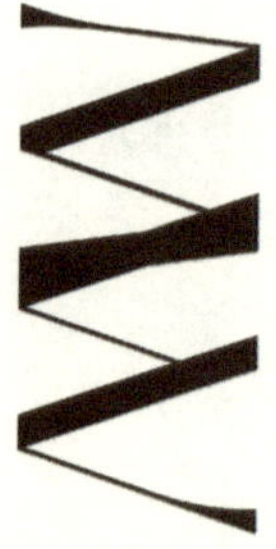

Published by: Moving Words Publishing

www.movingwordspublishing.com

Copyright © 2024 by Willa Drew

Cover: A Fabulous Production

(@afabulousproduction on Instagram)

Artwork: María Peña

(@me.me.pe on Instagram)



ISBN: 978-1-957897-11-0

Second Edition: July 2024

**The story so far...**

In Part One **Kisses, Lies, & Us**, a film student, Nick Stavros, finds himself at a swanky bar in LA on Christmas Eve. While his father is in a meeting, Nick orders an old fashioned cocktail using his fake ID with the name Shawn Rosstav. The bartender and aspiring screen writer, Sarah Connor, who serves him inspires Nick to drop his hockey-jock persona and be his true self. Aside from the fake name. Sarah and Nick spend Christmas Eve together eating tacos, talking movies, and sharing a romantic kiss, but are torn apart before exchanging contact information.

In Part Two of **Kisses, Lies, & Us**, on the way back from Toronto, where Sarah attended her grandmother's funeral, Sarah's plane makes an emergency landing. Sarah not only finds herself in Chicago on Valentine's Day, but she discovers Shawn Rosstav's ID in the leather jacket he placed on her shoulders on Christmas Eve. With his address and time before her flight back, she decides to take a chance on love and surprise him. Unfortunately, the address on the ID belongs to Nick's ex-girlfriend who greets Sarah at the door. No matter how quickly Nick realizes what happened, he doesn't catch Sarah as she runs away, but he catches her Toronto Maple Leafs hat she leaves behind. Certain that the guy she kissed on Christmas Eve hid having a girlfriend, an upset Sarah flies to LA alone. Both Sarah and Nick are notified they have been accepted into the Starlight Foundation's Film competition that begins in the summer in LA.

In Part 3 of **Kisses, Lies, & Us**, Nick's lie is exposed on the first day of the Starlight Competition. In front of Sarah, who's a screenwriter on the project, Nick, the director and leader of the Blue Team, is introduced under his real name. Sarah and Nick are forced to work together as they write, direct, and film a short movie. Between work at the coffee shop and the competition, Nick doesn't have enough money to live by himself, so he stays with his father. Their relationship grows colder as summer progresses. Sarah calls a temporary truce and asks Nick to be friends. In hopes of getting Sarah back, Nick agrees. Just as Sarah is giving in to her attraction to Nick, her friend outs more skeletons in Nick's closet. In a heartwarming grand gesture, Nick films himself telling all the lies he said over his lifetime, to prove to Sarah he doesn't want to hide anything. Sarah's kiss breaks the friend zone. When Sarah's roommate leaves and Sarah offers Nick to move into her apartment, Nick is certain that next to his girlfriend, his life is going to be perfect.

# CONTENTS

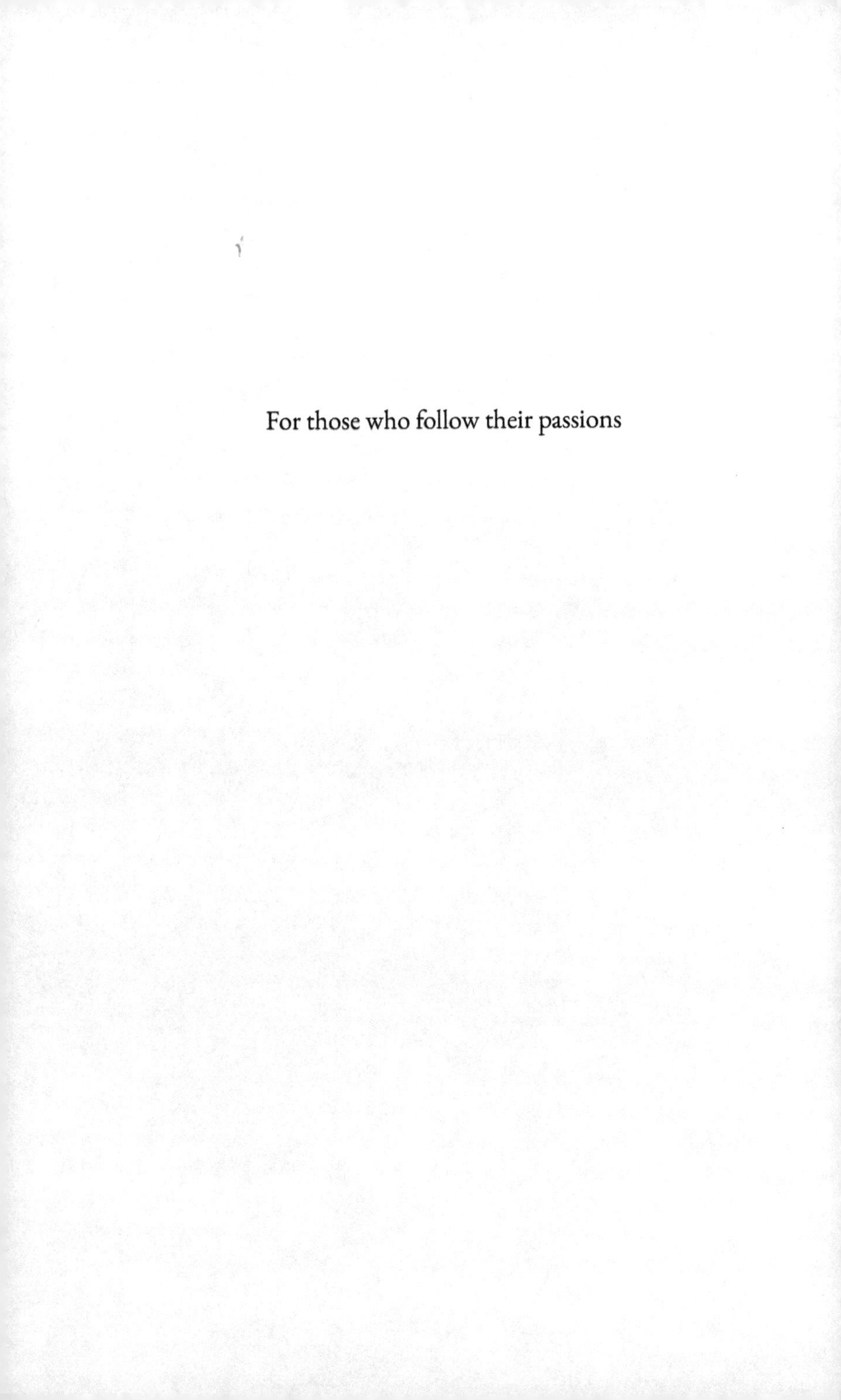

For those who follow their passions

# ONE

## *Sarah*

I CLING TO THE last shreds of my willpower and run my hand over the steamy mirror in the bathroom. The glass fogs. Again. Everything is out of my control. Again.

What will tonight hold?

When the nominees were announced weeks ago, I was thrilled Nick made the list for potential Best Director. *Indigo* as Best Picture and *Our Lines* as Best Song also made sense. My nomination came as a surprise, and while I've been trying to play it cool around everyone, this win would mean a lot.

The Starlight Foundation's awards gala has the potential to change everything, be the validation I need. If our movie wins, or if I win for best screenplay, job offers are almost a guarantee. If that doesn't happen . . . what will I do next? How long do I cling to my hopes before I accept I'm not made for Hollywood?

A win would prove to Mom I'm making the right choice staying here.

My towel slides off my head and releases the damp wave of my blond tresses. The sweet aroma of strawberry conditioner emanating from them reminds me of home and dulls the shards of anticipation coursing through my body. Mom's care packages always contain things I miss from Toronto, but the fruity conditioner Mémère and I found while roaming around Kensington Market is a must. I need to remind Mom to send me another bottle. I run the towel over my hair then wrap it around my body.

I open the bathroom door and slam into a broad chest.

"Thought you'd never get out of there." Nick's hands find my waist, and his mouth finds my lips.

I sink into the kiss. More calm. More comfort. More of the support I crave tonight. His body and mine press together, and I dig my fingers into the silky brown waves I love. Since his mother cut his hair last week, it's far too short for my liking, but the style accentuates his cheekbones and gives him a polished, professional look. Adding a tuxedo will be a dangerous combination. A different kind of anticipation washes over me. I can't wait to see him all dressed up.

Nick's hand heads south. He creates the perfect angle, and the kiss is no longer flirty: it's ambitious and beckons me to step over the line we've agreed not to cross. Not until tonight. Not until he's no longer the leader of Team Blue. With the Starlight Foundation competition complete, Nick will stop being the boss I have to work with. He'll be the man I want to be with. My boyfriend in every sense of the word. At last.

As much as I don't want to, I have to cool this down.

"Just a few more hours"—I twist away from his mouth—"and our pact is over."

Heat flares on my collarbone. I'm not sure I can hold out much longer. The way Nick presses his forehead against mine, I can tell it's getting near impossible for him as well. "Whose stupid idea was this pact, anyhow?" Nick's voice rasps against my ear.

"I believe it was you?"

He might not have been serious when he teased that I shouldn't sleep with my boss. But I didn't want to be known as someone who sleeps her way up the ladder. Not doing what I always do—jump into bed with the guy I like—seemed like a good idea at the time.

The front door slams, and Nick and I spring apart. I grab my towel before it reveals more than would be visible in a bathing suit.

"Oy, I'm home," Siobhan announces. She's so loud our neighbors above and below probably hear her. "Hands off each other."

Nick drops his hands but leans in and hovers his lips over mine. "Does she have a sixth sense for when I kiss you?"

He takes a step back, rakes my naked shoulders with his stare, and walks around me into the bathroom.

Heat floods below my navel. I should be grateful to Sio for halting Nick and me when she did. The only reason we haven't broken our self-imposed pact is that between Nick's new responsibilities as morning shift manager at Blend, my late hours at The Diamond Club, and our ever-present roommate, Nick and I have barely had a moment alone together in the apartment. I wanted to rent a hotel room for tonight but neither of us can afford one. Hopefully I'll have a screenwriting job by his birthday. Extra money for a night alone would be heaven.

"You're never going to believe this." Sio strolls in holding an extra-long garment bag.

"What's that?"

"Mrs. Marino lent me a dress for tonight. Look at this stunner." Siobhan runs the zipper down the black cover to reveal a swath of gold beaded material. The owner of The Diamond Club and Siobhan are the same height. Tall. Well, everyone is tall to me, but either of them could've been a model. "It has a thigh-high slit. Move over, Angelina Jolie. This is my opportunity to show some calf candy."

"The dress is beautiful. Can't wait to see you in it."

"Let me wash off the grime of old men drinking scotch first—"

"Totally." I wince. "But Nick's in the bathroom."

"You have to tell him to stop steaming it up. It's like I'm back in Ireland sharing with my brothers. Do I have to remind the Prom King about the five-minutes-per-shower rule?"

I nudge her shoulder. "Be nice."

Chimes bounce off the walls of the open-concept living room and kitchen.

"You gonna answer that?" Siobhan knows my mom's ringtone.

"I better." Mom won't stop until I answer so I hit the green button.

"Which dress did you decide on?" Mom's voice erupts through the phone speaker. No hello. That's my no-nonsense mother.

Right. I was supposed to send her a photo. This is not an emergency, but now that she's on the phone I can't not reply. "Hang on. I'm about to put it on." In my room, I switch the phone's camera off and change.

My dress is sparkling, short, and tight. The miniskirt makes the most of my legs, especially paired with the one pair of high heels I own. I spent a whole night's tips on the stilettos, but they give the illusion that I'm average height. Nick won't have to practically bend over to kiss me tonight. I turn the phone's camera back on and move it up and down. "What d'you think?"

Mom insisted this was the best of all the options I tried on at the second-hand store. It's both retro and back in style, and friendly to my budget.

"A vision in silver." Her smile is wide and genuine. "You'll need to put your hair up for it though."

"That's the plan." I set the phone in the holder on my dresser and brush my smooth locks.

Mom's face sours. "I'm sorry the family can't be with you tonight. Even though we're not there, remember, you always have us. A home, a job, and people who love you here. Win or lose." Tears are visible in her eyes.

Emotion from my mom is all or nothing. Today it's all, and the force of her words tugs on the longing to come home that always lingers in the background. It would be so easy to stop struggling in LA and go back to Toronto. "Mom, don't cry. I know you guys love me. I appreciate it. I really do. But this has been my dream for so long."

"I know." Mom wipes at her cheek. "We support you. Mémère would've been so proud of you for getting where you are." Her smile returns. It's a different kind, but better than watching her cry and not being able to hug her.

"I've been thinking about her all day." Mémère is never far from my heart. It's been less than nine months since her death, and I see reminders of her everywhere. When I pour a glass of sherry at work, when I shift Betty into fifth on the highway, when Nick laughs at my corny jokes.

"Wherever she is, she's thinking about you too." Mom's voice is wobbly.

"We're rooting for you." Dad appears behind Mom's back and kisses her on the temple. "Text us as soon as you know."

"Love you, honey," Mom and Dad shout in unison.

"Love you too." Their faces disappear from the screen, and I hunt for the clip I want to use to hold my hair up.

"Are you almost . . ." Nick's head pops into my room, his damp hair a contrast to the tux. With the silver tie loose around his neck he could be on the cover of GQ. Heat blooms in my stomach and obscures whatever thoughts I had. Nick's eyes drink me in from my head to my toes and back again. We might be on the same page because I read his desire to remove the dress I just put on. The fire spreads from my core and rushes over my skin. I need Mom to call me again or I'm going to make us late by peeling the suit off him.

I know I'm playing with fire, but I put my hand on my hip. "See something you like?"

Nick's pupils dilate and cover the brown of his eyes with the inky glimmer of desire. "Do I ever."

A silent conversation courses between us. This happens a lot these days. Like I can read his mind, and he can read mine. Both of us agreeing we want to act, close my bedroom door, and devour each other, but also agreeing we can't.

Nick lowers his eyes to the floor first and breaks the trance. "Who were you talking to?"

"Mom and Dad apologizing for not being able to make it today."

"Your parents are sweet." He leans against the door, not daring to cross the threshold. "Don't think I've ever heard my dad say I love you to me or anyone."

"He'll get there. You still have a lot to learn about each other. At least he's coming to the Gala. Is he riding in the limo with us?"

Wil opposed the limo idea, grumbling about the expense, but Nick never went to prom and never got the experience. I want him to have everything, so I arranged it with the company that provides car service at The Diamond Club. With everyone on the team chipping in, it wasn't too unreasonable.

He continues to scrutinize the faded herringbone design of the parquet. "You know Dad. He's not going to hang with a bunch of young people. He'll meet us there. We'll have plenty of time together at the Gala."

"Maybe this'll help you and him to get closer."

"You'd think spending two months on his couch would be enough." He pushes off the doorframe. "But I'm not going to complain. He's in my life. And that's more than he's done for ten years." I have trouble grasping what it's like to not have a father around. His older brother Mike played the role and from what I gather, he was good at it. "I've always wanted a dad. A dad who wants me. Who's proud of what I'm doing with my life."

"Nick." I wait until his gaze finds mine. "I think Theo is. He's just not great at showing it."

"Your parents are the best. Can't wait to meet the legends who inspired our movie."

"A few more weeks." I was nervous asking Nick to come home for Thanksgiving in October. Flights to Canada from LA are expensive, but the way his eyes lit up and the instant yes erased all doubt. "Now shoo." I wave my hairbrush at him. "Let me do my hair or we'll be late."

# Two

# Sarah

Nick is holding my hand under the table. My shoulders relax, and I'm grateful for his strength. I need a little too much of it tonight in this ballroom abuzz with Starlight Foundation winners and hopefuls. I'm in the hopeful category.

"You've got this," Nick whispers in my ear as the crowd's attention moves to the stage where a buff guy in a classic black tuxedo is reading the list of my fellow nominees. Adrenaline spikes, and my tapping on the chair leg resembles Mémère's whisk hitting the bowl of cream she preferred to whip by hand. Nick pushes with our joined palms on my knee, and the weight holds me in in place, fusing us together.

"And the Star goes to . . ." Butterflies the size of elephants swirl in my stomach. As if looking at the presenter might jinx me, I close my eyes and hold my breath. Please, let it be me. Nick crushes my hand in a silent 'you got this,' and I squeeze back, a silent 'I got this.'

"Karina Appleton."

What? Applause erupts, and I unwind my fingers from Nick's. Following the expected routine, I clap for the winner and take a sip of champagne, but the taste of disappointment overrides the fizz and sinks into my stomach like an oversized ice cube. I didn't win. No marker to validate I'm worthy. I can practically sense the job offers drying up.

I track Karina, who looks dazzling in her blush-pink off-the-shoulder gown that complements her light-brown skin. Her teammates shout their congratulations as she makes her way onto the stage. I try another mouthful of the bubbly alcohol, but it only irritates. The applause, the lights, everything is irritating. I should be happier for Karina. For my friend. Because she is my friend. Alongside Sio, Ryan, and Nick, Karina made her way into my very selective friends category.

These last few months of laboring together over our scripts during the competition, I found first the critique partner I enjoyed working with, and then a friend whose company I loved. But Karina already has a position as junior writer with a small studio. I have nothing connecting me to the career I want. No fallback plan. I needed this. Nausea hits me. Partly because I struggle to imagine what's next for me. Partly because I hate to be a person who's jealous of a friend's success.

From the stage Karina thanks her parents, teachers, and friends, and her smile is infectious. It melts the ice of my disappointment. I swallow my defeat and rise to join in the applause.

Nick follows suit. He towers over me, standing close behind. The heat from his body seeps through. I lean my back against him.

"It should've been you," he says.

I shush him as I nudge his shoulder. I want to kiss him, take solace in the lips that always make me feel better, but we have a strict no PDA rule. For now. We take our seats. I interlace my fingers and tuck them under my chin, resisting taking Nick's hand again. I don't want to be too needy. He slings his arm over the back of my chair, and I take in a lungful of his aftershave. Nick's scent, touch, and presence calm me. And I borrow from him the strength I lack. My pulse is pounding in my ears, and I'm willing it to slow down. I can figure something out. Our movie can still win. There still might be job offers. It's not over.

Karina's back at her seat. She's breathtakingly happy. The only thing I can do is step over my jealously and guilt and go talk to her. "I'll be right back."

I tug at the short hem of my dress as I wind my way through the tables. Karina's face is glowing when I reach her. She catches sight of me, and her grin widens. "Can you believe this?" She holds up the trophy.

"I can." I wrap my arms around her and squeeze. Her joy swirls around us, and I smile into her shoulder, for the first time truly happy for my friend. "Congratulations."

"I couldn't have done it without you."

"Me? I doubt that." I keep my hands on her and fight the tears that threaten to ruin my makeup. I'm not crying for myself. These are for Karina, her success, and her talent.

"No, I'm serious." Her deep brown eyes implore me to believe her. "You're the perfect sounding board. You pushed me to cut out all that dialogue in the spacewalk scene and let the camera do the talking."

Karina and I do work well together, and I don't want this to be the end. "Well, there's more where that came from. I'm always here to lend my judgy eye." I wink at her. "But today is not about working. It's a celebration."

"I'll drink to that," an unfamiliar man's voice says behind my back.

I spin to find a man in his early thirties, jet-black hair tousled a little too professionally, one curl begging to be tucked back into place. "Sarah, this is my boss Rod Varma. Rod—Sarah Connor. She was also nominated tonight."

Rod extends his hand. "Karina mentioned you were the one to beat."

His hand is clammy, but his grip is firm.

"Apparently not." I shrug.

He chuckles at my joke, releases my hand, and offers Karina a quick hug.

"But if it had to be one of us who won, I'm glad it was her," I say.

Rod smirks at Karina. "Don't let this win go to your head. We still need you in the writers' room bright and early tomorrow."

"I'll make it a triple espresso then." Karina pretends to write a note on her palm.

Rod tilts his head to address me. "This one cracks me up. I need it after today's session." He regards Karina. "The execs want a big action-packed scene for episode eight, and every idea was complete and utter shit." He glances at the ceiling. "What I wouldn't give for an original idea."

"They say there are no original ideas." The words fly out of my mouth. "Only different twists."

"True." Karina backs me up. "Aren't there like only seven storylines and three motivations: love, hate, and money?"

"Someone's done her research." Rod crosses his arms. "Listen to a lot of podcasts on writing, do you?"

"Sarah's big on research. You should see the detail she went into for her movie. It took place in the '90s, and she figured out what kind of security system a car of that time would have." Karina wraps her hand around my waist and pushes me a little bit forward, as if she wants Rod to pay attention to me.

"Not that hard. I've always been into cars." I offer him the everything-is-great smile I've perfected in my years of bartending. Rod's gaze is intense, and my cheeks flush, like I'm being inspected. A new flock of giant butterflies is wreaking havoc in my stomach. I scramble for something to break the tension. The stupidest joke my dad told me last week springs to mind. "What type of car does a dog hate?"

His eyebrows rise, and I'm sure he thinks I'm an idiot. "I don't know. What type of car does a dog hate?"

"A Cor-Vet." I mentally add the cymbals crash. There's a moment of silence. What is wrong with me? This guy must think I'm drunk or something.

"Cute." His lip curls to the side. "Corny but cute."

"Sorry, I have a million car jokes." Now my cheeks must surely be blazing. "It's a competition between my dad and me to one up each other."

"Well, should I ever need a bad dad joke, I'll know where to look." He nods at Karina. "Glad we have another award-winning screenwriter on our roster, but I need to get back to my table. This event is about schmoozing just as much as about the winners."

I give Karina another hug. "I better get back too, before Nick sends out a search party." Though I might not have won the trophy I came here for, I'm taking home the grand prize. A wave of longing crashes from my heart to my belly as I make my way back to Nick. I'm not going to be Team Blue for much longer, but after tonight I'll be Team Nick for a long time.

# THREE

# NICK

Laughter and chatter swims around our silent table. First Wil moved to Mateo's group after El didn't show up to accept the award for their song *Our Lines*. Then Siobhan ditched us to talk to the Foundation's guest of honor, Asher Menken. Dad and I ran out of small talk, and Sarah has been holding us together all evening. Now Sarah's gone to congratulate Karina. Which leaves Dad and me sitting a foot from each other. Alone. The worst combination.

Dad hasn't said anything in five minutes. I've emptied and refilled my water glass twice. If Mom suggested I give my plus-one ticket to him because she thought it would get us closer, she was wrong. My hope was Mom could extend her stay and come. Having her here for two weeks was amazing, surreal, and a piece of home I didn't want to admit I was missing. But she had to fly to Chicago. Sarah asked Siobhan, and Wil naturally invited

El. I called Dad to placate Mom but expected he wouldn't be interested. Yet here he is.

"Theo Parker?" An older woman with a short bob leans over the back of the chair next to Dad. "Is that you?" Dad stands and embraces her.

"Colleen, I didn't know you were going to be here."

Her gaze trails over his trendy black suit, cufflinks, the classic haircut Mom gave him that highlights his graying temples. Dad is the picture of ease and wealth. Looking at him you'd think he's a successful titan of industry. "Nice to see you in a suit. Must've been at least ten years since we've attended something like this."

She's about Mom's age but nowhere near as beautiful. Dad's meaty palm lands on my shoulder. "You remember my son, Nick? Nick, this is Ms. Hansley."

"Nick Stavros." I stand and shake the woman's hand.

"Stavros not Parker?"

"Mom changed our last names to her maiden name after the divorce and . . ."

"Yes." She puts her hand over her heart. "That must've been a dark time for your family. The media didn't make it any better." She leans closer and whispers, "Not sure if I'm allowed to say it, but I voted for the *Schools in Chicago* short you submitted. By far the most unexpected and well-done documentary I've seen in a while." She puts both hands on my forearms and scans me, as if she's seeing me for the first time. "Little Nicky." I wince at the name. "Last time I saw you, you were this high." She holds her hand at waist level. "All grown up now."

"He's my youngest. Mike, my oldest, is a successful engineer in Chicago," Dad says it as if he had something to do with Mike's life, as if we are his pride and joy. Not a tone I'm used to hearing from him. "Ms. Hansley and I worked on the TV show *Bridges of Our Town*."

She puts a hand on Dad's arm. "Ah, those were the days. We were not much older than Nicky here. Wearing our under-eye bags as badges of honor after sleepless nights to find the perfect cliff-hanger for each episode. We thought the world was our oyster."

Dad's lips tighten. His oyster turned into five years in prison for fraud and tax evasion along with an eviction from our mansion in the hills. Dad dragged out in handcuffs. Mom crying. Mike punching. And now he's in his fifties, living in a shitty one-bedroom. Good times indeed.

The lady ignores Dad's change of mood and addresses me. "Call me Colleen. I'm mentoring with the Starlight Foundation these days. Sharing my decades of screenwriting knowledge with the new generation." She tilts her head. "Are you working with your dad?"

My neck tenses. I open my mouth to speak, but Dad beats me to it. "No, better. He's at UCLA studying film." If I didn't know any different, I'd believe he's impressed with me, maybe even proud. But this is Dad. This display is part of the show, the farce for the sake of others, not a reflection of his feelings about me. "He's nominated tonight for Best Director and Best Picture for *Indigo*."

"Dad, she knows this. She's on the committee."

Ms. Hansley gives a series of nods as if she, too, is impressed. "So hard to reconcile the excellent work you're doing at such a young age and the little kid I remember you as. Your movie has all the winning ingredients."

I straighten my shoulders and don't let my smile betray the havoc her words wreak on me. The higher their expectations, the farther I fall. I was a hundred percent certain Sarah would win. Of all the awards I expected us to win tonight, I was positive she would walk away with one. If she didn't win, what chance do I have? "It's not just my film. Our team was amazing. I think you had Sarah Connor in your sessions. She's our screenwriter."

"She's one to watch. Her and Karina"—Ms. Hansley gestures to the stage that still has Karina's name displayed on the screen—"were by far the two best writers this year. I read both their scripts, but as their mentor, I wasn't allowed to be one of the judges." The corners of her mouth fall as she frowns. "Too bad Sarah didn't win. They had to choose one. I'm sure it was a tough decision. But Sarah will go far. I have no doubt."

"Her script was beautiful. Nick and her work well together." Dad's words surprise me.

Ms. Hansley gestures behind her. "I still need to run to the ladies' before the break is over, but I'll be rooting for you to win, Nick." She smiles at Dad. "We'll talk soon, Theo."

"Yes, yes. Let's get in touch."

Dad takes his seat, picks up his glass of wine, and drains it. I search for Sarah and see her heading back to our table. She gives me a quick peck on the cheek and sits down. A thrill courses through me at the contact. Tiny tingles sprout on my cheek and expand into a field of desire. We've kissed hundreds of times in the weeks since I moved in, but her lips touching my skin is still a treat. She sends my heart drumming, sets my chest on fire, and makes my fingers crave to never separate from her. Will I ever become indifferent to her touch? I hope not.

Sarah bounces in her seat beside me as they read out the names of the nominees for Best Director. I hope Sarah won't be too disappointed in me when I lose. The pounding in my ears almost drowns out the presenter's voice as my name is listed last.

"Nick Stavros for *Indigo*." Why did they say my name twice? Confused, I turn to Sarah for guidance.

She has her hands over her mouth, her eyes wide as saucers. "You won," she screams.

What? I won?

A hand lands on my shoulder, and Dad beams at me. "That's my boy."

This can't be happening. Sarah stands and tugs on my arm. I join her, and she pushes me toward the stage. I stumble a few paces, then come back to her. I bracket her radiant face in my hands and break our no-kissing-in-public rule. She melts into me, not shying away from my kiss, boosting it, infusing me with confidence and pride. Her fingers dig into my arms, and this moment is another one going on the highlight reel. Too soon she pushes against my chest, breaking the kiss. "Go get your award."

Somehow, I end up onstage. A statue with my name on it in my hand. I press my fingers over the little engraved plate. Best Director. Best Director. I won Best Director.

I take a deep breath and lower my head toward the microphone. "I accept this award on behalf of the amazing team that made *Indigo* come to life." I take the microphone out of the stand and straighten to my full height, lifting the star above my head. "In our movie, you've already heard the now award-winning El sing the song she and Wil wrote, and you've seen how our set designer, Riyaz, transformed LA into Toronto, Canada. An ironic reversal I understand." A few chuckles answer me.

"Our costume designer, Bri, who scoured second-hand stores to find the perfect nineties retro looks. The world they created is what set the stage for our success. However, for me as a director this whole journey started with one person. Without her, I wouldn't be standing here today. She challenged me. Dared me to dream . . . and she is a dream come true. Sarah, this is for us. And it's only the beginning."

I peer in the general direction where Sarah is, but the lights are too bright. I do hear her distinct holler. My chest expands, and I'm not sure my heart can get any fuller. Polite applause greets the end of my speech and I shuffle off the stage, heading straight for her. She meets me partway, embracing me like it's the most natural thing to do. "You're my dream come true too."

There's a rush of congratulations: from my dad, from my fellow directors. Palms are pressed and words are spoken. But it's all a blur. The golden trophy statue in my hand is not that heavy but the meaning behind it is—I have a promise. There is a future for me in Hollywood, or New York, or Toronto, or wherever I end up living with Sarah. This is proof I'm good enough. As a director at least.

The stream of handshakes stops, and I fall into my chair, still in a daze. Riyaz and Bri stagger back to the table with Wil in tow and deposit him into his seat. Best Picture is next, and Team Blue is ready to accept the award. I find Sarah's hand under the table, and we resume our silent support by not letting go of each other. *Indigo* has Best Song and Best Director under its belt.

Best Picture would make a hat-trick and the entire team's dreams come true. We listen to the announcer, eyes trained on the stage. He rips the envelope open, and my heart sinks. *Indigo* is not the movie that starts playing on the screen behind him. Ice forms in my veins. The elation of winning earlier is drowned in my shortcomings. I've failed Sarah. She's not going home with a trophy. I don't understand. How could I win for Best Director and the movie I directed not win? What did I do wrong?

My chest aches as I watch my disappointment reflected back at me in my teammates' faces. We lost.

Dad slaps me on the back. "Ah, you win some, you lose some."

That's my dad. Full of compassion. "Thanks, Dad."

I'm afraid to look at Sarah. Will she regret being on my team? This probably explains why she didn't win. She pulls on my hand, and I'm sure she's going to let go. Instead, she brings our entwined fingers to her lips. I glance at her face, expecting tears, but she looks back at me with defiance in her eyes. "We made a great movie. And we'll make more."

The lump of angst in my chest evaporates. I kiss her nose. "I'd like that."

"Then it's a deal."

As one pact ends, another starts. I like this one a lot more. A lifetime of making movies with Sarah. Count me in.

She grins, a glint in her eye. "I do have something that might make the loss feel better."

"You out of this dress?" I brush my fingers down from her exposed shoulder to her wrist.

"Better." Sarah snuggles into me. "Siobhan won't be coming back to the apartment with us."

I catch Siobhan walking out the side door, Asher Menken regarding her like she's a shooting star. No Siobhan. Sarah and me alone in the apartment. All night. This might be better. "Really?"

Sarah drags her finger along the collar of my jacket, and my entire nervous system comes to life. "Yep. She's found somewhere else to spend the night." Her breath tickles my earlobe as her dress scratches my palm.

I need to get the silver distraction off her, remove all barriers to her skin. "What are we waiting for?"

# FOUR

## Sarah

I'M ACTUALLY HAPPY WE couldn't afford a limo ride home for the team because I get Nick to myself. The flutters in my stomach rev. I clasp his hand in the back of the cab. Or he clasps mine. Our fingers are entwined, and we fit.

Nick's speech tonight shattered the precious glass container that held my love for him. I hurt in the best way imaginable. I'm attached to this man. In a way like no other. His actions, words, emotions affect me, will raise me up or tear me down. No matter how dangerous this is, how vulnerable I feel, I abandon the final layer of caution.

I want to expose my soul and experience everything with him. It's time. This is right. This isn't a rash decision, a momentary flirtation to make myself feel good. This is real. My body longs to be next to his, and my skin prickles with anticipation. But my heart yearns to be part of the action as well and express to him in other ways what he means to me. How he is my dream come true.

Time to turn the dream into reality.

His hand lands on the small of my back as we climb the four flights of stairs to our empty apartment. The punches of my pulse against my ribs quicken. Nick's lips press against the side of my neck while I rummage for my keys. My skin is ablaze. He slides his fingers up my spine and rests his palm on the back of my head. The trail of his fingers sets fire to my core. His hands will be my undoing. Will I ever get used to his touch? I hope not.

The key slides into the lock; the bolt clicks open. I can't resist any longer, my body twisting to award Nick's lips a proper place to land—my mouth. My heart thumps against my insides, impatient for Nick's hands, skin, tongue to travel across my body without obstacles, borders, hesitation. This night is ours. This life is ours. He's the partner I've dreamed about but never truly believed existed. Mémère was right. When you know—you know. And I know. I saw Nick for who he is the first time we met, and I trust him more than any guy I've ever been with.

Trust is the aphrodisiac I've been missing. Nick's lips traverse my clavicle and linger in the tender spot beneath my ear he discovered our first week together. I can't suppress my moan. And realize I don't have to. We're alone in the apartment. I can scream his name if I want to. I moan louder.

His lips leave my skin. "I love it when you make that sound."

"Don't stop," is all I'm capable of uttering as I thread my hands into his hair and place his lips back where they belong. I can sense his smile against my neck and give in to his demands, arching my back for better access.

My fingers find the buttons of his shirt, fumbling to undo them. One. Two. I want access, too. His lips find mine, and I forget about the buttons, clutching at the fabric instead, pulling the shirt from his pants. When my hands finally press against his hard abs, I swallow his groan. I try to throw his words back at him by my lips refuse to leave his.

Cold air hits my back as Nick's hands leave me. Disappointment stings, because I couldn't tear myself away from him like that. But I forgive him when he quickly undoes the rest of the buttons and discards his shirt and jacket.

Shirtless Nick is hot. I can't keep my hands off him. But I force myself to back away and spin around. "Undo me."

Nick's nails scrape against the skin above my zipper as it takes his shaking hands a few tries to start. My dress is hard to peel off, but his eyes eating up every inch of my skin is my reward for reducing my dress to a shimmering puddle by my legs. My prize is better. Nick picks me up, and I wrap my legs around his waist. His hands around my waist were the first thought I had about him when we met. My legs around his waist is the current thought I'm stuck on.

My feet touch the comforter on my bed. Nick and I are eye-to-eye. Gone are the puppy-dog eyes women swoon for. The molten chocolate that burns in their stead dissolves my insides. The way he's looking at me, it's like he can see my soul.

"Sarah. I . . ." His Adam's apple bobs as he struggles to speak.

I press my forehead against his. "I know." I know what he's feeling because I'm feeling it too. It's more than just crossing the line from girlfriend and boyfriend to lovers. This is an accumulation of what we started on Christmas Eve: the first touch, the first kiss at Griffith Park, the missed moments on Valentine's Day, the friendship we created as I sat on his shoulders watching the July Fourth fireworks. This is us. And this is so much more than just one night. This is the start of something that is going to last forever.

His fingers skim over my back, my shoulders, leaving goosebumps and taking my breath away. He inhales and exhales in short, rapid bursts. I put my hand on his chest, his heart beating like the pistons in an engine racing down the highway, and I wrap myself around him.

Our clothes are gone, the condom is on, and I get what I want. All of Nick. The last remaining distance between us disappears.

My bedroom has seen a fair share of our touches, but tonight we lie bare, and Nick is the best view I've seen in this room. In my life. The movements and words I performed with other nameless, faceless guys take on a new meaning with Nick. The actions are no longer routine, a means to an end. Nick doesn't only take care of me, he erases the awkward first times with previous partners. Every step of the process is both new and familiar, comfortable and hot, aching and sweet. We don't play against each other. There is no winner. No race against time.

"My girl." His voice is thick. "Sarah."

I try to say his name, express what I'm feeling, but at this moment I can't tell where Nick ends and I begin.

I resist opening my eyes. My mind knows it's morning; I can feel the sunlight streaming through the window on my skin. The warmth is nothing compared to Nick's touch. My heart wants to go back to last night. I know he's not here, not lying beside me in my bed. Life had to return to normal. It's a regular Friday for the rest of the world, where people go to work and coffee shops have to be opened. But the world has changed for me. For us. I want to stay in this little moment a little longer.

Someone in the apartment above starts a shower; the groaning pipes break the last remnants of the spell, and reality forces its way in. Time to get up.

The dress I wore last night is neatly folded on the bed beside me, my clutch sitting on top. There's a note.

*Check your phone.*

*Nick*

My stomach flips. I snap open my purse and fish out the phone. The device flashes low battery, and I plug it in and open my text messages. There are a few from Sio, one from Ryan, and there it is at 5:37 a.m.—text from Nick.

Nick: Morning, beautiful. I hated leaving you this morning and couldn't bring myself to wake you. Although I wanted to. I wanted to kiss you, hold you, repeat our night together over and over. You're the words expert, but I had to try to find a way to say what I couldn't. What you mean to me. You are a dream come true. I miss you already.

I hold the phone against my chest, over my heart as if his words could touch me. As I take a deep breath to steady my shaking hands, the hint of coffee and bergamot reminds me he's real. My heart overflows with this wonderous emotion I'm not ready to name.

When my fingers are capable of typing, I hit reply.

Me: The only thing that could make my morning better would be if you were still here. With me. I like being called the word expert, but I don't know if I can beat your perfect message. I'm not sure there are enough words in the English language to come close to expressing how amazing it was to be with you. You make every day better, every hour happier, every minute worth holding on to forever. I can't wait to see you at the apartment tonight. I can't wait to see you every night.

# FIVE

# NICK

My night with Sarah was everything I wanted and nothing I expected. Dating MacKenzie should've prepared me plenty, but I was not the same person with my ex as I am with Sarah. The fakeness bled into everything in my previous relationships. The reality transformed my experience with Sarah into a gift I wouldn't have thought possible. I watch my fingers on the lever of the coffee machine, and an image of them on Sarah's neck fights its way into my mind. I swallow the rising heat.

"Add a splash of cashew milk to the espresso," Wil shouts over from the register. Two days without seeing El and happy-go-lucky Wil got up and left, replaced by grumpy-ass Wil.

El not showing up at the Starlight Gala caused some riff between the two of them. They're talking but not talking. I can't imagine not talking to Sarah again. "You and El are still performing at The Devil's Martini, right?"

"That's the plan. At least for another month." Frown lines form on Wil's forehead.

"Got it." I pour the two shots of our signature blend into a to-go cup that's smaller than my hand. The tiny container sends me into the memory of holding Sarah's slender wrists in one hand above her head, trailing my lips down from the juncture of her jaw and neck to the rounded slope of her shoulder. My throat tightens.

"Wake up." Wil takes the coffee from me and passes it and a reheated quiche to a girl who's in my economics 101 class.

I tried to sign up for mostly film-specific classes in my first semester but there are some bullshit ones I have to take to fulfill my course requirements.

"I'm gonna take five," I shout over the hiss escaping from the steaming wand.

The lunch rush is over, and Wil can handle anyone else who comes in.

"Take ten, you look like you need it." Will turns on the water and washes the blender I used for the order I messed up earlier. "But you're the manager."

I am. Managing the morning shift works perfectly with my course load. I shut the door to the storeroom that reeks of the pumpkin spice syrup Wil broke this morning. My knees ache as I pull them up to balance on the rickety stool in the corner. I breathe out, looking for some calm. I want to sit still, close my eyes, and replay every second of last night. To commit it to memory. To etch it into my brain, so no matter how much time or life try to erase what happened between us, I'd have a perfect image to hold on to. To return to again and again, because it happened. The proof is in my hand. I open the text she sent and reread her words.

*You make every day better, every hour happier, every minute worth holding on to forever.*

My heart and head buzz. I make someone's life better. Not a burden or someone they have to look after. I let the confidence of Sarah's confirmation of what last night meant to her settle into my skin, my soul. This is real, not a dream. She's not going to disappear or change her mind. Sarah is my girl.

I scroll through a collection of texts. Mom congratulating me. Mike's jab with a picture of my old room saying, "Looks like you're not going to need this anymore." A string from Dad asks to meet today. Last one's from a couple of hours ago. My shoulders tense as I push the call button.

"Was working the lunch rush. What d'you need?" I listen to a loud murmur of voices behind him.

"I'm on your campus. Okay if I come by?" Dad's asking me for permission? Something is off. "When are you done?"

"Another hour. I won't have too much time. I have to go meet Sarah."

"I'll be right there." He hangs up, and my mind searches for what could be so urgent and private that we need to talk in person. Is it related to Mom? Why didn't she say anything? A rock sits in my stomach as I stand and make my way back out front.

The shift ends with me sweeping the galley, restocking the cups, and pouring more beans into the metal contraption that grinds and measures the perfect amount for each shot. The afternoon barista arrives on time for once, and I punch in my shift hours on the tablet by the employee exit. Morning shift over, and I can put my hands where they belong, on Sarah's skin.

"Two lattes and . . ." Dad's voice sounds from the till. I pull my backpack from its cubbyhole, fill it with two sandwiches and some day-olds I'm bringing Sarah for our lunch together.

With a deep breath, I steel myself for a conversation with Dad and exit the storeroom. Ms. Hansley is scanning the pastries and cakes in the glass display like she did to me yesterday. She looks younger without the heavy glam makeup, but also less imposing. Dad asks her, "Have you decided?" He sees me exiting and acknowledges me with a lift of his eyebrows.

"A slice of the carrot cake, please," says Ms. Hansley.

Tea bag in my travel mug, I fill it with hot water. "I'll be at the table over there." I point to a corner out of the way, and Dad nods.

I blow on the steam rising from my cup as Dad and Ms. Hansley pull up their chairs and sit.

Seeing the two of them together raises the hairs on the back of my neck. When I went over to Dad's place for Mom to cut my hair, the couch was made up and a book she was reading lay on the bedside table in Dad's bedroom. I was right worrying about Mom getting back together with Dad. If he wants me to cover for him and not tell Mom about his relationship with Ms. Hansley, I'm not doing that. I never wanted to believe Mike and think bad about Dad, but he can't play with Mom's heart. She went through too much during the divorce for me to let him trample over her again.

"What d'you need?" I sound worse than Wil did this morning, but since I've stopped playing Nicky around everyone, including him, shielding my emotions is harder.

"Don't sound so thrilled." Dad puts up his invisible hackles, and we are at the standstill we always run into when we try to have a serious conversation.

"I can't believe I've been to Blend hundreds of times and probably even had you make my latte for me but had no idea you were Theo's son." Ms. Hansley seems nice, but if this is her way of buttering me up for the "I'm dating your dad" speech, I'm not interested. She glances between Dad and me. Here it comes. "Gotta love life. Most definitely stranger than fiction. I'm so glad I connected the dots. You're exactly who I'm looking for."

Okay. That was not what I was expecting. The muscles in my shoulders ease a little.

Ms. Hansley rifles in her purse and puts a stack of stapled papers on the table between us. "This is the proposal I've been working on. If you agree, you'll need to start right away."

Whatever she's talking about, I'm not following. I slide the pages toward me and scan the title. "Second Chances: Life After Prison, A Documentary."

"I'm confused. Wanna catch me up?" I address my question to Dad, who's been avoiding looking at me since he sat down.

"You know I spent five years at Terminal Island." His voice is quiet and reserved. He says it like it's a piece of trivia and not a life-changing circumstance.

"I wrote to you every month." I tighten my grip on my mug, concentrating on the warmth and not the icy resentment churning in my gut.

"Right." He dismisses me with a nod and shifts his gaze to Ms. Hansley. "Colleen has a passion project, a documentary she wants to make on life after prison. The concept is for me to conduct four tiers of interviews. First while they're getting ready to be released, second on the day they're out, third a month after they leave the institution, and maybe round it out with a six-month follow-up."

"Cool project. What's it got to do with me?" I'm still talking to Dad, but Ms. Hansley answers.

"The prison where your dad runs this outreach program"—Dad runs a prison outreach program? He never mentioned anything about it—"is one of the institutions that agreed to the filming, but we can't have a large crew. And I don't have a lot of money. With your dad involved, I thought you might take on the director and cameraman duties. I can't pay much, but you will get credit as director and, say, associate producer?" Ms. Hansley puts a hand on Dad's arm. "You get to work with your dad, which I thought would be an awesome experience."

My thoughts are racing. My heart tries to catch up with rapid beats against my sternum. Credit as a director on a funded project, not just a competition? That's gold. Joe Berlinger got his break this way. The project's totally in my wheelhouse. Documenting the lives of people and using it as a way to educate others about the realities they would otherwise never know about was the reason I did my *Schools in Chicago* short.

I glance at Dad, who's studying his coffee cup. Some of the excitement leeches away. How am I supposed to work with Dad when he can barely stand to be in the same room as me?

"Are you interested?" Ms. Hansley's hazel eyes are full of hope.

"I am. But what's the . . . downside?" There must be something I'm missing.

"Hopefully it's a win-win-win." Ms. Hansley points at each of us. "I get to make my passion project; your dad shows the industry he's still best-in-class; and you"—she smiles—"well, it's a chance to get valuable experience and credits. Something I'm sure your classmates will be envious of."

I've been around Dad long enough to know when someone is selling me something.

"But all things come with sacrifice." Ms. Hansley gives me an apologetic smile. "The prison will only let us in on weekends. Like I said, budget is limited, so I can't pay you much. Think about it as volunteering, with a benefit. We'll provide your equipment, reimburse your expenses, and make something that could change people's lives, starting with yours."

"Are you okay with doing it with me?" I ask Dad, because he's awfully quiet for someone who wants to be part of this project.

"I was the one who suggested we hire you." Dad rotates the coffee cup in his hands. "But you don't have to say yes for my sake."

He's still not looking at me. Logically, this is an awesome opportunity, but I have to fit it in between class and working at Blend. It means less time with Sarah. I want more of that, not less. But I selfishly and childishly want to spend time with Dad and see what he's like, even if he's forced to be around me because of the project. I need him to see me for the man I am and how he inspired me to be part of the film industry.

I'm not like my brother. I don't blame him for everything bad that's ever happened. To me, Dad's scheme to borrow against the pension fund was a way to keep our family afloat when the movie he invested in fell apart. He paid for it with years in prison. That one failure doesn't define him. I learned that the worst way, and I know my criminal record is not who I am. It's who I was for a brief period in my life. I'm no longer that person. Dad is no longer a criminal. My dad is a brilliant screenwriter and producer whose movies I've rewatched a thousand times. I want a real relationship with him instead of a mosaic of images from hazy childhood memories.

"Give me today to think it over," I say. "If I agree, when do we start?"

"I understand we sprung it on you, but I do need your answer by the end of the day." Ms. Hansley tightens her lips.

Dad's gaze meets mine. "We start next Saturday. I can pick you up, and we can drive to the prison together." The corner of his eyes crinkle, and giddy excitement brews inside me. Will he be happy if I say yes?

"I'll text Dad, but I have to run." I roll the stack of papers into a cylinder in my hand. "Can I take the proposal with me?"

"I brought this copy for *you*," Ms. Hansley replies for Dad again. "If you're in, I'll send you the details." She smiles and lifts her cup of coffee. "I hope we get to work together."

I lift my cup and stand. "Thank you for thinking of me."

"If you are even half as good at this as Theo, the project will be up for an Oscar next year." She raises her palms. "You might just be the next young director making blockbusters studios fight over. I can see that for you."

Ms. Hansley sees a lot more for me than most of the people in my life. Except Sarah. If she were here, she'd probably agree with her. I wave at Dad and Ms. Hansley and type a text to Sarah as I weave between the students and frisbees.

Me: I've got a job offer. Not a job-job, but I could be directing a documentary and get credit as a director.

I'm sure Sarah would want me to go for it, but after what happened last night, my life is no longer about me. It's about us.

# Six

# NICK

The Diamond Club is quiet when I arrive. Still too early for the have-to-be-seen crowd and too late for the business lunch bunch. I spot Sarah's golden-haired head huddled with Ryan behind the bar where I first met her.

She glances up and a glorious grin breaks across her face. "Mr. Old Fashioned."

My heart pounds, and I quicken my step as she bounds my way. I bury my nose in Sarah's hair. She always smells like strawberries, and living with her now, I know it's the conditioner she uses, but I choose to forget that's the source of the scent. I take her face in my hands and kiss her, because there is nothing to stop me now. PDA galore. Her fingers grip my shirt, tugging me closer as her tongue sweeps over mine.

"You smell like coffee."

In my rush to catch the bus, I forgot to change. I think the other students in my classes leave hungry because I force their noses to think about food. Wil suggested I leave some clothes at his frat house, but I fear Mateo would try to charge my jeans rent. "Sorry. But I brought food."

"My boyfriend is the best." Her praise settles in my heart. I open my mouth to compliment her back, but she's talking. "Come see what Ryan did."

She leans over the bar and flaunts a gold trophy on a black shiny plastic stand. Looks like one of the athletic awards that litter Mike's room. But this one has a white label over the original engraving with "Best Screenwriter of All Time" scrawled in black marker.

Guilt kicks my stomach. I should've thought of something like this. All I brought for her is day-old sandwiches and pastries. "Cool."

Sarah clutches the trophy and smiles as Ryan makes his way over to us. He nods at me, his eyes barely meeting mine.

I nod back. His apology to Sarah was the right thing, but all I got was a text. Maybe I'm oversensitive, but would saying sorry for digging around in my past and outing me without warning kill him? I flex my toes in my sneakers. Sarah's explanation for Ryan's absence at *Indigo*'s screening and the Starlight Gala revolved around how busy The Diamond Club was, but I know the true reason. I bounce my backpack on my shoulder.

Sarah's gaze flits between the two of us. "Everything okay?"

"Sure," Ryan offers as I say, "Yep."

She rolls her eyes, grabs my hand, and addresses Ryan as she pulls me out of the bar. "Taking my break."

With her hand in mine, I forget about Ryan and calculate whether to stop her for a kiss here or wait until we get to the storage shed the employees use as a break room. As soon as we're out of sight of any customers, she makes the decision for me, jumping into my arms. Air whooshes out of my lungs. My heart leaps to greet hers. Lips firmly attached to Sarah and one eye on the pathway, I carry her the rest of the way. Once inside, I press her against the door and try to stop her hands from ripping my shirt off.

"We only have half an hour." She bites my ear, and electricity courses through me. Much as I want a repeat of last night, this shed is a little too public for me.

I gently set her down on a stack of crates and pry myself from her. "Then you'd better eat." Backpack open, I offer her a choice of ham or turkey sandwich. She pouts but takes the closest one.

"There's root beer in the cooler." She points to a silver container on the floor. "Mrs. Marino has a new contract with this local microbrewery, and they have the best vanilla root beer I've tried in my life."

I snag two bottles and sit beside her. Sarah snuggles against my chest proving she's not mad at me for denying her what she originally desired. I sling my arm around her shoulders, and relief crackles across my scalp. I want to have her as close as possible. Having the right to touch her is addictive. For as long as I can remember, holding hands seemed cheesy and only a thing teens in Disney shows do, but these days I'm all in. With Sarah I love handholding, hugging, kissing, and having her sit on my lap no matter where we are. My lips stamp the top of her head. She's perfect.

"Hey." Her free hand finds mine like she can't stop touching me either. "Tell me about this job."

I glide my fingers through her hair. "I still can't believe it. My dad showed up at Blend with Ms. Hansley—"

"My Ms. Hansley?" Sarah pushes away and stares at me like I can't be right. "From the Starlight Foundation?"

"The very one. I met her at the Gala last night when you were talking to Karina." I tuck a lock of hair behind her ear and graze her chin with my thumb. "She's producing a documentary and wants me to direct."

Sarah's eyes sparkle. I love the way they do that when she's excited. Like they did last night. "That's awesome. What's your dad got to do with it?"

I shift on the hard crate. "The film is about convicts getting out of prison. Dad and Ms. Hansley —Colleen—know each other from way back, and she contacted my dad to work on the project. The prison she's working with is the one he . . . spent time at."

"Oh." Sarah gnaws on her lip. "How do you feel about working with your dad? Going to that place with him?"

I hadn't stopped to consider I'd be walking into a prison with Dad. I begged Mom to take me there before we moved to Chicago, but she refused.

"Not sure." I uncap one of the root beers and take a swig. The sweet, malted taste hits my tongue. Sarah's right, this is good.

"Maybe I get him to talk about what he was up to during the ten years of my life that he missed. Honestly, I think it'll be weird."

"But it could be good. Maybe give you two a chance to find some common ground."

Movies were supposed to be our common ground. Mom insisted on seeing *Indigo* before she left. Dad sat and viewed it on the couch with her, while I paced back and forth. Watching Mom watching what I created was nerve-racking and exciting at the same time. After Mom wiped away a tear as El's voice held the note I lined up with the lead character walking out the door, saying goodbye, I could finally stand still. Mom went on and on about how good *Indigo* was while Dad nodded. He never said whether he liked it or not.

"So, you think I should go for it?"

"Think? It's a no-brainer." Sarah wraps her arms around me and nestles back into our embrace. "Of course you should."

Her voice vibrates through my T-shirt to my heart, where I hear and feel her confirmation.

I pull out my phone and text Dad. "I'm in. What's next?"

"I'll pick you up at seven a.m. next Saturday." His reply is instant. Maybe he is interested in working with me. Or impressing Ms. Hansley.

I stuff my phone in my pocket and settle my hand on her lower back. "Dad says we start next Saturday."

Her head pops off my chest, something like distress swimming in the pools of her irises. "What? It's Thanksgiving next weekend. Remember? Canadian Thanksgiving is on the second Monday of October. We're supposed to fly out next Saturday."

I slap my forehead. "Fuck. I didn't think." I ball my fist. Her gaze falls, and she pulls away from me. My body aches at the lack of her, and I run my hand along her spine, wishing she'd come back. "I'll call Dad right now and tell him I can't take it."

"Don't." Her shoulders slump, and she picks at the wrapper of her sandwich. "You can't say no to a great opportunity like this. You should stay."

When Sarah invited me to go home with her for Thanksgiving, we talked how their Thanksgiving is about food and family just like ours. While making *Indigo*, I learned everything about how her parents met, heard nostalgic and outright funny stories about her Mémère's cottage, and saw photos of her two younger brothers Taylor and Grayson. The offer to meet them scared me more than when Sarah suggested I move in with her and Siobhan.

I want to see them. Sarah had dinner with Mom, Dad, and me, and they were just as in love with her as I am. She's hard not to love—smart, outspoken, beautiful, talented, and kind. I doubt her family is going to be enthusiastic about my sorry poor student self attaching to their daughter. Especially if I don't show up as promised.

I place the bottle on the floor and reach for my phone. "No. I'm calling him now. Maybe we can start a week later. Or—"

She places a hand on mine, halting my typing. "No, Nick. This is more important. There'll be other chances to meet my family." The sugar from the root beer churns in my stomach. I've let Sarah down. Fuck. I'm such a loser. How could I have forgotten?

"Are you sure?"

"Absolutely." A peck on the cheek from her and I almost believe she means it. Almost.

"I really do want to meet your family."

She tears open the wrapper on the sandwich. "And they want to meet you."

"I'll be there next time. I promise." She takes a bite of her sandwich. My appetite has dried up. I hate myself for disappointing her. "I'll miss you."

She nods.

"Just me and Siobhan in the apartment is going to be a disaster." I try to lighten the mood. "Siobhan will probably start rationing not only the shower water but the amount of air I can breathe on the premises."

I get a little smile and the vise around my heart eases. "She's not that bad."

"Only because you're her friend. She's scary to everyone else." Even Riyaz preferred meeting at Blend and not the apartment, because at the sound of Siobhan's name his three-word sentences shortened to one-syllable utterances.

"I'll tell her to behave. It'll just be three days. Maybe have Ryan over. He's a great buffer."

Ryan is *her* friend, but I'm not sure where we stand right now. I don't want to tell her that I'll be okay, because I won't.

I'll miss her like the sun. We've not been apart for this long since before the first day of the Starlight competition. And with over a month of living with her, three days will be torture. "I'll think about it."

"What time is it?"

I look at my phone. "Ten to."

"I have to get back." She rewraps her barely touched sandwich and hands it to me. "I'll wake you up when I'm home."

"I'll be dreaming about it." A stab of longing lodges between my ribs. My time with Sarah never seems to be enough.

# Seven

# NICK

Dad's Toyota follows the Gerald Desmond Bridge and leaves Long Beach behind. This is not a location I envisioned for a prison, so close to LA. In my imagination prisons are set in desolate unpopulated areas, not on an island less than an hour from UCLA. I open the car window to film the contrast between the highway and the shoreline. My phone captures the glitter of light on the water and the distant barking of the seals. The sun is already up, and the view of the ocean as we cross the turquoise bridge is spectacular. This is what I fantasized driving to a Sunday beach outing with Dad would have looked like. Instead, we're off to interview inmates at a low-security facility.

"Did you get visitors when you were here?"

Dad flicks the turn signal on. "No."

My tongue itches to ask more, but I can tell by the way he spat out the small word, this is not a topic for discussion. The weather? Yes. Did I bring free coffee? Yes. His days in prison? Hard no.

Dad warned me to wear a T-shirt without any logos or markings and approved of my black jeans that have no rips or holes that could cause us to be stopped at security. We follow a one-lane road lined with wire fences, cars, and potholes between industrial-looking structures. The almost-yellow building by the front gate says Correctional Institution in large brown letters and in a smaller font Terminal Island, CA below. The fenced gate and warning labels give no illusion of what we are entering.

I lock my backpack and the camera bag in the trunk. We got the approval to bring my camera and tripod, but it's the only special authorization we received. I insisted we would need a mic, but the answer was clear: nothing that an inmate can touch is allowed. We'll be maintaining our distance. Talking and filming inside specifically designated rooms is allowed, but that's the full extent.

"Morning, Guzman." My dad puts his wallet into a small plastic tray, and the short but sturdy corrections officer pats Dad down. "This is my son, Nick. He's got permission for the camera."

Guzman's gaze scrutinizes me, and I feel like he can tell every crime I've ever committed or even thought about. I swallow and try not to fidget.

"Sign in here." Dad points to an iPad. I fill out the info and scan my ID, my real driver's license. Guzman runs his hands over my body, and his firm pats make my skin itch. I would not want this man's job. He takes my camera and the tripod, runs them through the scanner, and gestures to follow him down a corridor.

The first inmate we're interviewing today is about Dad's age. His buzz cut betrays mostly gray hair, and the beiges of the uniform wash out the light brown of his skin. His expression is neutral, and I know this time doesn't count as work or education for him. I'm still unsure what benefit these guys get by agreeing to these weekend interviews, but maybe having their story out there in the world will bring them the closure their sentence could not.

On the car ride over, Dad and I worked on the questions. We landed on five core ones, and I wrote them on the blue index cards like he asked. Sarah always uses green index cards to map out her scenes. Are all screenwriters obsessed with index cards or have I found the only two?

Dad and I have an hour to see each person today and for me it's all about introductions, establishing rapport.

"Could you introduce yourself?" Dad sits across the table from inmate 9190, and I place the camera on the tripod behind his left shoulder.

"Erik Julio Sanchez." His gaze finds the camera, and I get the feeling it's not his first time in front of one.

"We're doing it interview style. Disregard the camera and just talk to me." Dad flips through the index cards with the questions.

"He's your son?" Erik asks Dad. I don't look much like Dad. My wavy hair, brown eyes, and height are the only recognizable features we share. I'd always been told I was Mom's mini-me when I was a kid. Her maxi-me now.

"We're working together." I can only see Dad's profile, but even that bit is enough to look intimidating. No tux required. My shoulders bunch up. Is he proud I'm here or am I projecting my need for a pleased father? The spike in my heart rate answers: I hope it's the former. "What's your sentence?"

"Five years for fraud and tax evasion," says Erik.

Sounds exactly like Dad's. My breathing matches the acceleration in my chest that's worse than during a rush to the net with the puck on my stick. Here we go. The chance I've been after to learn more about my father. I care about Dad's reactions more than those of our interview subjects.

"And you're out soon?"

What? Not sharing anything about himself? Not even a glimpse into his life before he and Mom reconnected last year? I cross my arms. I'm such a dumbass for expecting anything.

"Yeah. Right in time for Thanksgiving. My wife has the menu planned: turkey, mashed potatoes." Mr. Sanchez smiles and leans back on the metal chair. "Been dreaming about it for weeks."

Leaving this place or the Thanksgiving meal? Dad guides Mr. Sanchez through the questions about the scheme he was involved in, taking over people's bank accounts following instructions that were shared on the dark web. How easy it was to change the addresses and phone numbers and move the small amounts electronically from the victim's accounts into his. He's not shy about admitting his crimes because of the immunity that covers his nonviolent crimes prior to the conviction. "I was a huge help, you know. Led them to a much bigger ring than mine. They were grateful."

Maybe the feds were, but I doubt the victims he stole the money from would agree. I think of Sarah and the scumbags who set up the front for the fake screenwriting program, took her money, and disappeared. I grind my molars. Erik's is a different MO, but I'm scouring for some feature, something that will show me how to recognize people like him.

"What do you regret?" Dad hits the first actual question on the index cards.

"I'm too old to regret things." Mr. Sanchez tugs on his ear. "Life turned out like it did. And I'm not saying I haven't done bad shit, but regretting is for the weak. I'm not gonna waste time on that. My focus is on the present, not the past."

I still frequently find myself in the past. Dreams of begging Mom in the first years of Dad's sentence to see him still haunt me. Old disappointment I thought I was over flares in hot patches across my cheeks. I lower my head to hide my reaction. Mom was adamant Dad had no one on his visitors list, so reporters wouldn't track where we are and come bother us. While still in LA, Mom got calls from the press, but once she changed her number and we moved, it was like Dad never existed.

I don't remember ever being called out as the son of that Hollywood producer who went to prison. Dad's appearances in court splashed across all major networks, and for the length of his trial, I clung to the fantasy of Dad's innocence. It *had* to be one giant misunderstanding, because my father was a good guy. A workaholic, yes, not someone I saw around too much, but he was not a criminal. The legal system proved me wrong.

Xavier is the next person we interview. In this all-male prison, the largest population is Hispanic, then white, followed by Black, and a small percentage of Asian and Native American inmates.

"Where will you live? Transitional housing? Or do you have a place you'll be renting?" To qualify for this documentary the subjects had to have no more than six weeks left in their sentence. Our interviews will follow our current cast of twenty, and we hope to end up with at least five stories that we can track for six months or maybe beyond.

"Couch surfing." Xavier rubs his shaggy blond beard and shifts his gaze away from Dad's.

"So, no place to stay?" I've never talked to Dad about where he went post-prison. For five years after he got out, there was nothing but silence. My blood roars in my ears. There's still nothing but silence.

Chris is our last interview of the day. He's smiley and does not look that much older than me. We have wavy brown hair in common, but his eyes are blue-gray and perpetually smirking.

He takes his seat on the chair with a swagger, and I get the vibe of my hockey teammates the instant he talks. "Can I get a Coke?"

Dad brought a Ziplock bag with quarters to potentially get some food, but Chris is the first one to openly ask for something. He's the only one who's here with some plan in mind, and the feeling of superiority that emanates from him is the same one my hockey buddies mastered by high school. An unmistakable self-assuredness that I didn't see in the two previous guys. I capture the upturned angle of his chin, the slight curve of his lip, the twinkle in his eye.

"Don't think we're allowed today, but I'm sure we'll figure something out." Dad puts his elbows on the table and interlaces his fingers.

"With your background, I'm sure you can find a way to persuade them into getting me a Coke." Chris mimics Dad in his posture. "Not like I'm doing this for nothing." Chris sets his jaw on his fingers and keeps watching Dad like a cobra.

Dad breaks their staring match and glances at his index cards. Not like him. There are no clues in his cool exterior. What's going on inside his mind? He knows the five core interview questions by heart.

What do you regret?

Where will you live?

What are your family's expectations for you?

What will you do for the next six months?

Where do you see yourself in five years?

"We're here to talk about your plans for after you're released." Dad shuffles the index cards, like they are a deck of playing cards. "But we don't need all the applicants. If you're not interested in telling us about your post-release plans, it was very nice to see you." Dad stands.

Chris glances at the door behind us. "I'll be staying with my sister in San Bernardino." The smirk and attitude are gone. Maybe Dad does know what he's doing.

"Is she your only family?" Dad sits back down.

"Yeah." Chris straightens in his chair.

"Has she been in prison as well?"

"Her? No." Chris gets defensive, as if Dad's trying to insult his sister. "She works at a bank. Started as a teller. She's a supervisor now."

Dad's tone changes. His voice is softer. "Was she mad when you got caught? What were her expectations for you?"

"She thought I was going to be like her. Start as a teller, have a career. And I was doing it. But I wanted to go to this concert with my friends, needed her to loan me some cash until I got my paycheck, but she said no." Chris glances at the ceiling and leans back in his chair. "I borrowed from the till. I was going to give it back the next day. Why do they care? They had stacks of money in there, not like anyone would've missed the five hundred if they didn't catch me."

Dad nods. Does he regret borrowing against the pension fund? Or does he only regret that he got caught? I bite my tongue. I wish I could ask him, but I know better.

We finish the interviews with the first five inmates on our list and get back to the car. The idea I had that I'd be learning about Dad from his words was wrong. But I have a different perspective. When I see the interior of the prison, when I see the people he was surrounded by for five years, when I imagine Dad in here, not a visitor from the outside, I'm both grateful to Mom she never took me to visit him and angry at her for not forcing Dad to see me. My hands curl into fists, but I stuff them into my pockets before anyone sees. Maybe Mr. Sanchez was right. Maybe I should focus on the present and not the past. And my present is with Sarah.

I retrieve our stuff from the prison guard and check my phone. Sarah's flight landed two hours ago. I hope she's having a better day with her family than I am. I turn on my phone and text her.

Me: Does the air at home smell better than LA smog?

Sarah: Just stopped at Tim Horton's. Everything is better with Timbits and a double-double.

Me: Miss you already. Sure I can't pick you up at the airport Tuesday afternoon?

Sarah: I'm sure. I'll go straight to The Diamond Club. But I'll see you Tuesday night. The three days will fly by. I promise I'll make our reunion worth the wait.

# EIGHT

## Sarah

IT'S BEEN LESS THAN twenty-four hours since Nick kissed me goodbye at the airport and I already miss him. I sigh. Still, it is good to be home. I wish Nick were here with me. But the opportunity to work with his dad, to have director credits, I understand how important it is. I gnaw on my lip. Hopefully he'll make the New Year's hockey game between the Leafs and the Bruins. Dad already bought the extra ticket.

Hockey is one thing Nick and I have in common and yet will never agree on. I don't regret getting him the tickets for the Kings the eve of his birthday, not that I'm letting my family know I'm going. If my plan works, I'll first share the excitement of the live game and then a luxurious bed at a hotel with my boyfriend.

"What are you smiling about?" Dad doesn't miss a trick.

"Happy to be home," I say. Dad and I are tight but not tight enough to share my plans for Nick's birthday.

Red, orange, and gold create a fall mosaic through the window of Mom's clunky Côté Fraises van that chugs up the 400 highway. We're spending Thanksgiving weekend at the cottage, and Mom and my brothers made the trek last night. As I drive, my shoulders lose the tension of six hours on the plane, and I relish the comfort of alone time with Dad. Time to get the real story of what's going on.

"How's Mom doing?"

"Oh, you know her. Burying herself in work. She fired another assistant. Not up to snuff, apparently."

"We all grieve in our own way." A hole in my heart that appeared after Mémère's death grows at the thought of being at the cottage without her. I wish she could've met Nick, seen me happy with him.

"Yes, but this is the third one since your Mémère died."

I glance at Dad, who stops his one-fingered typing on the phone. "The first year is the hardest. The first of everything." A Timbit gets stuck in my throat. I cough. In LA, it was easier to almost believe Mémère was still with us. My brain knows she's gone, but my heart can't accept it and smarts with regret. I still pick up the phone to tell her the news whenever anything good happens.

"Honestly, I think she's having trouble adjusting. She needs to grieve. Properly." He's watching the road ahead. "She's using work to avoid her issues."

"I get it. We're more alike than she thinks." I laugh without humor and take my foot off the brake. The apple doesn't fall far from the tree. I've been picking up extra shifts at The Diamond Club to forget that I'm the only one on Team Blue who didn't get a job offer.

"Maybe you could spend more time with her this weekend? Talk?"

My fingers curl around the steering wheel. "I talk to her on the phone every week."

"You update her on your life. You don't talk." Dad takes his eyes off the road to look at me. "She needs someone who's going through the same thing, and you know your brothers and I don't have the emotional intelligence to imagine what's going on in her head."

I almost laugh. My dad has more emotional intelligence than most of our family put together. Having lived all around the world growing up, he experienced things Mom, me, and my brothers can't fathom in safe, secure Canada.

"I'll try." I clench my teeth. I'll stop sending Mom's calls to voicemail and avoiding conversations on how serious I am about staying in LA.

As soon as we hit the side road that leads to the cottage I roll down the window and suck in the fresh country scent. Home. The last vestiges of tension evaporate. The air is clean and sweet with just a hint of dampness to warn of things to come. Summer is gone, winter is coming.

Mom's in the garden picking herbs when we pull up. She wraps me in a big hug and holds me longer than usual. I let her. She needs the comfort. I take her warmth, she takes mine. We miss the affection of a third embrace. Mémère should be here. She should be roasting the turkey. She should be making the pecan pie. She should be . . .

But she's not.

Heat prickles behind my eyes and I untangle myself from Mom's arms.

"You look tired." Mom touches my hair, my shoulders, as if surveying for damage LA life has inflicted on me. "Taylor, Grayson, come get Sarah's things."

"Yes, Mom." My brothers groan in unison as they mock-drag my tiny carry-on.

I snap a picture of the cottage Mémère and my grandfather bought before they had a house. My grandfather was in love with the Canadian countryside. I send the pic off to Nick.

Me: Here's our cottage.

Mémère was always happiest here, surrounded by memories of her husband playing his annual Boxing Day hockey game with the other cottagers on the lake.

Me: Maybe we can play hockey here on Boxing Day.

He replies with a picture of our kitchen table covered in books and notepads.

Nick: More fun than slogging through my Economics 101 notes. Was I asleep when I took them?

His schedule is getting out of hand. I tap my thumb against the back of the phone case. This documentary will screw with Nick's only chance to sleep in. Mr. Parker better not dash Nick's hopes again or he'll have me to answer to.

A notification covers the screen. It's from the Veritas Agency about junior writing jobs. The "Thank you for your interest but . . ." preview line kicks me in the stomach with another dismissal. That makes eight this week. I pop my lips. A nice, even number of rejections.

I've been applying anywhere and everywhere but I can't even get to the interview stage. No bachelor's degree. No experience. Winning Starlight was my last chance to get people to notice me as a screenwriter. My gut fills with lead. Is bartending in LA all I can get as a job?

Everyone tells me it'll come, but as each day passes, and I get farther and farther away from the competition, a blade shaves off a sliver of hope from the illusion I created that I can make it as a writer. In LA, time is both longer and shorter. The effect of taking part in a notable movie at the competition is limited. I rub my eyebrow. If no one has shown interest in my work for over a week after the Gala, I doubt I'll hear from them.

I'm never up this early, but the lake is beautiful at sunrise, so I get out of bed and head to the dock. Mist is rolling off water so calm it looks like a sheet of glass. I stretch my arms over my head, light and refreshed, my brain clear after a night away from the buzz of the city. A loon warbles a hello, and I curl up in my favorite Muskoka chair. I pull out my phone, snap a picture of the peaceful setting, and send it to Nick. He's three hours behind but already awake, waiting for Ryan to pick him up for the surfing outing I set up for them.

Nick: We must film something there. A cinematographer's dream.

Me: Bring your camera when we come up in December.

It sounds like an order, but I'm sure he'd love to visit the cottage, play a game of hockey on the ice with us, and indulge in the Canadian countryside. Three dots are wiggling on my screen, so I type quickly.

Me: I miss you

The dots stop, then start dancing again.

Nick: I miss you too. Hard to sleep without you.

My heart melts. Ever since we came home from the Starlight Gala we've been sleeping in the same bed. Nick's room is basically vacant. I should ask Siobhan about adding a fourth roommate. The extra cash could be handy.

Nick: Siobhan is driving me nuts. Everything I do is wrong when you aren't here.

I feel for Sio, having been in her place less than a year ago. One perfect night with the most amazing person and then he ghosts her? Sio's not a long-term relationship person, but Asher and her looked so enamored when they left for his hotel after the

Starlight Gala. She was full of plans when she told me about their night together. Yet he never messaged her back. Asher might be a film star, but that's still unacceptable. I had to stop her from storming down to Asher's parents' place and banging on the door. She wants an explanation, and I don't blame her.

Me: Give her space. Spend tonight with Wil at the frat house.

Nick: I'll think about it.

I hear footsteps on the wooden boards behind me. The only person in this household who gets up this early on the weekend is my mother. "Morning, honey. You're up early."

I motion toward the lake. "Couldn't miss this."

Mom settles into the chair beside me and hands me a mug. "It is breathtaking. This is my favorite time of day here." She looks at my phone. "Can't you put that thing away?"

The smell of coffee reminds me of Nick. Everything reminds me of him. My skin longs for his touch. "Just sent Nick a picture of what he's missing." I type out a quick *Mom's here, gotta go* to Nick and place my phone, screen-side down, on the wide wooden arm of the chair.

"Ah, the new guy in your life. I thought you were bringing him to meet us."

I shift in my seat. "He had to work." Not a lie. But not the whole truth. But then Mom and I rarely speak whole truths. I don't tell her about my job hunt, and she doesn't share her opinion on LA . . . much.

"Tell me about him."

"What do you mean?" I watch her face for clarification. "You know everything. He's from Chicago, played hockey, wants to be a director."

My mother lays her cool fingers on my arm. "No, not the facts. Tell me why he's the one for you."

"Oh." A flutter flies through my heart. I play with the tie on my fleece pajama pants. I wasn't expecting this. "You've never wanted to know about any of my boyfriends."

"You've never sounded this excited about anyone before." Mom's thumb rubs back and forth across my wrist. "There's something different about this boy."

"You're right." Would she think I'm moving too fast if I tell her he's the one? "Nick is kind and passionate. He has the best smile." My chest warms with the thought of his goofy grin. "He makes me laugh and he . . . well . . . he cares about me. We're a team, you know?"

Mom's gaze finds mine. "I do, honey. I felt the same way about your father."

We sit there, both of us letting the ramifications of her words settle into the misty morning air around us. The sweet song of two loons echoes over the water and hints at a world where I too can have a partner for life.

Karina's ringtone cuts through the air, scaring the loons and making me jump. It's far too early for her to be up. Or has she not gone to bed yet? "Sorry." I hit cancel and put the phone on silent.

Mom and I walk back to the cottage. The aroma of bacon draws us to the kitchen where Dad is flipping a pancake and shaking his butt to music from an ancient stereo set. Mom kisses Dad on the cheek and tries to steal a strip of bacon. "You know you have to wait until the boys are up. We eat as a family."

Dad puts down the spatula and wraps an arm around Mom's waist, swaying her to the half-beat of the music. "How's my luv this morning?"

Will that be Nick and me someday? I walk away. "I'll go wake up Taylor and Grayson."

Before I do what I promised, I walk into the guest bathroom and check my phone. There's a text from Nick, three missed calls from Karina, and a voicemail. I listen to the voicemail first.

"Sarah. Call me ASAP." Karina's excited voice blasts in my ear. "I have the offer of a lifetime." I dial her right back.

"She actually threw their coffees into the trash in front of them. Rod fired her on the spot. I couldn't believe it." I'm not sure Karina has taken a breath in the last sixty seconds. "She was escorted out of the building and everything. Didn't even have a chance to get her coffee mug from the kitchen."

"Harsh."

"I'm glad though. She wasn't just messing up everyone's orders after a month. Her notes were crap, and she had no ideas to pitch, just told everyone how great theirs were. I know us women are supposed to support each other, but she was not even trying." Karina lowers her voice. "I think her daddy got her the job, and she thought her name would be in big letters on the screen. But until you're full-time, you don't get a credit."

"Sounds like she didn't really want to work for it." I'd work my ass of if I were given half that chance.

"Enough about her. She's the past. You're the future."

I reposition the phone closer to my ear. "Sorry?"

"Are you not listening to me? There's an open spot." Karina squeals. "I recommended you to Rod."

I stare at my reflection in the mirror. And blink. "Me?"

"Yeah, you. He remembered your Cor-Vet joke from the Gala and heard an earful from Ms. H about your *Indigo* script. He wants you to come in. It's only a trial basis for three months. If you impress him, and I know you will, he could hire you full-time."

My skin tingles. I tighten my grip on my phone to keep it from falling. A writing gig. It might be about vampires, but it's a real writing gig.

"It doesn't pay much. Don't put a down payment on a mansion in Malibu. And it's not like in the movies. We get shit jobs like cleaning the writing room and keeping them caffeinated."

Her description doesn't quell the electricity coursing through my veins. I'll be in a writers' room. Have the chance to write. I force myself to calm down. "Sounds like what I do at The Diamond Club."

"Yeah, that'll come in handy. The hours are similar. No early mornings, unless you're sent on set. But late nights are a guarantee. An occasional weekend as well if we're on a deadline. I haven't seen the sun in over a week. But what you write might be streamed by millions."

The reality of what Karina is offering sinks in. Shivers ripple across my skin and awaken my dormant  career opportunities. This is the chance of a lifetime. I'd be foolish not to take it. "When and where?"

"You'll have to start right away. Rod's expecting you at the studio tomorrow at noon."

Tomorrow? No. It's Monday. It's Thanksgiving. My heart plummets. Mom will kill me if I bail on her. Plus what about my shifts at The Diamond Club this week? Mrs. Marino is expecting me Tuesday afternoon straight from the airport.

"You'll be here, right?" Karina asks.

I glance at the photo of Mémère and me. I'm twelve and we're building a sandcastle at the beach up the road. Both of us grinning. I wove a story about the princess who lived in the castle waiting for her prince to rescue her kingdom. Mémère whispered in my ear that my princess was strong and did what she needed to do to save herself and her people.

"I'll be there." Mémère's hopes for me strengthen my resolve.

A text notification pops up.

Sio: I hate the early shift. Three cups of espresso and I'm now jittery yet still can't keep my eyes open. Can't wait until you're back on Tuesday to deal with Layden. He's still useless.

Me: I'm coming home tonight but I'm not sure about Tuesday.

Sio: That bad with your mother?

Me: No.

Me: Yes.

Me: It's not about her. I got a job. Junior writer on a TV show!!!!!!

Sio's ringtone trills, and I hit answer.

"EEEEEEEE!" we shout in unison.

# NINE

# NICK

THE PARKING LOT IS empty except for a van with a small group of surfers who, unlike me, appear to know what they're doing. I scratch the stubble I didn't have the time to shave. Why the hell did I agree to this? Ryan pulls into a spot, and I climb out of the passenger seat.

One perk of opening Blend every morning is that my body is now awake at five a.m. even if it's Sunday. Without Sarah's compact body beside me, I didn't get a good night's sleep. How someone so small can hog half her bed, I'll never know, but a quarter of a bed with her is better than a king-size one by myself. After tossing and turning most of the night, dragging myself into the gloom of the new day was the last thing I wanted. What won't I do for Sarah? This playdate she set up for Ryan and me is not something I'm excited about. Surfing or not.

The sunset we filmed for *Indigo* at this beach on Ryan's recommendation was gorgeous, but the sunrise might just be a good enough reason for me to enjoy this outing. I wish I had a real camera with me. Someday I'll be able to afford the latest model phone but even without the upgrade, the picture filling my screen doesn't need a filter. Panoramic views, tight shots, angling the camera up from the sand, sideways into the sky.

"Are you actually interested in surfing?" Ryan's face is flat, missing its usual carefree grin, and a muscle ticks in his jaw. Still, he's the poster boy for a surfer dude.

"Interested?" I close my camera app. "Sure."

"Then let's get out of the parking lot." The top of his wetsuit is undone and tied around his waist.

Maybe I need to resume my visits to the campus gym. I tug at the sleeves of the spare suit Ryan lent me, trying to get it to cover some of my forearm. It's both too wide and too short for me. But even at the second-hand store the ones that fit me were unaffordable. Spending money for a one-time outing to placate Sarah is not worth the waste. I'd rather splurge on a dinner that doesn't involve eating french fries out of a cardboard box.

Two gleaming surfboards bracket Ryan. For a bartender with a wage lower than Sarah's, he owns too many wetsuits and surfboards. Never mind the expensive electric SUV he drives.

"What do I do with my phone?" I wave the most expensive thing I own in the air.

He offers me a board in exchange for my phone. "I'll lock it in my car." He taps a button on his watch and the car's lights flash. He always has the latest tech. How can he afford it?

"I'd like to dig into your background," I say under my breath. Like he did mine. Find some dirt to smudge his perfect face.

"Excuse me?"

Crap. I didn't mean for him to hear. "How do you afford all this? Do you have a second job? Digging into people's backgrounds for cash or something?"

"I thought we were past that." Ryan leans his board against the locked car and zips himself up with much more grace than my comical five-minute show of doing the same thing.

"Past what? An apology?" I head to the steps that we used to get us to the beach during the shoot.

"Not there. That's for experienced surfers," Ryan says and points to the opposite side of the parking lot. "We're going to start with the more . . . gentle side for your first time."

"Didn't know you had one." At least not where I'm concerned. I kick a pebble out of my way. Is he pitying me? I half-expected him to throw me into the biggest waves and let them pummel my ass. Then both of us have a legitimate excuse to tell Sarah why I'm not returning to surfing any time soon.

"Fine." He pauses in the middle of the wooden planks that lead to the waves. "I'm . . . no. I'm not sorry. I hate lying. I would have done it all over again. I was clear from the start I'd protect Sarah, and I've known plenty of charismatic swindlers who appear to be genuine but are there only to take advantage of whomever they can. I refuse to apologize for caring."

"For friends, aren't you caring a bit too much?" The smoldering headache I woke up with flares into flames behind my eyes. A familiar sign of trouble. I rub my forehead to force myself to keep calm. "Isn't it my role to care for her now?"

"Are you for real?" He stops and spins, the long rays of the morning sunrise casting an orange glow on his skin. "Do you not have friends? It's not like you're limited to one person who can care about you."

I stare at the sand, struggling to keep hold on the fire that's spreading to my neck. Of course, he's right.

"Sarah's the reason I didn't get sacked when I started at The Diamond Club. She covered for me, taught me everything I know, and I'll never forget that. Boyfriend or not." He steps closer to me. "Do you know how many so-called boyfriends our friendship has lasted through?"

Low blow. Sand forgotten, I glare at Ryan, make sure there's no doubt he understands me. My chest burns. "I'm nothing like them. What we have is real. And serious. And I'm not going to let you stand in our way."

"If there is anyone standing in your way, it's your overinflated ego." The orange glow looks more like flames of anger. "Instead of being jealous of her friends, figure out what it is she sees in you, and hope that it'll keep her interest."

His words slice through my skin like a hot knife through butter. I toss the anger back at him. "You didn't manage to do that."

"And it took me months to get over it. Over her. But I am over her." Ryan draws in a deep breath. "We are friends. Just friends. And as a friend, I'll keep an eye on her."

His stare dares me and instead of punching him, I clench my free hand and head back to the car. While his perfect face could use some rearranging, I won't do anything to hurt Sarah.

"Is this how you deal with honesty?" he says. "Run away?" I keep walking, putting distance between my fists and his jaw. His words are the kindling to the inferno raging inside me.

"You don't deserve her then," Ryan shouts after me.

The orange sky drowns in red, along with the sand and ocean. In a few strides I'm nose-to-nose with Ryan. The surfboard is unforgiving under my fingers, and I clench my free hand at my side. I will not hit him. "Don't ever say that again. Or I'll be the one teaching you how to punch and kick, and it won't be gentle. She. Chose. Me."

"I'm sorry. Okay?" Ryan takes a step back and holds up his free hand. "I only want Sarah to be happy."

Regular hues of orange, green, and blue return to the world with his apology. I pry my fingernails from my palm and let the ocean breeze blow out the blaze that almost consumed me. "She *is* happy."

"Now that is the truth." He runs his hand through his blond hair, and his shoulders drop. "Really dude, I'm sorry. I have a tendency to dig for the worst in people. Before Sarah and Siobhan, I . . . well let's just say any so-called friends I had never cared about me."

His confession tugs on memories of my so-called hockey bros. I figured everywhere Ryan went people would be lining up to be his friend. My ribs tighten. I shift the surfboard. "What did they care about?"

Now he studies the sand, running his toe in it. When he looks up at me, his face is resigned. "What I brought to the table. Mostly money." He squints at the sun over my shoulder. "My parents come from money, and the rules of that world are very different. Nothing like what you live by."

"Are you going to complain about being rich?" Just when I was beginning to like him.

A tiny smile graces his lips as he dips his chin down. "No, dude. I'm trying to apologize."

"You're not doing a banging job of it."

"Not something I do on the regular. I'm usually right." The ego on this guy. "People are usually as bad as I think they are. Or worse."

"Do you do a background check on everyone you meet?" My imagination conjures a secret server with terabytes of data.

Ryan studies the sand again.

My brain catches up with my gut. "Damn. You do. Don't you?"

"It's how I get to know people." Another drag of his toe over the sand.

"Dude." I toss his favorite word back at him. The smoke from my rage settled, I see another side of Ryan. "You could try the old-fashioned way. Get to know people. Ask them questions."

He shakes his head slowly, like I'm some child who doesn't get that there isn't any ice cream left. "You know nothing about me. You can't give me advice from your high horse. Not everyone's life is a good as yours."

I bark out a laugh. "As good as mine? Poor. Growing up with a father in prison. Stealing cars. Having a mom who works herself to the bone to support me and my brother. The brother who's so perfect, anything I do can never compare. How exactly is that the picture of perfection?"

"You have people who love you, you dumbass." He moves his surfboard across his chest like it's a shield. "Your parents, your brother, Sarah. Can you even see what you're taking for granted? No one loves me."

That's impossible. I want to mock him, but his face is stoic, serious.

"No one has ever loved me," he says. "Even Sarah. She cared about me, still cares about me, but I would've given all the money I had for her to look at me the way she does at you." His fingers are white where he's clutching the surfboard. "Damn it. I *am* jealous. But not because Sarah loves you. Because you have so much, and you don't appreciate what you've got. Money is not everything. Trust me."

I take a step forward. "I don't know who messed you up, but that sucks. I accept your apology." I offer Ryan my hand.

He lays his surfboard down and grips my palm.

"Friends?" I offer.

He stares at our handshake, twists his head toward the beach, then meets my gaze full-on. "Only if you mean it. I don't need any phonies in my life. I don't have any more money to offer. But I'll always have your back."

"Much better than you stabbing it." Ryan tries to jerk his hand out of mine. "Hey. Joking here. Tell me stuff to my face the next time you have something to say, and we'll be good."

His hand relaxes in mine. "I promise."

"Good. Do we still have time to surf?"

The smile that splits his face is brighter than the rising sun. "You still wanna?"

"I'm already wearing this getup. Might as well."

The waves that make a beautiful contrast to the sun are harder to control than I remember. Mike and I tried surfing when I was in elementary school, but the ten years between then and now erased any skill I might've developed. I fall. And I fall. And I suck in lungfuls of cold salty water. And I fall some more.

Ryan's watch beeps. "That's it for today, dude. I gotta go."

Small mercies. My legs are shaking from my failed attempts at getting up on the board. "Hot date?"

"I wish." Ryan and I bend to pick up our boards. His boards, I guess. The rich family tidbit explains a few things. "Apartment hunting."

"Looking for a new place?"

"Not because I don't love my place. But . . . change of circumstances." His mouth forms a line. "I've seen two rooms this week. One was smaller than a closet and the other was in a basement without any windows. The roommates seemed like nice people, but the smell of weed was overpowering. Probably because there were no windows to air the place out."

"Yikes. Glad I didn't have to apartment hunt."

"Yeah, dude. Like I said. You're lucky."

# TEN

# NICK

Surfing in the morning. Three more interviews at the prison. Sunday may be a day of rest for some, but not for me. Tomorrow starts with another morning shift at Blend. I dump my camera bag at the front door and head for the fridge, exhausted.

Siobhan bounds out of her bedroom, and her face transforms from gleeful to grumpy. "Oh, I thought you were Sarah."

"You've got your days mixed up. She's not coming back till Tuesday." I grab a Coke and crack it open.

"You're behind the times, boyo. She's coming home tonight."

The sugary liquid catches in my throat and I sputter. Sarah's roommate always has to be right. Even when she's dead wrong. I almost regain the ability to breathe again when the front door opens and Sarah walks in.

Siobhan smirks. "See?"

The taste on my tongue turns bitter. Is it because Siobhan is somehow right this time? Or because Sarah told *her* she was coming home early? Not me. I go for my phone to see if I missed a message, but I was texting with Ryan on my walk up to the apartment. There was nothing from Sarah.

"Am I glad to see you." Sarah crashes into me, and my free arm encircles her. "The flight was awful."

I place the bottle on the table and hold onto her, not sure what's wrong or even what's going on, but I can't deny her a hug. I'd do anything to erase the strain from her voice. "You're home now. It's okay."

Her fingers press into my back. "No, it's not."

Dread crawls up my spine. What the hell happened? Why am I the last to know?

"No one can cover for me Tuesday night." Her words are muffled against my chest.

"Sorry?" I feel like I missed the opening scene in a movie and a few vital clues. "What are we talking about?"

"My shift at The Diamond Club. Everyone I called is busy."

"Okay." It's not like Mrs. Marino to switch Sarah's shifts last minute. I rub her back. "Well, did you ask Ryan?"

"He's working the same shift." Siobhan cocks an eyebrow. "Don't you know her schedule by now?"

I press my lips together to keep from snapping at Sarah's friend. I concentrate on the girl in my arms instead. "Hey. Did Mrs. Marino ask you to work a different shift?"

Sarah stiffens in my embrace.

Siobhan snickers and plods down the hall. "You two need to talk."

What the heck is going on? My girl unwinds herself from me and raises her fingers to her mouth. I tug at her hand. "Tell me, what is it?"

The muscles in my shoulders tense at the idea of there being something wrong. I brace for the bad news.

"Nick." Her voice is thick. "I'm so sorry. Everything happened so fast. First the call, then I had to break the news to Mom. She locked herself in the bedroom when I told her I'll be missing Thanksgiving dinner. Didn't even say goodbye. I cursed the speedometer on Mom's van that wouldn't go past a hundred kilometers. By some miracle I managed to make it to the airport before they closed my gate."

Her anxiety infects me. My pulse quickens to match the words tumbling out of her. But I still have no clue what I'm supposed to be anxious about. "Slow down. Tell me what happened."

She takes a deep breath. "I got a job."

It takes a few seconds for the words to sink in. "Okay." I still don't get what upset her. "A promotion at The Diamond Club?"

"No. A real job. Karina recommended me for a junior writer's position on *Vampire Club*." Her lips curl up. My head hurts trying to put the puzzle together, but my heart reacts to her happiness. This sounds like good news. Not something to worry about.

"It's only temporary, but it could be a full-time placement." Her smile wanes. "I have to be in the writer's room ten a.m. to at least eight p.m. starting tomorrow. That means I can only work nights at the club and need to switch out of the morning and afternoon shifts."

The outline of what she didn't share with me comes together. She got a position in the business like she wanted. And she didn't tell me. Or did she forget to tell me? Do I only exist when I'm by her side? My throat burns. I look at my empty arms.

I spent this weekend worrying she wouldn't be able to find anything in the business and was going to ask her if I should email Ms. Hansley in case she had something for a screenwriter. Sarah keeps up a brave face, but I know she's been unhappy. Bri got a paid internship with El's cousin, Zoe Yilmaz, an up-and-coming designer. Wil joined Mateo and me at UCLA. Riyaz signed a contract to start work in December. And Sarah doesn't think I'd like to know when she finally gets a job?

This should be good news, why is my blood boiling with irritation? What kind of a boyfriend am I if I can't be happy for her? She sacrificed our weekend away so I could start my director's gig, and she was excited for me.

I lock my unhappiness away and focus on celebrating with her. I will be the boyfriend she deserves.

"That's amazing." I hope my words sound genuine as I kiss her on the forehead. "How did this happen?"

"I'm replacing a girl who got fired." She takes a seat at the kitchen table. "Rod, that's the head writer, he remembered me from a joke I told at the Gala."

I take a seat beside her, hold her hands in mine. "I'm so happy for you. A real writer's room. That show is getting a lot of buzz. I overhead a group of girls taking about the lead. Kyle somebody."

"Kyle Bardot." She nods. "They say he could be the next Chase Stokes."

"That's good. If he has a growing fan base, they'll put money into the show. It could run for years."

Her eyes light up. "Don't get too excited. I have to prove myself."

I wave a hand between us. "No problem. You're the most capable person I know. You'll have them eating out of the palm of your hand in no time."

"Maybe."

"No doubt about it."

Sarah's hair is still damp when she climbs into bed and tucks into my side. I inhale her fresh strawberry scent and know I'll have no trouble sleeping tonight.

"How did it go with Ryan this morning? Are you officially a surfer?"

I laugh and it hurts. "Every muscle in my body aches. But we caught a few good waves. Well, he did. I swallowed a lot of saltwater."

"I'm glad it worked out." She hooks her leg over mine. "Ryan needs a few more friends in his life."

Now that I know a bit more about him, his protectiveness over Sarah doesn't grate as much. "Did you know he's looking for a new place to live?"

"No. Why?"

"Sounded like they raised the rent on his current place or something. He can't afford it."

She chuckles. "He should move in here. We could use the extra cash." She pulls my chin to look at her. "It's not like you're moving back to your room anytime soon."

Never, if I have my way. I take her mouth with mine to prove she's right. My fingers find familiar and new places to caress, and my body starts aching in a different way. It feels so good to have Sarah in my arms. My blood simmers from our actions instead of her not telling me she was coming home early. Forgive and forget. I'm just so glad she came home. To me.

The cares and concerns of the day fade away when we move together as one. We try to keep things as quiet as possible, aware Siobhan is sleeping behind a thin wall. The rhythm of her hips answering mine is now comfortable. I've discovered how to coax out the little gasps and the tightening before she crosses her finish line. Knowing these things about her is the opposite of mundane. The movie of Sarah comes together frame by frame.

Her name on my lips, I brace myself on my elbows and keep up the tempo even though I can barely hold on. She gives into me. I watch my favorite scene as she comes undone beneath me. This is because of me. Because of us. My heart captures her every flutter, squeeze, quake, aftershock. Her eyes fly open. Gaze on gaze. The impossible blue is my undoing. I give way to her and soar to my climax. My name on her lips.

I hold her close as we catch our breath. For the millionth time I wish I had money so I could spoil Sarah, give her everything she desires. Including a home with a huge bed and no roommates.

She draws little hearts on my stomach, her head resting on my chest. "How did it go with your dad?"

"Okay, I guess. It was weird seeing him in that place. The guards all know him, and a few of the convicts too. He . . . I don't know, fits in there. But also, he doesn't."

Thinking about Dad as a former prisoner still comes as a surprise. Maybe it's because I've never seen him in prison. Or maybe because my vision of what prisoners are like is always at best what *Orange is the New Black* showed and at worst *Shawshank Redemption*. Neither of them fit Dad. He's smart. He's a good person. He's . . . a former prisoner. An ex-con?

"Well, he volunteers there, right?" Sarah's hand pauses. "So, that's to be expected."

"I guess. It was almost like he commanded their respect. Not sure how I feel about that."

"What do you mean?"

On the ride home I tried to work up the courage to ask Dad about what life behind bars was like for him. But I couldn't get the words out. The silence stretched between us, and the farther we got from the prison, the harder it was to start the conversation.

I rub the stubble on my chin. "I guess I thought it would be different. These inmates, it's not like you'll see them in the store or on the street and say, 'That guy is bad, he's taking the last dime from his retired grandma and her bingo friends.'"

"None of them looked evil?"

"Not in the slightest." The faces I zoomed in on and examined on the screen, looking for micro-expressions that would tell me a story different from what their words were conveying, didn't reveal anything. "Hustlers, maybe, but there's nothing that I could detect. This last guy, Chris—"

"You're allowed to share their names?"

"Well, this is not investigative journalism. I'm not protecting my sources or anything like that." I had a thought about doing something along those lines, but I'm much better with the visuals than words. "They agreed to have their first names listed as part of the documentary."

Sarah's palm rests over my heart. "So, what about Chris?"

"He wasn't what I'd imagine someone who's ready to go straight would be like." Her skin begs to be kissed and I'm eager to help. I sink my fingers under the strap of Sarah's tank top. Although not same as sex, the ease with which we talk about our day and share our innermost feelings lights me up inside.

Whether it's through touches or words, I can be open, and honest, and myself with her.

"What does a straight and narrow life after prison look like? Did you ask your dad? He seems to be on it."

"I should." Why have Dad and I not talked about it? I haven't asked, and he hasn't offered. Not like we had lengthy heart-to-hearts while I was staying with him. "But you've met Dad. He's not one to chat. I've learned more about his life from the questions and answers during these interviews."

Last year brought so much change it might as well be a lifetime. Ten years without Dad. One year with Dad. My life has sped up since he called Mom and asked to talk. If not for Dad trying to reconnect with us, I would've never thought of spending Christmas in LA last year. Never met Sarah. Never known what giving my heart to a girl means. The love I've made fun of with my hockey bros in movies is a thing that happens. Hits you over the head. Steals your breath. Hurts you and heals you.

"Parents are tough sometimes." With her ear over my heart, she can hear every erratic beat, and I'm not embarrassed. "The closest people we have and yet complete mysteries. Things didn't go so well with my mom either."

"Why not? Isn't she happy for you?"

"Maybe." Sarah snuggles closer and my hand slips to her waist. "But I missed our family get-together. She made it seem like I was abandoning her."

"You couldn't pass up this chance."

"Exactly. But I'm glad I went. Seeing them, seeing the nature around Mémère's cottage, my soul is fuller. I'll find a way to make it up to her."

With an alarm set to wake us up with plenty of time for her to get to her new job on time, Sarah sleeps in my arms, and I fall into the best slumber now that she's back by my side.

# ELEVEN

## Sarah

Two black coffees, a vanilla chai latte, a cappuccino, and three lattes leave one spot on the two trays I balance in my hands. The third coffee run of the day makes me wonder what the staff writers' salaries are, because I for sure can't afford spending five bucks a pop three times a day on fancy drinks. Maybe they get a caffeine allowance no one has told me about. Another thing no one has told me about. If not for Karina, I'd be crying every night after work.

"Don't forget to put your phone on do not disturb," Karina whispers as I hand her one of the black coffees. Yesterday after coming back with their lunch orders, Nick called in the middle of a heated discussion about the viability of our female lead being able to swing a broadsword, and everyone stared at me. Rod ignored me for the rest of the day.

I get a nod as I place Rod's latte beside his laptop. "We need something sexy. Something the fans will tweet about. The exes need a splash to get the show renewed for season two."

With the rest of the drinks dispersed, I take my seat and open my laptop.

Mémère trained me how to be a server the summer after my thirteenth birthday. Tending to our regulars at the little café attached to the bakery was my way of pacifying Mom's need for me to be part of the family business. Plus, the tips paid for my movie marathons at the Cineplex Odeon. I continued appeasing Mom by going for a Small Business Management degree at Humber College. She was thrilled I'd be able to learn valuable skills I could apply to running the bakery.

My mornings and afternoons were for school, so I switched to bartending in the evenings to get cash. Dad's friend hired me without even an interview. I'm a quick study, but he was an excellent teacher. He loved to experiment, and his guidance is the reason I can pour a perfect pint, mix an Old Fashioned, and create a million other concoctions.

No one is guiding me here. Everyone assumes I know what's expected of a temporary junior writer. How to take notes. Where to procure new markers for the dry erase board. And how to call a zoo to find out what a lion's diet is like. Googling the random pieces of trivia for the show is not enough. When the writers want some information verified, I must go to credible sources, not online blogs. To experts in the field, not Wikipedia.

Rod points to Karina. "Look up the top ten most shocking scenes in TV history."

"Just type anything they say, and we'll sort it out later." Karina speaks out of the side of her mouth at me as she taps on her laptop.

I scan the notes she took for me while Rod paces, waiting for an answer. The room listens as Karina reads out the list, including a shootout, a wedding massacre, and a plane crash. The last one makes the hair on my neck rise as bile swirls in my stomach. I still have disturbing dreams about my Valentine's Day flight. This is not what I imagined I'd be doing at nine in the evening on a Friday night.

"No, those are all overdone. We need to make Kyle look like a movie star." Rod looks around the room at everyone but me. "C'mon. Give me something people."

"How about a car chase?" Rod's stare makes me regret speaking. Not the time, Sarah. Not the time.

"Too expensive." And I'm dismissed. "Let's not make this more complicated than necessary." He stretches. "That's enough for today. I think it's time for me to get something alcoholic into my system." There's a round of cheers from the other writers.

Rod throws the mostly full coffee into the trash. The lid flies off, and the milky liquid sprays out of the can and on the floor. "Clean this up, Connor, would you?"

Once again, the after-work drinks invite does not include me. Or Karina, as she hangs back and helps me clear the table of any sensitive material that can't be left lying around. "Are you still happy I recommended you for the job?" Karina collects the assorted sticky notes off the floor from under the rolling chairs.

"Of course I am." I use my excited-to-be-here voice to not appear like an ungrateful brat.

"You don't have to pretend around me." Karina waits for me to finish taking the pictures of the whiteboard I'll have to translate into words before Monday morning. "I'm two years into working in the biz, and the two words I wrote that made it to the screen were 'merci beaucoup' because I was the only one who took French in high school and could spell it."

"You've been working for two years?" I ball up more napkins and mop the now-cooled spilled coffee. Although Karina's win hurt because it was not me, her screenplay was excellent. I read it in one evening and took notes on some of the things I could've done better. Sucks that her director messed a lot of it up.

"I started in high school. My performing arts school had agreements with several studios for internships." Karina sorts the stickies by color.

I wipe the final traces of Rod's scrawls off the whiteboard. "I'm so behind. I'm about to be twenty-three, and I'm at the first rung of the ladder." My hand shakes. My voice mimics it.

"Sure." She leans on the table and crosses her arms. "But you're on the ladder. You know what you want."

One of the things that drew me to Karina in the first place is her optimistic outlook. She reminds me of Mémère. Mémère came in a tiny package like me, whereas Karina is tall and lean with flawless brown skin worthy of a modeling career. "I want my characters to come alive on the screen and for the audience to believe they are real people. Because they are real to me."

Karina pushes off the table and swings an arm around my shoulder. "I'd drink to that."

"That's a good idea," I say. Nick won't be home for another hour or two. He's over at the frat house with Wil and Mateo bingeing some new car racing video game Mateo got an advanced copy of. Not my thing. I prefer real streets in a real sports car. "I'm too wound up to go home. Wanna grab a drink?

"Best idea you've had all night." She elbows me gently. "Where to?"

"Mind if we drop by my other job? Ryan's been texting me about moving into the apartment."

"Ryan?" Karina adjusts her glasses. "I thought Nick was your boyfriend. And he already lives with you."

"Nick *is* my boyfriend. Ryan is my work friend. Nick's moving into my room, and Ryan is taking his."

"And how is Ryan related to drinks?"

"He bartends at the same club I do. I can drive us there, and we can drink, talk, and pretend we are the screenwriters of our dreams."

❋   ❋   ❋

"This place is swanky." Karina stops to take a selfie by the illuminated blue of the pool with the shimmering lights of the hotel behind. "Do you get to use the facilities?"

I take her phone and snap a few pics of her with the cabanas as a backdrop. "One of the perks of working here. That and the tips."

"And the coworkers." Ryan, with a tray of drinks balanced in his hand, appears next to me.

"How could I forget? The coworkers are probably the main reason I've stuck around for so long." Unlike my current job, Rod might be regretting his choice. "We'll be at the bar." I give Ryan an awkward side hug, careful not to touch the arm that's holding probably over two hundred dollars' worth of booze.

"*That* is Ryan?" Karina ogles Ryan as he strolls away. "Are you a lamp that attracts hot guys? I know Nick is cute and all, but Ryan is a lot more my type."

"Ryan is . . ." Blond, blue-eyed, well-built, above average height, nice to look at. The main reason Mrs. Marino probably hired him in the first place. Most definitely not for his bartending or server skills. ". . . a good guy."

"Is that a do-not-touch warning for me?" Karina threads her arm through mine. "Just say the word. I'm good with girl code. Not going to try for someone who's off-limits."

I laugh. "Nothing like that. We used to . . . sorta date? But go for it."

"You make it sound like I won't get far with him."

I steer Karina toward two seats at the end of the bar. "It's just that I have not seen him with anyone since we switched to being friends. Every day multiple girls try."

Karina glances over her shoulder. "D'you think he's still carrying a torch for you?"

"He's not. No worries there. Just don't get your hopes up. Ryan is a good guy, but he's complicated." Aside from the lack of dating, there are other aspects of Ryan I've never addressed, including my growing suspicions that he's a lot smarter than he leads people to believe.

The poolside bar is mostly empty. Although the heater lamps are out and there's no wind today, the balmy upper fifties are not cozy enough for most patrons to stick to the outdoor seating. Makes sense why Ryan is running the drinks to the restaurant. As if on cue, Ryan reappears with an empty tray.

"Can I talk to you?" He indicates the end of the bar.

I step away from Karina and follow Ryan. "Is it about the move?"

Ryan leans in. "I might need to pay the rent a bit later than I promised," he whispers. "But I can score you and Nick a free hotel room for his birthday as a temporary payment, help free up some cash."

"Sure. Don't worry." I nudge his shoulder. This I can do. The first thing I don't have to worry about botching today. My head is lighter. "Once you're back on your feet we'll get even."

Ryan's eyes fall to his hands. "Ah, your friend is staring at me."

"Sorry. Karina-Ryan, Ryan-Karina." They nod at each other. "Karina is the one who got me the writing job."

Ryan gives Karina an appraising look. "Karina . . . what's your last name?"

"Would you like my address and social security number as well?" Karina plays with her dangling earrings made from actual pencils.

He misses the flyball Karina sent his way. "I can get those myself if you give me your last name." Ryan tends to blurt out the truth in the most awkward way. He'll probably be able to get me a whole dossier on her by tomorrow.

"How about you give me your phone and I'll add my first and last name?" She gives him that eye twinkle thing she does. "Oh, and my number, and IG handle, so you can DM me any time. "

"I'm not on socials. And I have a great memory." Ryan's still smiling at Karina from over the bar, but he's caught on now. Just like with countless girls before, he's not interested, and he's making it politely but very clearly known.

Karina rattles off her phone number, which I'm confident Ryan will remember but not ever use. "Got all that?"

"Yup." Ryan taps his temple. "Locked away."

"I wish I had your brain." I mimic his tapping but on *my* temple. "I'd be able to work so much faster."

"'Cause you need to memorize Rod's coffee orders quicker?" Karina snickers.

I look at her. "Because I've decided to start working on my next screenplay. I've been thinking about the scam I lost money to when I arrived and decided I can channel what happened to me and use it to write a script."

"OMG, Sarah." She places a hand on my arm. "That's brilliant. You could totally fictionalize it, and that could be like an awesome thriller or something. Love that for you."

We order drinks and spitball scenarios for my new screenplay. Karina and I talk over each other as we brainstorm what our heroine does when she finds her money is gone. We argue over how she'd choose between giving up or trying to make it in LA. Would she decide to return home or keep following her dream?

I pull out my phone to take some notes about the idea, and the additional romance plotline Karina assures me is a must in any blockbuster. A series of texts from Nick and three missed calls from him are the first thing I see. Shit. I forgot to remove the do not disturb. I check the time. It's almost 1 a.m.

His last text was at 12:15 a.m..

Nick: Hope you're not working too hard. Going to bed. Wake me when you get in.

Guilt colors my world, knowing he stayed awake and will be up at five a.m.. My finger hovers over the call button. If we talk now that'll help me feel less in the wrong, but it'll rob him of much needed sleep. I set my alarm to five to wake him up with a kiss and remind him why I'm not the worst girlfriend ever.

# Twelve

# NICK

Every interview session at Terminal Island brings us closer to the end of the first phase of the documentary. We have three more people to go, and then we wait for them to be released. To go home. Or to transitional housing. I won't get multiple takes of them walking out of this place. Can Dad use another camera? Or maybe Sarah can run it if she's free for any of the releases. I zoom in on Nazhir, the tall thin man doesn't look like someone who steals other people's identities. Or did. He insists he's reformed now.

"What are your plans for the first month after you get out?" Dad's back to his interviewer pose: fingers interlaced, eyes trained on the inmate across the table.

I still haven't worked up the nerve to ask Dad about what his life was like in prison, never mind what he did when he got out.

The words catch behind my teeth. Why did it take him five years to reach out to Mom and me?

"Visit my parole officer?" One side of Nazhir's mouth hooks to the left: half smile, half grimace.

"Good plan." Dad leans in, and his profile catches on the corner of the frame. I adjust the camera to center on Nazhir. "Do you have a support system outside? The first few weeks out . . . can be difficult."

My ears absorb every word Dad says. Questions remain trapped in my mouth like fish in a net. Difficult how? What was his release day like?

Nazhir sniffs. "Some relatives in Eureka."

"Any work lined up? A way to make money?"

"My former classmate said he'd find me something at an auto shop. I'm handy. And the classes here were good."

"Don't be too picky," says Dad. "Money is money. Take whatever you can at first. You can switch later."

"Is that what happened to you?"

Dad sits back. "We're not talking about me." Crap. His refusal hardens the hope I'll learn more into a ball of defeat at the base of my throat. Just when we were getting somewhere. "You're out . . ." Dad checks his index cards. Aside from the questions, he's also created one for each of the inmates we've interviewed. Key information like family associations, living arrangements, and release dates. ". . . on November first, right?"

Nazhir nods. "New month, new life."

"That's one way to look at it." Dad pauses, and his head shifts ever so slightly in my direction. "But the things you've done, the . . . mistakes you've made, they're on record now. A part of you."

"I paid my debt to society." Nazhir shifts in his seat.

"Sure. But you don't get a clean slate, no matter what they sell you in the brochure. Your record will follow you wherever you go and tinge everything you do, every relationship you have, with the stain of your past. No amount of soap or penitence can wash it off. Your friends, your family, they will never look at you the same way."

Is this what Dad really thinks? He must know it's not true. Ms. Hansley doesn't seem to mind his past. She seemed almost eager to help him out, give him a second chance. If Mom were here, she'd hug him. I still my arms from reaching out to him. I'd hug him too if he'd let me. She's already planning to come to LA for Thanksgiving to be with both of us. I'm not sure who she wants to see more, me or Dad.

I've forgiven him, haven't I? The thought rolls around in my head, searching for confirmation. The calm beating of my heart when I think *forgiven* reassures me that Dad and I are in the clear. Maybe I haven't exactly told him, but I moved to LA to be closer to him. Okay, to Sarah now as well, but originally—for him. That must count for something.

Nazhir looks like he might throw up. There's a knock at the door, and Guzman barges in. "Time's up."

I have no sense of time inside the prison. Sometimes minutes seem like hours. Today hours seem like minutes.

We repack our stuff at the security check-in and pile into the car. Dad doesn't say a word. The drive to Sarah's apartment isn't that long. My chest tightens and I adjust the seatbelt, but it's not the problem. I want to ask Dad so much, but I don't know where to start. Looking for a perfect time hasn't paid off. I rub at the knot in my middle. We're trapped in his Toyota for a while longer. The worst thing he could do is shout at me or continue with his silence. It's now or never. "What did you do your first month out of prison?"

One hand on the steering wheel, Dad rubs his chin with the other. "I . . . I don't remember. It was a long time ago."

That's a crock of bull, and he and I both know it. I straighten in my seat, breathe into the pain his non-answer is inflicting. He all but admitted to Nazhir he had a hard time when he got out. "Did you have a support system?"

"Sure, kid."

Who were they? Not Mom. Not Mike. Not me. Why not us? "Why did you wait to reach out to Mom until last year?"

"Nicky, why do you drag up that shit? Can't we just focus on the future?"

"Sorry I asked." The swirling under my ribcage goes from a dull ache to sharp pangs. He can be honest and open with a total stranger. A criminal. But when I want a morsel of truth, emotion from the man, I get the brush-off. I pinch the bridge of my nose hard enough to override the tsunami in my chest. "It's Nick, not Nicky."

"Right. I forgot."

He drops me off at the apartment, and I take the steps two at a time to the fourth floor. All I want is to wrap my arms around Sarah and not think about prisons, or coffee orders, or the test in film history I have tomorrow that I'm not ready for. That's a lie. I know most of the movies already, even though memorizing the dates is something I need to work on.

But not tonight. I'm buzzing. Maybe if I get up at four a.m. tomorrow I can study. Tonight is about Sarah. My heart beats faster. Between her new job and the few weekend shifts she switched to at The Diamond Club, we've barely seen each other. She crawls into bed at one or two in the morning, and I crawl out of bed at five a.m. to open Blend. We've been like ships passing in the night. But I checked, and tonight we're both free. My fingers tingle at the promise of touching her. We'll order in, watch a movie, and make out. Or just make out. I'm good with that.

I near the door to our apartment, and my hopes of alone time with Sarah waver at the cackle of Siobhan's laughter. I walk into a scene from a sitcom: Siobhan, Karina, Ryan, and Sarah are sitting around the kitchen table, bottles of beer circling the now-empty bag of chips I bought for us yesterday.

"And then he picks his nose with the same finger." Karina holds a digit in the air, and the occupants of the table roar with laughter. Sarah is in tears. My irritation at finding her surrounded by a crowd of people wanes. She looks so happy, having a good time with her friends.

She sees me, and my heart skips a beat as her eyes light up. "Nick." She tugs on my shirt for me to dip down so she can kiss me. I happily oblige. Her lips taste of beer and salt. I savor her.

"Good timing." Siobhan takes a swig of beer. "We just finished moving Ryan's stuff in."

I unlock my lips from Sarah's but can't quite let her go. I glance at my surfing buddy. "You found a place? Where?" I keep my arm around Sarah's shoulders, pinning her to me.

She pulls me over to the table, sits me in her chair, and climbs on my lap. Blood rushes to parts of my body I was planning to use when we're alone. "Your room."

I rewind to a sleepy conversation in bed when I was definitely not thinking about Ryan. We joked about me forgetting what my room looked like but didn't talk about renting out my space. Annoyance resurfaces and drags down the lightness of seeing Sarah laugh. "My room?"

"Yes." Sarah drapes her arm around my neck. "Remember, we chatted about Ryan looking for a place to stay?" I crumple the empty chip bag in my fist. Why do I feel like a squatter in an apartment I pay my share of rent for? Sarah draws circles on my bicep. "I moved your stuff into my room."

She moved me into *her* room? Me in her room . . . this was not part of the plan. I'm mad at her for not asking me first, but the end result is something I can't be too upset about. I tuck my exasperation away. Even though I've spent every night since the Gala in her bed, today she made it official. There's no way she can get rid of me now. This new living arrangement holds a whole other level of wonders and possibilities. I bite my lip to stop my smile. "Our room then?"

Sarah beams.

"Thanks, dude, for letting me crash." Ryan tips his Coke in my direction.

"Yeah. Happy to help." Being closer to Sarah and making her happy—that's what counts.

"Karina was just telling us about the one time they let her on set and one of the extras was picking his nose on camera." Siobhan imitates by thrusting her finger on the outside of her nostril and mimicking excessive digging.

"And it wasn't part of the script." Karina takes a breath between her giggles. "Awkward."

"Reminds me of the teenager who had the hots for Sarah." Siobhan wiggles her eyebrows, and Sarah squirms in my lap. I'm a teenager for a couple more weeks. I still and try not to let the irritation that was heating up earlier escape.

"Dude tried everything to ask Sarah out." Ryan twists one of the silver rings on his hand.

Sarah hides her nose in the crook of my neck. "So very awkward." I hold her closer, protect her from the story she doesn't want to hear. But she's laughing along with them. "After I said no a million times, he'd sit at the end of the bar, nurse his Coke, and try to accidentally bump into me."

Ryan snorts. The most uncool thing I've ever seen him do. "I had to go into my bodyguard mode and escort him off the premises."

They swap more stories. Some are funny, some are only funny to them, all of them have nothing to do with me. Sarah remains on my lap, sipping her beer and running her fingers through the hair at the nape of my neck. I caress her hip, soaking up the chance to touch her. My stomach growls. "We should order food."

"Oh." Sarah's hand halts. "We already had dinner. Ryan brought sushi. I saved you some. It's in the fridge."

Ryan looks up. "A thank you to the girls for letting me stay here on such short notice." The girls and me. I live here too. Hot bubbles of annoyance surge back up. "It's their fave." Ryan gestures a thank you in Siobhan's direction.

Don't I know it. Sarah and Siobhan eat sushi like I used to eat Mom's chicken souvlaki—any chance I got. I've never eaten so much fish in my life. And especially not raw fish.

"Thanks." I lift Sarah off my lap to find a Coke in the fridge, but there's nothing except ginger ale. "Did you move my Coke too?"

"Sorry, dude, Sarah said I could have the last one." Ryan stands and stretches, his shirt rising to show off his perfect six pack. First, she gives him my room, now she gives him my Coke. The simmer of emotions I've been pushing down heats to a rolling boil.

"Remember the elderly guy who only drank vodka?" Ryan watches Sarah and Siobhan exchange oh-no glances.

They launch into another story I know nothing about. I slam the fridge and walk past the laughing group. I'm going to say something I'll regret if I don't leave their little private party now. "I need a shower."

If anyone is listening, they don't acknowledge it. I switch on the shower and hope the hot water hitting my back can counterbalance the steam gathering inside me.

# THIRTEEN

## Sarah

"So, what do you think?" Rod yells in my ear over the chatter of the crowded bar as he slides into the empty space in the booth beside me.

It's the first time he's invited me out for the post-writing-room drinks, and I hate to admit I'm freaking nervous. I have no idea what Rod's referring to. I rub my finger against the seam on my jeans. Confident Sarah hasn't been around much. Everything I do lately feels unfamiliar and off. The rough ridge catches on a crack in my nail. I tuck my thumb inside my fist. Does he mean the round of martinis he bought the gang? The karaoke place he insisted we try? The other writers who are crooning Sinatra classics?

I go with honesty. "About what?"

Teeth that glow in the murky light of the bar flash at me. "The show. The job. The other writers. What we wrote today. All of it. I want to know what's going on in there." He taps a finger against my forehead, and I resist the urge to swat his palm away.

This guy holds my fate in his hands. As head writer, he has the power to extend my contract and keep me on the show. I've been trying to find a way to impress him for days, but whenever I speak up, he always shuts me down. Karina says Rod was the same with her.

Yet here he is, asking me what I think. Should I do what the other writers do and kiss his ass? The truth worked a moment ago, so I go with it again. "The show is smart and funny while still managing to make the lives of a gang of vampires seem real."

He nods and sips his martini.

"The job is great. I love it." Okay, I go with a little ass-kissing. So far, I've basically been doing more of the things I do at The Diamond Club, just add in notetaking and take away the tips. I get coffee, clean up after the team, and watch others do the thing I want to do.

I survey the table of people around us drinking, and laughing, and chatting. "It's a good team. Everyone seems to gel and feed off each other."

"Yeah, they're good eggs." He crosses his arms and slouches in the booth. "They'll learn to accept you. It just takes writers a while to warm up to someone new. They want to know you're in it for the long haul. That you're going fit in."

"Haven't you heard? Good things come in small packages. I may be tiny, but I have big ideas." This is my chance, so I go for it. "Like in the scene we wrote today. I think it's a mistake to go with the giant SUV for Kyle's car chase." Despite the fact that I suggested a chase scene last week, the room got excited when the idea came up again this morning. Seems Rod liked it better coming from one of the other writers. "It's just . . . not sexy."

"Interesting." He puts down his drink and angles toward me. "That makes sense. But we don't have the budget for the big names. There's insurance to think about. If Kyle or one of the crew gets a scratch on one, it could shut us down."

"I think we could find an older muscle car. There are a number of classic car groups in LA, and they might lend us one." I think about Mateo. He might loan us his car. "Corvettes are so recognizable, have tinted windows, and it'll give Kyle more personality. He's a hundred-year-old vampire, he can't drive around in a boxy SUV."

Rod looks interested, so I keep going. "Plus, think of the cool close-ups of Kyle where we can play up that he's not actually twenty-five. He appreciates the best of each decade he's lived through."

Rod beams at me. "Look who's thinking through the back-story."

His admiration gives me confidence. "Don't we have to? We need hooks to play with in future seasons. These . . . trophies Kyle keeps, they can have an impact. Like the mockingjay pin Katniss receives as a good luck charm at the beginning of Hunger Games. It's in every book, pinned to her chest, and then it plays a key role in the finale. We want that payoff."

*Careful, Sarah, don't get ahead of yourself. He hasn't agreed to even keep you on past this season.*

Rod bumps my shoulder. "I think you're going to go far, Connor."

Riding high on the conversation with Rod from last night, I get into work early and set up the room. I know where the markers are. I made enough copies of the new version of the script, and my laptop is on, ready to track the changes. Coffees are sitting in front of each of the writers' favorite spots around the table as everyone mills in.

Rod is the last person to arrive. "Okay, folks, settle down. We have a lot to get through today. We need to map out episode twelve. That's a high-voltage scene, so we need to have fun and games. Also, I wanna take a look at what we wrote yesterday with the chase. I've reconsidered the car we have Kyle driving."

I sit up straight. Did he just use my idea? My heart gallops as I wait for him to ask me to explain my suggestion to the group.

"We have a hundred-year-old vampire, turned right when cars became all the rage, and he drives a boxy SUV. We have to make sure the stuff he surrounds himself with matches his backstory. Think big picture here, find a way to seed the older items he collected over his life as a vampire. Hook them into future seasons." It's my exact words coming out of Rod's mouth. I can barely sit still with excitement.

Rod surveys the room. His gaze falls on me last. Here we go. He's going to give me credit. "Connor, be ready to take notes. I want this documented."

No, he didn't. Acid burns in my gut. My fingers shake as they hover over the keyboard. What is happening? Is he stealing my idea? Right in front of me?

"You got that?" Rod dares me to speak up and claim the idea as mine in front of the group.

My throat is dry, and I try to get my mouth to open and say something. Say anything. I fail. All I can do is nod.

"Okay then." He turns back to the others. "Before we start, we'll be working through lunch. Everyone, text your orders to Connor."

When I get home, Nick is lying on the couch in the living room. He jumps up as soon as I enter. I place my hand on his chest and tug on his shirt. He immediately dips down to my level so I can kiss him. He doesn't hesitate, and his lips are like a balm for my mood. I give in to his touch, letting it consume me.

Stale coffee cups, stolen scripts, and a storm of dissatisfaction fade away in the arms of my favorite person. I shouldn't give

Nick this much control over me, but at this moment, I just need him. He's always here for me.

As if he can sense I need a little more than our usual hello kiss, he wraps his arms around my shoulders and engulfs me in a cocoon of security. The pressure of him against my skin intensifies as my back hits the door, and I'm completely sheltered from the world by the wall of Nick. This is where I want to be.

Even when the kiss ends, his arms don't let go. He tucks me into him, his chin landing on the top of my head. "How's my girl?"

His words break the bubble of denial, and the truth is on the tip of my tongue. I want to say, "Shit. My boss stole my work. He hates me, and I'm never going to make it in this business." But I don't intend to waste our precious time together complaining about my supposed dream job. I don't want to burden him with my silly worries.

I take the pain, angst, and doubts, roll them into a little ball, and tuck it away behind my heart. I focus on the good. "Much better now I'm with you."

"Did you eat?" I feel the words reverberating through his chest where I'm pressed against him.

"I had a bag of chips around three o'clock. Does that count?"

He kisses the top of my head. "No. You have to eat properly." Another squeeze, and I almost forget about my shit day. "Good thing I made us dinner."

I push away from his chest and look up, way up, into his soft eyes. "You did what?"

"Don't look so shocked. I'm capable of boiling water, throwing in pasta, and heating up a jar of tomato sauce. Didn't even call Mom for instructions." He grins. "It's nothing fancy, but it's food. I stopped at the farmers' market on campus and picked up some veg for a salad. Plus the fresh country loaf you like."

"You are the best boyfriend ever." Nick's eyes shine at my words, and I want him to be this happy forever.

"That's the goal." He takes my hand and leads me to the kitchen table set for dinner, including napkins and a vase with sunflowers.

"Did I miss something? Is it our anniversary or something?"

"No. I just felt like spoiling you." I do feel spoiled. Since moving out on my own, I've had to do everything by myself. Love for Nick seeps deeper into my heart. His care nourishes me just as much as the food he prepared. Nick pulls plates from the cupboard. "Both Siobhan and Ryan are working tonight. I think this is the first time we've been alone in . . ."

"Forever?"

His smile is infectious, and I feel the woes of the day slip away. "Dinner was the best I could come up with."

"It's exactly what I need."

A plate of piping hot pasta arrives, and Nick pulls up a chair beside me. "Tell me about your day."

"Same old." I twirl the pasta on my fork. "Are you free Friday night?"

Nick pauses his fork midway to his mouth and nods. "Yup. Date night?"

"Not exactly. It's my boss's birthday, and we're taking him out for dinner. I thought you could come."

"Weren't you out late last night?"

"The whole gang goes out after work almost every night. I've finally been invited to join, and it's kinda unofficially mandatory. A lot happens after hours." Like hitting me up for ideas and then stealing them. Anger bubbles back up but I push it away. "I don't wanna miss out."

"If it's a work thing, does the company cover the expense?"

"I wish. But Karina says it's like when you pay for parking. Part of the pleasure of doing business." I bite the piece of bread. The buttery flavor melts on my tongue and my heart flutters. Nick made the extra trip just for me. "I spent sixty dollars last night on drinks and food. The bartender did a half-ass job on my Ramos Gin Fizz. That it lacked the fizz was the least of the problems. But I don't get to control where we go. I suggested The Diamond Club, but Rod didn't want to drive that far."

"He's missing out. I happen to know The Diamond Club has the best bartender in town." I smile at Nick's compliment, but it makes my heart ache. Is that all I'm good for? Mixology and small talk?

"So, you'll come?"

Nick takes my hand in his. "Anything for you."

# Fourteen

# NICK

The table is on their sixth or seventh round of drinks. I lost count after Rod, the birthday boy, or man, I should say, made a face and insisted everyone have sake with their sushi.

"No way. Vampires can't get trunk…" Sarah giggles. "I mean drunk." She leans in and lifts a tiny glass I didn't think capable of doing so much damage in such a short time.

"Oh, do you know any personally?" Rod taps his glass of alcohol against hers.

I stare at the three tiny bottles of Coke in front of me that cost as much as the sake but doesn't have the same kick. The sugar isn't helping me stay awake, but I'm not missing a minute of Sarah and me being in the same place. Even surrounded by all her coworkers, at least I can hold her hand.

The server puts the bill on the table.

Rod extends his hand as Karina tries to capture the little black plastic tray. "You can't pay for your own birthday dinner."

Rod snatches it up.

Some of the folks make a weak protest.

"Who says I'm paying for it?" Rod smiles at the table. He hands the folder to Sarah. "Last one in has to pay." My fingers curl into a fist under the table. He's been monopolizing her all night, drawing my girlfriend into conversations and drinks I can't be part of. Now he wants her to pay for this ridiculously expensive dinner?

"Oh." Sarah moves for the bill, but her fingers miss the folder. I've never really seen her this way. There's alcohol in the apartment, but maybe because of me she rarely drinks.

She narrows her eyes and tries for it again, but Rod pulls back at the last moment. "Kidding. Clear Productions owes us all a night out after how hard we've been working. They got this."

The table cheers, and I play along. The salmon nigiri Sarah insisted I eat churns in my stomach. The urge to get up and leave rolls over me, but I'm here with her, for her, and not these inebriated writers. I zero in on the feel of her skin under my palm. Old Nicky knows how to fit into a group and get along with everyone. The persona is like a dark cape I put on, but it doesn't make me a superhero. More like a villain. Can't wait for this dinner to be over, so I can rip it off and get back to the real me. The next barrage of jokes rounds the table, and I chuckle like I give a damn.

"Let's do karaoke!" Karina bounces up and down after sliding out of her seat. The others cheer, and I suppress a groan. I want to go home. I'm opening Blend in less than seven hours and need to get some sleep.

"Great idea." Rod pushes away from the table. "You in, Connor?"

Sarah threads her fingers through mine and tugs on my shirt. Our sign for me to lean in for a kiss. I happily oblige, and she pecks me on the cheek. "Can we?"

Warmth spreads across my chest at her use of "we." We are in this together. Of course, we are. I may've been feeling like an outsider tonight, but I'd do anything for Sarah.

Like sing karaoke, apparently. I stifle my yawn. "I'm in if you want to."

Her bright slightly glassy eyes sparkle in the low light of this overpriced sushi bar. "It'll be fun. You'll see." Sounds like she's done this before. The ease I felt a moment ago seeps away and my stomach flips back to turmoil. Is this how she spends her nights relaxing after a script session?

The air outside is surprisingly balmy for mid-October, and even though it's past eleven p.m., we dodge cars to cross the busy Westwood Boulevard. A whole new breed of people come out after eleven in West LA. A breed of people I don't see because I'm usually in bed.

Rod, Karina, and the other writers are laughing and shouting in front of us. As we make our way down the crowded sidewalk, Sarah leans on me. Parched for her nearness, I gulp these few moments with her, just the two of us. She's my drink of choice.

The minutes of her undivided attention are intoxicating yet fleeting. There's never enough time.

Magenta neon frames the entranceway to The Pink Flamingo Karaoke and Kraft. So does a wall of muscles I tower over but wouldn't want to go up against. Everyone files into the place, but a meaty hand on my chest stops me. "ID."

Sarah comes back. "Kurt. This is my boyfriend, Nick." Kurt? Sarah knows the bouncer's name? Sharp prickles radiate from my heart into my chest. How often do they come here? "He's not twenty-one, but I promise he won't drink."

Kurt looks me up and down. I should do something to smooth over this situation. Nicky would know what to say, but the oily words stick to my tongue. It's like the bouncer is assessing my qualifications as Sarah's boyfriend, not my age. The brawny man frowns. The lump in my throat threatens to suffocate me. Did I just fail?

"Connor." Rod stands half in shadow. "You coming?"

Sarah's hand slips from mine as she aims her sunny smile his way. "Be right there."

"I can't sing *I Got You, Babe* without my singing partner." Rod waves at her to get in.

If I have my way, he won't be singing with her at all. Even if I have to get up and embarrass myself and her by what Mom calls my "toneless renditions."

"Can't let the underaged in past eleven," says Kurt.

I shuffle my feet and look at my hands. My stupid nineteen-year-old hands that can't go into a bar with my girlfriend.

"Come on." Sarah leans against the wall inside the entrance, Kurt between me and her. She does that thing I've seen her do at The Diamond Club to appease customers who are being unruly: tilts her head slightly and looks into his eyes, her fake smile offering encouragement. "Can't you make an exception this one time? Please?" She puts her finger on the center of Kurt's chest and draws a heart over his heart.

I grit my teeth and swallow the lump in my throat. Sarah shouldn't have to do this for me. I'm making things worse.

"Are you in or are you out?" two girls say from behind me, snickering.

Time to admit I've failed. I pull Sarah to the other side. "You go. Have fun with your friends. I'll head home."

"No." My Thumbelina stomps her foot and pouts. "I want to sing with you."

My jaw relaxes at her whining. I must admit it's kinda cute. She's cute. "I don't have a good voice. You need to make nice with your boss." I point my chin in the direction of the bar. "This is your chance. Go have fun, and we'll sing together next time."

Sarah shakes her head at me and disappears into the gloom of the karaoke club. Every cell in my body yearns to follow her, but Kurt raises his eyebrow in a don't-even-think-about-it way. The laughter of another group of customers entering the club grates at me, and with a nod at Kurt, I leave to go home. Alone.

I pull out my phone to call a ride-share. It's a thirty-minute wait. Great. What am I supposed to do now? I lean against the window of a closed clothing shop and stare up at the starless sky. My body aches from moving boxes of coffee this morning and general lack of sleep. Sarah likes to sleep on the side of the bed against the wall, but it leaves me on the edge. If I'm not having a nightmare about falling out of bed, it's actually happening. Like this morning.

"Mr. Old Fashioned." Sarah's skipping down the sidewalk. Her golden hair is like a halo around her beautiful face. She slams into me, and I wrap my arms around her to keep her from falling. "Where do you think you're going?"

I steady her on her feet but keep her close, welcoming her softness. "What are you doing? You can't leave Rod and the gang."

"I can. I want to spend time with my boyfriend." Her words are a bit slurred, but they slide into the little crack in my heart, filling it with joy. She chose me.

"Are you sure?"

Sarah's head jerks back, and it takes a moment for her gaze to focus on me. "Never been more sure." Does she mean tonight, about missing the karaoke, or is there more to her words? I want there to be more. There's more for me. I'm sure about her.

I lean down, press my lips against her cheek, then hide my face in her hair. Strawberry aroma invades my lungs. Her tiny frame melts into me, and my worries, concerns, and frustrations of the day evaporate. There is nothing like holding Sarah. "I'm sure too."

Her hands dive into my hair, and Sarah's mouth finds mine. I taste the sting of the sake and the sweetness of her that I'm addicted to. She takes me from a one to a ten on the desire scale in less than sixty seconds, and I'm lost in her smile, her kiss, her curves.

"Get a room." A gruff voice breaks the spell Sarah has me under. We are making out on the sidewalk of Westwood Boulevard. I pry my lips from her sweet skin. A room sounds like a great idea to me.

"I wanna dance." Sarah announces as she lets go of me. She puts her finger on my chest and draws a slow line until she finds the waist of my jeans. Her digit slips inside, and she tugs me off the wall. "Let's go dancing."

My stomach lurches. I doubt there's a club in town that will let me in. I wish I had my fake ID right about now. I've never wanted to be twenty-one more in my life. In a few days I'll turn twenty, but that's not close enough. Once I'm legal, nothing is going to stop me from giving Sarah everything she wants.

"We can dance at home." I tuck her hair behind her ear.

She pouts. "Nope. I want to dance where everyone can see my sexy boyfriend."

I try to suppress a grin, but it's so hard when she says things like that. Girls in high school told me I'm handsome, but she makes me feel like James Bond or Captain America.

Her eyes gleam with mischief. "I know. Let's go to the pier. They have music there."

My smart, smart girl. The pier is open to the public. No age restrictions. How did I ever get so lucky? "It'll take a while to get a ride-share."

"We can walk." She links her arm through mine and pulls me along. A wicked grin crosses her face. "Or dance." She takes my hand, holds it over her head, and twirls herself underneath it.

When she stops, she sways back and forth, and I put my other hand on her waist to steady her. The contact with her skin sends tingles up my spine and into my heart. "Maybe we wait until we get there for the dancing bit." I grin at her. "Walking is enough for now."

Her head rests on my chest, and her slender arms wrap around me as she lets me take the lead. Bubbles of joy, comfort, and lust fizz across my collar bone. There'll be no sleep for me tonight, and I don't care. Sarah wants to dance, and I can't say no to her.

# FIFTEEN

## Sarah

I've forgotten how different attending a real hockey game is. No announcer giving you the play-by-play. The sounds of the skates scraping the ice. The whistle of the referee. The collective stillness of the crowd as a player flies toward the net. The roar when he shoots and scores.

"Yes." Nick jumps to his feet and claps for Chicago as they increase their lead by another goal. He takes off his black hat featuring the red and white stripes of his team and waves it like a flag. I opted to leave my Leafs attire at home—no need to cause confusion. I do go as far as to stand and cheer. He hollers in celebration, and I whoop, brimming with his joy. Girlfriend duties.

Nick folds himself into the stadium seat, his knees pressed against the plastic seat of the fan in front of him. I couldn't afford the best seats at the Crypto.com Arena, but we are mid-ice, so the view isn't that bad. Back home we have the perfect seats for our annual Leafs New Year's Eve game. They are in the golds, so not as expensive as the platinum, but right behind the goalie. I love the view from there.

"Mom and Dad say happy birthday, by the way."

"Oh." Nick's intent on the puck as a forward makes a break-away.

I wait for the play to end. The ref's whistle. "And I'm going to be naked."

That gets his attention. Goosebumps sprint under my sweater. Big brown eyes size me up as if he's deciding if I'm serious. His oh-so-delicious hands bracket my face, and he presses a kiss against my lips. "I love your sense of humor."

If he only knew.

"Get your beer here. Ice cold beer." My tastebuds salivate. Beer and hockey go together like strawberries and cream, but instead of flagging the vendor down, I wrap my hand around Nick's. He'll turn twenty tomorrow, not twenty-one. No beer for either of us.

"Do you want a beer?" Nick asks.

I shake my head. "But I'll take a pretzel."

The Kings win in the end, but Nick doesn't seem to be disappointed. "Those were great seats. Mike and I never got to see an NHL game as kids."

We file out into the corridors of the stadium. Outside, the press of the crowd pushes us, and I can't see a thing. I crush against Nick. His tall form breaks the flow, creating a space for me as people advance around him.

Someone steps on my toe. "Ouch." I know I'm small, but I'm not invisible.

"What's wrong?" Nick weaves us around a garbage can overflowing with used cups and half-empty bags of popcorn.

I get jostled by someone else and bump into Nick's chest. He pulls me against a wall, creating a pocket and bends down, pointing to his back. "Climb on."

Nick hoists me into the air for a piggyback. As I suspected, it's a whole other world when you're tall. My body buzzes, alive, sure, and brimming at our connection. We even each other out. With his support I can see over everyone's heads. From up here the crowd is jovial, people cheering and singing.

Unlike the last time he let me experience life as a tall person on the rooftop on the Fourth of July, I can enjoy running my finger along the stubble of his cheek. The rumble of his laugh reverberates through my chest.

I duck my head down as we go through the stadium doors into the fresh October night. Nick heads toward the subway. "Wait." My heart hums with anticipation.

"Something wrong?"

I nuzzle the hair at the nape of his neck, hoping to ease the concern in his voice. I tug on his ear with my teeth and whisper. "Everything's great. But we're not going back to the apartment just yet."

"Okay." Nick repositions me on his back, and for the briefest of moments I'm weightless. Strong arms support me as I settle back against him. "Where to, then?"

I point in the opposite direction. The best part of the night starts now. "Over there."

We wind our way down the street, the crowd of hockey fans petering out the farther we get from the arena. There's a small ledge outside the Indigo Hotel. When Ryan had told me the name of the hotel, I laughed. It was too perfect. "You can put me down."

"But I like carrying you."

"Don't think we can make it through the revolving doors like this." Nick sets me on the ledge. I use his shoulders to steady myself, and we are almost eye-to-eye.

His hands wrap around my waist, and he kisses the tip of my nose. I sway. "Why are we going into the hotel?"

"I got us a room for tonight," I say. Nick's eyes widen, and I bounce up and down. "Happy Birthday."

"What?"

"I know we're doing the group dinner thing tomorrow, but I thought you and I could start your birthday early. Just the two of us."

A slow smile spreads across his face and sends my stomach fluttering. "Isn't this a bit . . . expensive?"

"Ryan found a discount code"—his smile slips a little, and I barge forward—"and upgraded us to a suite. It has a Jacuzzi tub."

The world slides sideways as Nick spins me around. He places me back on the ledge, looks up at the stars, and hollers, "I have the best girlfriend in the world."

A passerby grumbles, "Get a room."

That's the point. We both giggle. I hop off the platform, grab Nick's hand, and pull him toward the entrance. My feet are too slow and can't keep up with my heart. "Stop wasting time."

The elevator takes forever, and if we weren't sharing it with an elderly couple, I'd have Nick half undressed by now. I rock back and forth on my heels, and Nick settles his arm on my shoulders to keep me from jumping out of my skin. They ride the whole way to the twenty-third floor and follow us down the hall.

My fingers don't listen to me as I jam the key card into the lock. The light blinks red. I repeat the motion, steadying my hand.

Red.

One more try.

I see green, and it's go time. I pull Nick through the doorway and slide my hands under his shirt. His skin's warm, and the hard angles make me consider abandoning my plan. He's the romantic, not me.

No. He likes to savor every step. Tonight is about him. I make myself slow down. We have all night. I pry my hands from his body, my lips from his, and back up. "Pretty nice, huh?"

Nick takes in the tiled entryway, gilded mirror on our left, another door on our right, and the lights of downtown LA twinkling behind the floor-to-ceiling window before us. "I could get used to this."

"Wait till you see the bed." I vibrate. This is it. I find his hand and guide him into the adjoining room where red rose petals pepper the biggest bed I've ever seen.

"Wow." Nick looks starry-eyed. My skin tingles. His joy courses through me and settles any doubts about splurging on this night. I might have done this right.

"There's more. Give me a minute." I pull the bathroom door closed behind me, slip out of my jeans and hoodie, and into a red lace teddy. My palms graze my thighs. Nick's mouth is going to be there soon. I pick up my phone and send a text to Nick.

Me: I want you to undress.

"Are you texting me from the bathroom?" he shouts from behind the door.

Me: There better not be another girl in your life asking you to take off your clothes.

Nick: You're the only girl in my life.

My toes might've just curled.

Me: Good. Keep it that way. Now, have you undressed?

I bite my lip, waiting for the dancing dots to appear.

Nick: Yes.

As if the puck landed between the goalposts, I pump my fist.

Me: Lie down on the bed.

Nick: Are you ever coming out of the bathroom?

Me: Are you lying down?

Nick: Yes.

I teeter on the brink of what I'm about to share with him.

Me: Do you know I think about you all the time?

I hold my breath.

Nick: No.

My phone shakes in my grasp. All our previous texts were child's play.

Me: I do. I find myself daydreaming at work about our nights together, both past, present, and future. Every time I mix an Old Fashioned my heart skips a beat knowing the classic cocktail brought us together. What would have happened if you'd ordered a beer, if I didn't have an excuse to ask you if you liked the drink? A reason to talk to you about music? The courage to ask you to come to a Christmas Eve party? What if you'd said no?

Nick: I could never say no to you.

If he only knew the power he has over me. It's me who cannot say no to him.

Me: Tonight, I want to make your dreams come true. The night is yours. I'm yours.

I hear Nick groan in the bedroom. I unfasten the latch on my heart, then the one on the bathroom door.

Me: Happy Birthday, Mr. Old Fashioned.

I turn off my phone, open the door, and make good on my promise.

# SIXTEEN

# NICK

"THIS IS WHAT IT'LL be like every night when we can afford our own place." Sarah's running her fingers along the lines of my abs, and I'm not going to need much longer to recover.

"A bed this big? Definitely."

She pinches my skin. "No. You and me. The freedom to do what we want when we want."

I roll over, sandwiching her between myself and softest mattress I've ever lain on. "I want you." I catch her mouth and taunt her until she's gasping.

This time I take things at a leisurely pace, exploring all my favorite places. Every slow caress pumps my blood faster. Her skin is so incredibly soft. I stamp kisses across her shoulder and down her torso. The pads of my fingers press into her hips to hold her still as I tickle her stomach with my lips. Sarah makes the little moaning noise I love so much. It lingers on my tongue. With each taste, sound, and feel, we gain momentum. The moans increase, and now is the time when I feel she's truly mine. No roommates, no family, no bosses, no responsibilities. It's just us.

I find her lips again and tease them as we move together. One and the same. Universes contract and expand in the endless sky of her eyes, and my heart is so full, I think it might burst. I make every moment last as long as possible, drinking her in, mesmerized by what my touch does to her.

The lovesick voice in my brain is screaming, "I love you. I love you." I want to say it aloud, but it's too soon.

She'll think I'm rushing, being too immature. My heart skips a beat. We haven't been together long enough for this to be love. But I know different. I know what this is.

I knew it the first time I kissed her at Griffith Park. I know it every time I kiss her. Every time I hold her hand. Every time she tells me about her day. Every time she grumbles in the morning before her first coffee. Every time she kicks me in the middle of the night. Every time she smiles at me. Every single second I'm with her.

Every time.

I love Sarah. If I had my way, we'd never leave this bed.

Reality has other plans.

Check out time is eleven, and even though I have the day off, Sarah has to go to work.

"What time is your dad meeting us?" Sarah's pulling her blond hair into a ponytail, and I have to stuff my hands in my pocket to not slide my palm over the long line of her neck. I had all night with her, and it's still not enough.

"He'll be there by eight." I pack her present to me. Now I have something to put on her dresser beside her picture of her grandmother. The real birthday gift was Sarah, but having my fake ID framed was a nice touch. I thought she threw it out after Chicago. Despite the lie the piece of plastic represents, this means what we felt at Christmas was real. I swallow a wad of almost-tears, turn, and wrap Sarah in the longest hug.

We walk hand-in-hand out of the hotel to the curb, where her lips meet mine. I take her sweet kiss and transform it into so much more, bending her backward in my arms. When we break apart, she's breathless. So am I.

"See you at the Club." She steps into the waiting car, and I attempt to get my heart rate under one hundred.

For the rest of the day, I work on the documentary, stitching together clips of Dad asking the questions I'm still dying to know the answers to.

At the lobby of The Diamond Club, Dad's pacing between the door and the reception. I don't even try for a hug. I sigh. He's here. Every time he shows up, I have to pinch myself to make sure I'm not dreaming. "Dad?"

He pulls me to the small sitting area off the walkway. "I, uh, can't stay." I jam my clenched fists into my coat pockets, trying to ignore the tension his words build between us. He can't even manage to spend time with me on my birthday. Am I that hard to be around? He scratches his chin. "You don't want an old stick-in-the-mud like me around anyhow."

I really do.

Dad hasn't been to my birthday party since I was eight. It was Captain America-themed, and at that time I thought my dad was a superhero. "Okay."

He shoves a white envelope my way. "Happy Birthday."

"Mr. Parker." Sarah click-clacks across the lobby in her heels and kisses Dad on the cheek. I cram the card into my jacket pocket. "You look dapper tonight."

Is he blushing? "Thanks, Sarah. You look lovely as well."

"Thanks." Sarah twirls in her orange sleeveless dress and rests her arm around my waist. The feel of her support takes away an ounce of the pain. "Shall we go in?"

I kiss the top of her head. "Dad can't stay."

Sarah's smile falters. "Sorry to hear that."

I throw my arm over her shoulders and lean into her.

Her grip on my waist tightens. "Are you sure, Mr. Parker?"

"Unfortunately." Dad offers his most professional stiff smile. "But you kids have fun." He pats me on the back. "I'll see you the day after Halloween. To interview Nazhir." And he's gone.

"Happy birthday, dude." Ryan grabs my hand and yanks me into a half-hug before sitting down beside Karina. Four months in LA, and I somehow collected enough friends to reserve a table for eight.

Back home, my birthdays consisted of Mom making my favorite meal, Mike not ordering me around for one whole day, and maybe a trip to the movies, if we had the money. Last year was the first time I celebrated with more than family. Clark hosted a big party in my honor, or so he claimed. I'm pretty sure it was an excuse to draw girls to his house. We drank way too much, and I had to hide my hangover from Mom the next day.

Raging parties are supposed to be what every teenager wishes for, but looking around at the small collection of people at the table at this restaurant, I think I prefer this. My chest is full. Their presence lights me up from inside. I know these people; they know me. Not Nicky the hockey player. They know Nick. Just Nick.

These are my friends. Unlike Dad, they want to be around me.

Mateo slaps me on the back. "Feliz Cumpleaños, mi amigo."

"Gracias." One of three words I retained after a semester of Spanish.

Wil shakes my hand. "El couldn't get away, but she wanted me to give you this." He holds out a small pink envelope.

I pull out a square with a rhinestone-encrusted birthday cake and candles. A gift card for some restaurant I don't know falls out when I open it. Printed inside is:

*Now I'm the only one of the gang left in their teens.*

*Here's to a year of happiness, health, and most of all—love.*

*Happy 20ᵗʰ Birthday,*

*El*

I grin at Wil. "Tell her thanks."

Siobhan lifts a glass in my direction. "Enjoyed the room last night?"

Heat blooms on my cheeks at the memory of the things Sarah and I did in the hotel bed, the Jacuzzi tub, and the shower this morning. "Didn't have to listen to you snore all night, so that was a plus."

Sarah jabs me in the ribs. "Play nice, you two." She wags her fingers at both of us. "Or no dessert."

I stare at Sarah's lips. I definitely want dessert.

"Want to split the veggie chili?" Sarah points to the item on the menu. "It's not too spicy."

I can't help but grin at her. She loves to make fun of my lack of enthusiasm for adventure when it comes to food.

"Or I could get the chili and you could get the salmon, and we could share."

Sharing. I like this idea.

We laugh. We tell stories. We eat. It's perfect. Well, almost perfect. I miss Mom. Even Mike. I breathe through the twinge between my ribs. Sarah made my birthday the best it could possibly be away from them.

SEVENTEEN

# NICK

SIOBHAN, RYAN, SARAH, AND I get back to the apartment after midnight. My birthday is over, and I'm ready for bed. Sarah and I escape to our room and we get rid of our festive clothes. I stick my jacket in the five inches of hanging space Sarah allotted to me in her closet and empty the pockets. The corners of the thick envelope Dad gave me are bent.

"What's this?" Sarah pulls down her tank top and picks up the white rectangle with my name in Dad's orderly print on top.

I roll my eyes. "Dad gave this to me."

"Are you going to open it?"

"Sure." I take the envelope from her and rip the seam open. The card has Happy Birthday written in gold letters and a picture of a slice of cake. It looks like the kind you pick up beside the register at the pharmacy. Cheap. I flip it open and blue index cards spill on the bed.

More of Dad's handwriting inside.

*You said you wanted to know. Dad.*

I scoop up the cards and exhale. Small numbers in circles in the top right corner dictate the order. I read one.

*Where will you live?*

One of the questions we asked the convicts. The one Dad refused to answer. I cough, as if I can dislodge the fear suffocating me.

"Nick?" Sarah crawls onto the bed beside me. "Is something wrong?"

I shake my head, unable to speak. My throat is thick with emotions. Yes, fear, but also relief. Dad wants me to know. He trusts me.

Sarah examines the cards. "What are these?"

I swallow and force myself to speak. "The questions from the documentary." And the answers.

The answers I've been waiting on for over ten years. The box I store all dad-related emotions rattles in my chest.

"The five you ask each inmate?" Her fingers feather my hair. Her touch should be comforting but every nerve is on fire. What I want to know is right here, yet part of me is afraid to look. Why would he write this all down? Why not just tell me in the car when I asked?

Sarah's arms encircle me, her body pressing closer. I can't seem to catch my breath, and my hands are shaking so badly I can't keep the lines still enough to read the words. I take Sarah's fingers from my neck and press the cards into it. "Could you read them?"

She shakes her head and offers the cards back to me. "This is private."

"I'm not hiding anything from you anymore."

"Are you sure?"

I place my head on her shoulder. "Please."

Sarah runs her hand over my back. "What do you regret?" Her voice is soft, her lips close to my ear. "I regret the years I didn't get to spend with you, Nick." She reads Dad's words in her audiobook narrator voice, the one she used for the read throughs of *Indigo*. "I regret not experiencing the joy of seeing you grow from a little boy with the perma-grin into the loyal young man you are today."

I exhale.

I exhale ten years of agony. Of doubt. Of dread.

This one sentence is enough.

I don't care about the rest. Dad didn't want to leave me. When he didn't reach out after leaving prison, I secretly convinced myself he got caught and didn't fight the sentence so he had an excuse to not be around us. Around me. I knew it was completely irrational, but I was young, and the idea germinated in my mind as months, then years, passed, and there was no word from him.

"Hey." Sarah kisses my temple. "You okay?"

How do I answer that? My world just shifted. I reach for the only solid thing in my life. I lift Sarah's shirt and press my palm against the softness of her stomach. She's real. I'm not dreaming.

"I think so."

"I can stop if you want."

But I want more. My lungs hurt. I know what the other questions are. I want to know why, if he regrets not being there when I grew up, why he didn't show up. What was he doing? "No. Keep going."

Sarah flips to card number two. "Where will you live? When I left prison, I had nowhere to go. No support. I lived in transitional housing with other convicts and recovering addicts. It was not a place for children. It was not a place for your mom. I never wanted any of you to see me living like that. I had to do better before I could try to get back into your life."

I release my hold on Sarah and put my head in my hands. I've lived with two images of my father: the successful busy film industry professional of my childhood, and the closed-up, sometimes angry man who both encourages me to follow the career I chose and refuses to talk to me about anything outside of that. Him living in a house with addicts cracks open the shallow caricature.

Sarah shifts her weight, and I curl on the bed, my head on her lap. The box I stuffed all my hurt and anger into dislodges itself from my heart. "We can read the rest later." Sarah massages my scalp. Her gentle pressure eases the building headache.

I unclench my jaw. "I'm fine. Go on. Please."

"Three. What are your family's expectations for you?" She pauses. My body tenses. How bad can it be? "No family. No expectations. I pushed you away." Her voice drops to a whisper.

"I thought it best to cut off all contact, all connection with you. The name Theo Parker was tainted. I filed for divorce from your mother to save her, and made her promise she'd change your names to hers. To protect you. From shame, from reporters, from my mistakes."

Another pause, and I think she's going to move on to the next question, but she doesn't. "I was petrified the people and families of those whose pension funds I borrowed from—no, stole from—would hunt you down for retaliation. They were so livid at my trial, shouting obscenities, threatening they'd make me or anyone I cared about pay. I didn't want my sons to pay for the sins of their father."

She stops again. "Is this the first time you're hearing about this?" She takes a deep breath and sniffles. I would cry too, but if I start, I might not stop. I tighten the lid on my emotions.

"Yes." I press my palms into my eyebrows, hoping the pressure might relieve the crushing headache that's building behind my eyes. "Please, go on."

"Card number four. What will you do for the next six months? The day I left prison I should have flown, drove, walked, crawled to Chicago to see you, to ask you and Mike to let me be part of your lives. I shouldn't have waited five years to reach out. But I had my reasons. They seem vain now." Sarah's caress slows. "I couldn't get a job until another guy in the halfway house relapsed, and his janitorial position at an office building became available. During the day, I wrote new screenplays none of my former colleagues wanted to get involved with.

At night, I mopped floors and scrubbed urinals. It took me three years, saving every penny, to afford a place without roommates. My own place. Somewhere I could imagine bringing the three of you into."

The one-bedroom with the pull-out couch I spent two restless months on. The small, crammed space I loathed and mocked as a step down for Dad. My chest aches at his determination. For me. To have a place for me to stay with him. Three years to get that crappy apartment, and I complained about him not having a two-bedroom, not thinking of me. The pain behind my eyes travels down to my heart. I've been such a jerk. All the signs where there, but I didn't see them. Didn't look. I wanted the perfect dad who met me with open arms. That was an illusion. The reality is, he's not perfect. But who is?

Sarah continues. "Last card. Where do you see yourself in five years?" I will myself to stay still, concentrate on her voice. She's telling me his story. "My plan was to get my life back. I was working hard to find a higher-paid job. Maybe teaching screenwriting or even writing copy for an agency. Anything that would make you proud of me, want to be near me. I thought it would take a year or two. It took two more long lonely years of scraping by, begging for jobs, rejections upon rejections."

I complain because my first movie didn't win Best Picture while he struggled for years to get anyone to even talk to him, never mind read his work. I chew on my lip. I've been so blind.

"Colleen took a chance on me. Backed me for a writing position. Ten years after you last saw me, I finally thought I was good enough to attempt contact. To see if you'd want me back in your lives."

Sarah's fingers leave me, and I feel adrift. Untethered. They find me again, and she continues. "I was scared you would hate me when you moved to LA. When you got here, I was always afraid to say the wrong thing, always did say the wrong thing. Perhaps being alone for so long made me think I was incapable of loving."

His words disintegrate the box of pain. No Dad. It's me. I'm a difficult son. I didn't make it easy on you.

"I know I'm not a good man. I know I don't deserve forgiveness. I just wanted you to know that I am incredibly proud of you, and of Mike. I'm so proud of what you've done with your life, son. I love you very much."

Sarah puts down the card, and I drop out of the world, swimming in a sea of relief, regret, and release. My vision is a blur but for the first time in a long time, I can see clearly. Illusions of the perfect dad, the perfect reunion, the perfect life are washed away with each tear. I have a dad who loves me, who wants to be in my life. That's more than enough.

# Eighteen

*Sarah*

I HOLD NICK ALL night. Somewhere around two a. m. his shoulders stop shaking, and his chest starts to rise and fall in a steady rhythmic fashion. I've listened to him talk about his dad for months now, but I don't think I ever understood what he had bottled up in that huge heart of his.

Sometimes I think I know Nick completely. This night, I learned I've only seen a portion of him, but not because he's hiding. Because we have many more months, years of figuring each other out. I want to discover every corner of Nick. His hopes. His talents. His fears. His regrets. This weekend was more than just enjoying his body or making his birthday perfect. Holding Nick on my lap, seeing him cry, his vulnerability . . . my support was the biggest present I could offer. And he'll always have that.

By Tuesday morning, the only reminders of Nick's birthday are the two cards he set on my dresser. They stand next to the photo of Mémère and me, in front of his Best Director award, the fake Best Screenwriter one Ryan made, and the framed fake ID I gave Nick for his birthday. The corners of my lips curl up. Seeing the pieces of my life and his standing next to each other, connecting us into one whole, makes me certain moving him into my apartment, my room, my life was the right decision.

I put my feelings about Nick away, close the laptop with the latest version of the scam screenplay Karina and I have been toiling over any free minute we get, and face another day of playing nice with the writers that are finally paying attention to the suggestions I throw their way. I walk into the think-tank with my head held high. I'm still taking notes and wiping dry eraser marks off the board, but I see the light at the end of the tunnel. A very, very long tunnel that'll take me years to get to the end of. But Karina was right. I *am* on the ladder. *And* my colleagues are no longer trying to push me off it.

"Everyone ready to work?" Rod covers his big yawn with the papers I printed out for him. My brain buzzes and I clasp my hands together, ready for my gold star. Today is my day. Today I'm going to show how thorough I am, and he'll throw accolades my way. Or at least stop glaring at me like I'm someone who's dragging the team down. "The finale can't tie up all the loose ends. We need to seed the new intrigue for season two, and Connor here has some ideas how we could do that."

The visions of a gold star disappear. "Ideas?" I sound like a rusty hinge. Ideas on season two? The tendons in my neck stiffen. That's not what I've been focusing on. My task was to research ways to make Kyle's life as a vampire who was converted in the twentieth century more believable.

"Why did we kill trees to print out whatever this is?" He shakes my research. I went to four antique shops and scoured eBay all night until Nick got up to go to Blend for those pages.

"I put together a list of treasures he's held on to." I remind Rod of the task he assigned me.

"What's the reason for them?" He thumbs the stack of papers. "And where is he storing them? If he moves and changes names, is he stashing them in a cave?"

Why is he treating me like we haven't discussed this? Like he didn't ask me to do the research? I want to roll my eyes at him, but I don't. "I mean, he has the money. He could probably pay people to keep stuff for him. Maybe there are vampire-run storage facilities?"

Someone chuckles at my joke, but Rod looks anything but happy. "Because that's sexy. No one wants to watch a show about vampires renting storage units." Rod throws the pages into the trash can, takes a sip of his coffee, and sends it flying the same way. Brown liquid spreads on the photo of Andy Warhol's soup can. "Anyone have any better season two ideas than employing Kyle as a landlord for people's unwanted junk?"

That's not what I said. Tears well in my eyes. This research was his idea. I bite the inside of my cheek and use the pain to try to suck the liquid back into my tear ducts. It's not working. I need to get out of here. Nobody can see me cry. I rub my head to cover my eyes. "Could you take the notes?" I whisper to Karina, and rush for the bathroom.

Tear tracks line my cheeks when I look at myself in the bathroom mirror. Halloween isn't until tomorrow, but I could win Best Costume for impersonating a raccoon. I haven't cried in public since the plane ride home from Chicago on Valentine's Day. The hole in my heart grows. I rip a paper towel from the dispenser and wipe my face.

I did the homework, made the list like Rod asked. This was supposed to be my moment to shine. But I don't feel like a diamond. Not even useful like a lump of coal. What kind of a writer am I if I can't come up with a viable idea on the spot? I dig my nails into my plan. Maybe I'm not supposed to be doing this after all. Maybe this is a wake-up call to show me I'm not special. Not a storyteller. I scrunch the smudged paper into a ball and toss it. The wad hits the rim of the trash can and plops onto the floor. Even that I can't do.

I can go to Mrs. Marino, ask her to put me back onto the schedule full-time. I gulp. I'm good at slinging drinks. My customers like me.

Or.

I can return to Toronto and forget about this rotten city. At the thought, breathing becomes harder. Me stuck behind the counter at Côté Fraises, flour in my hair. Days in the bakery. Nights in the club. It wouldn't be that bad. At least I'd know what I'd be doing. Plus, I'd be keeping the family business alive, like Mom wants.

But what about Nick? I can't leave him. I can't breathe at the thought of not being with him.

Mom's ringtone disrupts the quiet of the bathroom. She's the last person I need to be on my case right now. I ignore her call and wipe my face with the paper towel again, erasing the traces of tears on my cheeks but unable to do anything about the red-rimmed eyes that stare back at me. I didn't even bring my purse to fix my makeup. Shit. Everyone in the room will know I've been crying. I blow my nose. Mom's ringtone makes a comeback. Her photo stares at me from the screen. I can't be a horrible writer and a horrible daughter. It might be important.

"Thank goodness you answered." My heart jumps into my throat. Something is wrong. "I need your advice." Mom's chipper voice is a vivid contrast to my current mood, and my jaw tightens in frustration. "I'm trying to figure out what to get your dad for our anniversary. Silver is traditional for a twenty-fifth. I can't decide between a picture frame for our wedding photo or cufflinks with his initials and our anniversary date on them. What do you think?"

By no means is this an emergency. "Your anniversary isn't for another month. Why are you really calling?"

Her eyes narrow. "You look like you've been crying. Are you in a bathroom? What are you doing crying in a bathroom? Whose bathroom is this?"

Why did I pick up? "I'm at work, Mom. We're planning season two. The show is getting good reviews."

"Here you go with your facts again." She shakes her head. "I don't care about the show; I care about you. Tell me why you were crying."

The dam holding my emotions at bay breaks. Weeks of feeling inadequate, fearing I can't do this, burst forth as tears and words fight their way out. "I don't think I can do this job. I can't do anything right."

"Honey." Mom's eyes watch me with the gentleness she usually shares through her touch. But she can't reach out and smooth my hair or dry the wet streaks on my cheeks. "You've been there how long?"

"A whole month." A loud whimper punctuates my answer.

"It's just your first month, honey. You can't go from zero to expert in a month."

"You don't understand. I've never worked this hard before, and I can't get my boss take me seriously." I verbalize my real fear. "If I don't impress him, Rod won't hire me. This is my trial, Mom, and I'm failing."

Mom sighs. "You are not failing. You are learning." I cover my face with my hand and sob about my wasted dreams. "Sarah." Mom's voice is firm. "Look at me."

I put down my hand and stare at the blurry screen.

"What would Mémère do?" Mom raises her eyebrows and tilts her head. "Would she be giving up now?"

Guilt twists my gut.

"My mother faced many challenges in her life," Mom says. "She left everything she knew to live in a foreign country, she had no support, only a husband who left her alone six months of the year to play hockey. She opened a bakery at a time when women couldn't have a bank account, never mind own a business. She taught herself how to drive, how to file taxes, how to perfect a strawberry tart. She was determined. Headstrong. A lot like her granddaughter."

Mom's glistening eyes implore me to be like Mémère. "If you were talking to her right now, she'd tell you to dry your tears, put on your stubborn face, and go conquer the world."

Mémère would definitely not be crying in the bathroom right now. She was a fighter. Even with cancer, she never gave up. "I'm scared I can't be the writer Mémère thought I would be."

"Mémère wanted you to be happy. She wouldn't care if your name is recognized around the world, or if you're someone who writes only for yourself. And your family loves you no matter what."

My heart swells. "You're obligated to say that." I wipe my nose.

"That doesn't make it any less true."

"What if I don't get hired full-time? What am I going to do?"

"You come home. We will welcome you with open arms. There is a business here waiting for you to take over."

It would be nice to not have to try so hard to make everything work out. The fog of despair clouds my mind. It's exhausting, struggling all the time.

"I know my daughter. If you go back into that working room—"

"Writers' room."

"Whatever you call it." Mom dabs a tissue in the corner of her eye. "If you go back in there and show this Rod the real you, you can't fail, honey. You stand up for yourself. Let them see the brilliant woman we know you are. Fight for what you want."

Maybe I need to call Mom more often. Her words are gentler than Mémère's, who was my first confidant. I've missed having her to talk to. But I need Mom in my life. I can't bear any more holes in my heart. I may be grown, but she'll always be my mother. We can both remember Mémère. Together.

# NINETEEN

# NICK

I DIDN'T EXPECT HALLOWEEN to be such a big deal at college. I expected parties, but not costumes during the day. The woman ordering a flat white wearing what I think is a Little Red Riding Hood outfit proves me wrong. Her friend in a Cinderella gown winks at me when I pass her travel mug back.

"You're coming tonight, right?" Wil drums his fingers against the counter. My friend is hyper AF today.

"Miss my opportunity to finally see WE perform? Not a chance." I pour two splashes of almond milk into a small house blend, snap on a lid, and add it to the tray for the big order we're preparing for Rocker Inc. down the street. "What's El going as?"

The grin that erupts on Wil's face is beyond goofy. "No clue. She won't tell me."

"Oh, thought you'd be doing a couples costume."

Wil pours the watermelon juice El ordered into a to-go cup and adds a butter tart to the box of pastries. "She's not my girlfriend."

I sidestep that comment. "I just meant because you are like a couple in a band. Thought you might do famous musicians or something."

"Nah, El's trying to keep a low profile."

"Right. I forgot." That girl's life is complicated. Being friends with her and Wil has opened my eyes to the downside of being a rockstar's daughter. I'm seeing a lot of things differently lately.

Sarah insisted I call Dad the morning after reading his birthday present index cards. Besides the physical and emotional hangover when I woke up, I told her I needed time to process what he wrote. He had five years. I should get five days. I pull on my ear. Dad would understand.

The longest sigh of relief leaves my lungs. It's so weird to think that. Dad would understand.

Ms. Hansley's text comes in ten minutes before my shift ends.

Ms. Hansley: Nazhir is being released at three p.m. Today.

That's a day early. And in an hour.

Dad: They do this all the time. We need to document it.

Nick: I don't have my lighting equipment with me, but if we're filming outside it should work.

Natural light is always preferable.

Dad: Can you meet me at the prison?

Me: I'll be there.

Ms. Hansley: You can expense the cab.

Dad: Thanks.

I stare at the word. I know now to pay attention to what my dad writes. I'm listening with my ears and my eyes. My thumb hovers over the keyboard.

Me: See you soon.

As the cab pulls up to the gate, I spot Dad and one of the guards standing by the entrance. He sees me and strides my way. "Just in time. He's about to walk through the gate."

I drop to my knee, unzip the case, and pull out the camera. The beating of my pulse against my temples grows louder. "I only need a minute."

"Fuck. He's here now." Dad motions for me to hurry.

Mike definitely gets the cursing gene from Dad. Both fall into it when emotions run high.

"It's okay, Dad. I'm ready." I hoist the camera onto my shoulder and find the entrance through the viewer. Dad's hand lands on my elbow, and a rush of electricity jolts through me. This man is proud of me. I take a deep breath to force my heart to stop galloping and fiddle with the lens.

Dad guides me forward, his grip firm on my arm, like I might float away in the breeze blowing in from the ocean. "Where do you want us?"

I peek out from the viewer and survey potential interview spots. The prison's main doors are too shaded in the afternoon sun. "Over there. See the exit sign?" To the left of the entrance, hanging on a wire fence, is a white sign with Exit and a big arrow printed in black. It's a bit on the nose, but it'll work.

"Got it," I say.

Dad lets go of me, and I catch him crossing into the frame, heading for the door where Nazhir is standing in a gray suit that hangs off him. I press record and watch the world through my lens. Dad shakes Nazhir's hand, and the newly released inmate looks relieved, like he's glad someone is here. That he's not alone. My chest tightens. I try not to think about what this day was like for Dad with no one to shake his hand.

Dad moves Nazhir to the sign. "You're free again. How does it feel?"

"Strange. I wasn't expecting to get out."

"Yeah. They released me a day early as well. My, uhm, place wasn't ready, and I had to use some of my release money on a hostel."

"Two hundred bucks is like a million right now." Nazhir holds up a manila envelope.

"It won't last long." Dad crosses his arms. "Did your classmate get you a job?"

Nazhir pushes a pebble around with his foot. "Nah. They aren't hiring right now."

Dad looks at the camera. Or me. I'm not sure. "Is someone coming to pick you up?"

"They called my sister. She said she'd come." Nazhir looks to the road. I zoom in and capture the concern etching his features. He almost looks scared. The muscles in my neck cramp. Shouldn't he be happy? He's free.

"Good." Dad nods. "What's the first thing you're going to do?"

"Was hoping to grab a burger." Nazhir looks over his shoulder. "The food in there sucked."

"The Ritz Carlton it ain't." The two men chuckle.

Dad asks a few more questions about where his parole officer will be, reminds him about the one month follow-up, and they exchange contact information.

Nazhir's head shoots up at the sound of a car coming down the drive. A female version of Nazhir climbs out of her Prius and flings her arms open. Nazhir falls into her hug. A hug that says so much more to me than words. I'm more of a voyeur than a cameraman capturing the touching reunion.

"Did we get enough?" The sound of Dad's voice is right by me.

"Yeah. I think so." Nazhir gets into the car, and I film them driving off. "Next time, maybe I'll bring Sarah or Wil, get some B roll, different angles. But we got enough."

Dad bounces on the balls of his feet. "Sounds good." He looks at his car. "Want a ride home?"

A smile tugs my lips. For the first time, the camera is a restriction, keeping me from the world. I swing it off my shoulder, place it at my feet, and throw my arms around him. He stiffens as I hold him. I grip tighter, and he takes a deep breath. He exhales and his muscles relax, a palm pressing against my back. "You are so like your mother."

"What d'you mean?"

"It was—is—always so easy for her to express herself. She'd make my favorite dinner, yell at me for screwing up, pepper me with kisses when I sulked." I do not want to think about my parents kissing. "A million little ways to show me she loved me. I'm not good at that."

I release my hold on him and take a step back. I've hugged him long enough. My cup is full. It's his turn. "You prefer written words."

His eyes search mine. He must find something he likes, because his mouth curls up, and he shrugs. "It's what I do. Paint a picture. It's easier for me to stay silent. Instead, I make my characters say what's in here." Dad points to his head. "And here." He points to his heart.

My eyes prickle. "Thanks for answering the questions." Somehow, it's easier to be honest with him now. Like I have the right to tell him. Which I guess I do. I guess I always did.

His gaze shifts to his hands. "I should've said something earlier. But we always put these things off. I never got a chance to tell my dad how I felt when he was alive. People said I wrote a beautiful eulogy, but what good did that do? He never knew. Your birthday seemed like the right time. To explain."

Looking at him, standing on the gravel, the yellow and gray prison behind him, the ball of tension I've felt around him for the last year no longer presses into my heart. It's not easy, but it's easier. "It helped. I . . . I didn't understand. I thought I was a burden. Something . . . someone you had to deal with because you were responsible for me."

His head jerks up. "No. Never."

"You are a good man." I've reread the last line he wrote over and over the past three days. Drinking in the notion he's proud of me, that he loves me. Letting it settle into the holes I carved out of my soul thinking I wasn't good enough. He shakes his head. "No, you are. Mom has always known it, and now I have proof. You did what you could to protect us from—"

"My mistakes."

"We all make mistakes, Dad. I've made so many, you have no idea."

"I'd like to." His words are quiet, but they bellow to me. My Dad is interested in my life. I could get used to this.

"You do deserve forgiveness. I forgive you. Can you forgive me?"

His eyebrows knit together. "What could I possibly forgive you for?"

"I've been a jerk. I created these huge expectations of what having you back in my life would be like. Ones no one could live up to, and then I blamed you when you didn't meet them. I'm sorry."

"Nick. Listen to me." He places his hands on my biceps. The same stance he used when he would explain why I should listen to my big brother when he left him in charge. "You have nothing to be sorry for."

"But—"

"Nothing. Do you understand?"

I nod. And I exhale. My doubts. My unrealistic expectation. I free the space in my heart for love.

He cocks his head to the right. "Really?"

"I want to."

"How about this?" He drops his hand and surveys the empty parking lot. "Let's consider today a fresh start for both of us. Our release from prison day. We've made mistakes"—I open my mouth to protest but he stops me—"both of us. We acknowledge them but agree to move forward. Find new ways to . . . connect. Be father and son again."

"I'd like that." I hold out my hand. He takes it in his, tugs at me, and I crash into his sternum.

It's brief, but I know it's huge for him.

He steps back. "Now I don't know about you, but that burger sounded good."

I can't keep the grin off my face. "I could eat." I text Sarah to let her know I'm grabbing dinner with my dad.

# TWENTY

## Sarah

THE WRITING ROOM IS a flurry of activity. The call came from the set five minutes ago, and everyone is acting like the president of the studio is on their way.

Karina got the honor of being the on-set writer for today. It was supposed to be a light day for the rest of us. Cleaning up some plot issues. Off at four. Plenty of time for me to go home, change into my Helen of Troy costume so Nick and I can catch Wil and El performing at Mateo's HalloRade, the Halloween bash he's hosting. My first real frat party in the US. Can't wait to see what an authentic one is like compared to what my fellow screenwriters make them out to be in the movies.

Apparently, coffee was more important than documenting the season finale structure, and when I get back with their orders, Rod's brown skin is a shade of red brighter than the strawberry lemonade in my hand. Not a look I've seen on him. "How the hell did this happen?"

The room falls silent, and the writers stare at their laptops. I tiptoe around the table and hand out coffee cups like the good little assistant I am.

"I asked a question." Rod slams his hand down on the desk, and everyone jumps. His stare pins me to my chair. Oh, shit. My teeth clamp down on the straw of my drink. What now?

"Well?"

I have no idea what he's talking about. I straighten my spine and channel Mémère. "I can't help until you tell me what's going on."

Rod's nostrils flare. Like really flare. I've written the words on paper before but never witnessed such an event. "We're talking about the fact that production has halted on-set this morning. Seems our action-packed, electrifying car chase scene has no action because the star of our show doesn't know how to drive a manual transmission car."

I choke on the icy lemonade that hits the back of my throat. Shit. Shit. Shit.

His eyes narrow. "Did you not do the research?"

"I did." I draw lines through the condensation on the side of my cup. I know I did my job. I still my fingers and return his stare. "His profile listed driving a stick shift as one of his skills." Along with horseback riding and surfing. I remember wondering if he ever surfs at the same beaches as Ryan.

"Well, actors lie sometimes. That's why we triple-check the facts." Rod tosses a marker across the table. "We don't just read a profile. We talk to their agent."

I wipe my wet fingers on the soft weave of my capris and raise my chin. "I did talk to the agent. They assured me he owns a manual transmission. I spoke to the dealership that sold him his Porsche 718 GTS six months ago, and they confirmed it."

Rod sits in the chair, looking . . . contrite isn't the right word. Neither is impressed, but it's closer. Close enough to plant a seed of confidence in my chest.

"That's good work." His voice is calmer. "You know a lot about cars."

"Not really. Just the basics."

"More than anyone in this room." Rod laughs but he rubs his chin. "Then why is he having trouble driving on set?"

"Is the car he's driving an older model?" I mimic Rod and sit back in my chair. "I'd suggested a sixties or seventies Corvette." Years of listening to my brothers argue over the best possible version of a Corvette finally pays off. "The clutch is a little looser in those."

He points a finger at me. "Well, it's about time we met the real Sarah Connor."

"Excuse me?" I look at the faces of the other writers. What am I missing?

"I've been waiting to see if you had what it takes to be on this team. Thought you were going to be like the last girl, too busy kissing my ass to do the work. Seems I was wrong."

Did he just say that? My palm flies to the collar of my T-shirt. He's been testing me the whole time, and I didn't see it? I rub my thumb against the curve of the S in my necklace. I thought

I was good at reading people. How could I be so off? "You were wrong. One thing I'm not afraid of is hard work."

"Okay, then." He steeples his fingers and settles his elbows on the table. "How do you suggest we fix this?"

All eyes in the room are trained on me. Am I pushing my luck? I move away from the table and stand. No. I'm proving myself. He wants to see the real Sarah Connor? I'm going to show him the Sarah who Mémère sent to LA to conquer it, not the Sarah who's been doubting herself ever since the scam fiasco. My hands land on my waist, and I face my coworkers and my fears. "Send me to the set. I need to see the car they have. Maybe I can help."

Rod digs in his pocket, pulls out a laminated card, and tosses it at me.

"Give them this at the gate. Head straight to Lot D. I'll text Karina to be on the lookout for you."

Lot D is in the back of the filming location. It's an intersection of two city streets that remind me of the part of Chicago Nick's ex-girlfriend lived in when I tried to find him on Valentine's Day.

After checking in at the gate and then again at the trailer on-set where they confiscate my phone, I spot Karina standing beside a late-seventies Dodge Challenger. Not the high-end vibe

I had in mind, but this vehicle still has the muscle car look. Deep turquoise, just like my younger brother's first car. Except this one is spotless: not a hint of rust. I giggle. Inside sits Kyle Bardo, looking as sexy as I imagined him to be when I originally wrote him in this scene. The costume designer has him in a classic white T-shirt, leather jacket, and aviator shades.

"Sarah. Over here." Karina waves at me. She puts her arm around my shoulders and tugs me away from the crowd. "So glad you're here. It's a complete mess. All these people and no one has any idea about manual transmissions. Kyle stalls the car every time. This is the tail end of the chase scene. We need him to drive the damned thing from here to the movie theater, stop, and get out. Who knew that'd be so hard to do? We tried pushing from behind, but we can't get enough leverage and not show people in the shot. The tow truck with the flat-bed is being used by another crew."

"Okay, Karina, breathe."

"Don't hate me, but can you find a way to . . . instruct these guys on how to get the damned thing into gear?" She leans in. "Without bruising their delicate egos." She glances at the star. "Especially Kyle's."

"I got this. I taught Grayson and Taylor in no time." I disregard the chill in my stomach.

"This is the first time we're shooting with a car. We'll have to rewrite this and three more episodes if we get rid of the driving scenes. Rod will kill us all. Please, help." Karina pulls me back to the crowd. My toe snags on the cable, my eyes too glued to the star of the show. I catch myself and straighten. She shoves me his way. "Kyle, this is Sarah. The girl I was talking about."

"I hear this baby is giving you some trouble." I'm shaking Kyle's hand. The star of our show. The heartthrob of our series. I get why the camera loves him. In person he practically glows: olive skin, dark hair, prominent chin, but those eyes. They're green and brown like the forest up at the cottage. I might be drooling. Karina kicks my shin, and the pain snaps me back to the professional I'm supposed to be.

"My Porsche has the shifters on the steering wheel. This one is old-school. And the clutch is wonky." He drops my hand and looks at the car. My insides spasm. Is he pissed? But he turns back to me and shrugs.

Like I thought. Kyle's Porsche doesn't have a gearbox like this car. "Dodges can be like that. My youngest brother had one"—I lean in—"and he stalled it all the time. I taught him a trick. I could show you."

Kyle's hazel eyes sparkle. "I knew there had to be a trick."

"Okay, everyone." Karina shouts. "Let's take twenty." She looks at us. "Holler if you need more time."

Kyle points to the driver's seat. "Shall we?"

I slip into the vintage car and Kyle takes the passenger seat. With the turn of the key, the engine roars to life. My pulse thrums. I press the clutch and release the parking brake. Kyle studies everything I do. I shift into first gear. "The key is to find the biting point of the clutch. In your Porsche, it's been pinpointed by the engineers. In these old cars, you coax it out of them. Learn their secrets."

"Like with a woman."

Is Kyle Bardo flirting with me? The double-time of my heart is about the car I get to drive, not the man next to me. "Yeah. My boyfriend knows mine."

"I hope to be so lucky one day." I catch a shadow of sadness in his eyes but before I confirm it, his movie-star smile slips into place. "What's the secret with this old girl?" Kyle pats the dashboard.

I slowly release the clutch. "Feel that? How the car responds as I ease off on the clutch?" The car purrs and begs for me to hit the accelerator. I hold it at the biting point for a flash, and the car inches forward. I press on the clutch, and the engine settles. I repeat the motion, look at Kyle, and twist my mouth to the side. "Get it?"

He puts his hand on the dashboard. "Yeah. It's like the car wants to move."

"Exactly. This car was meant to fly. You just have to give it the freedom." I ease off the clutch again. "This time, I'm going to give the car a little gas as we hit the biting point." The revs lower, and I tap the gas. The car accelerates, quicker than I expected. Betty is good, but she doesn't have the muscle this thing's tricked out with. The rumble of the engine travels through the steering wheel and into my fingers. I tighten my grip, stop the car, and put on the parking brake. "Wanna give it a try?"

"Sure."

We swap spots. "Just try to find the biting point first. Don't bother with the gas." He stalls it a couple times, but on the fourth try he gets the car rolling. "That's it."

"I felt it." He smiles at me. "You're right."

"Let's try with some gas this time." I figure he needs to at least get into third gear to make this look real.

Kyle gets the car going.

"Give it gas now." He does, and the car gallops. The RPM gauge jumps, and the engine screams as it begs to be shifted into second. The whine of the pistons compels me to move with it. "Now shift."

"What?" Kyle looks at me like he doesn't know what I'm talking about. "Press the clutch in." He does, and I grab the stick shift, slamming it back into second. The dissonance in my ears ceases. "Clutch out and more gas." He follows my instructions, and the car continues to accelerate. He turns the wheel, and we careen down the next street.

"Need to shift into third."

"You do it," he shouts over the roaring engine.

I feel the deceleration as he presses the clutch, and I move the shifter into third. "Gas. Now." The car shoots forward.

"This is working." Kyle's smiling like a little kid who's enjoying his ice cream. I mirror his glee. He takes another corner, and we nearly hit a wall. We jerk forward as he slams on the brakes and the car stalls out.

"That was good." Better than Taylor's first try. At least we're halfway to the theater.

"I get the biting point thing. The shifting is different."

"Let's try this. You work the clutch and the gas, and I'll do the shifting."

"You sure?"

"Yeah. I do it all the time." I squirm in my seat. Little white lie. I haven't done it since I was a kid. My dad would let me shift while he was driving. It was a game almost, to see if I could shift at just the right revs so the clutch wasn't necessary. I think that's where I first got my love of driving manual cars. The feeling of being in control is heady. I still try slip-shifting with Betty on long road trips.

We practice a bit more, and Kyle and I get into a rhythm. We take a corner, and Karina is all smiles as we stop in front of her. "Kyle, you rock." She mouths thank you to me. The confidence I felt in the writing room doubles.

"I want Sarah in the car with me." Kyle leans on the Dodge's roof as if he's been the one running and not the car. Beads of perspiration on his forehead warp his image of an old, cold vampire.

Karina's smile fades. "Um . . ."

Kyle gives me a please-make-this-work-look. I tap my foot on the pavement as my brain scrambles for a solution. I huff and catch Kyle's eyes. "You'll have to practice and do it by yourself for the next scenes, but today I'll spot you." I return my gaze to Karina. "I'm small. I can crouch in the footwell of the passenger seat, and no one will see me."

"I'll speak to the director." Karina leaves in a whirl of her green hobo-chic tunic.

We repeat the scene over and over. Ad nauseum. My legs and back ache from sitting curled up on the floor of the front seat. Once Kyle gets out of the car, I stay tucked there as they film the rest of the scene.

At last, the director calls the day to the end.

"Good job, girl." Karina pulls me into a hug. We head to the trailer to pick up our phones. Without the bright lights illuminating the set, the sky is dark. Really dark. "What time is it?"

Karina checks the watch on her wrist. "Ten thirty. I've officially been on this set for over fourteen hours. And no, there is no overtime pay."

Shit. The high of the power I wielded in the writer's room and on-set vanishes. The HalloRade party started at eight, and there's no way I'll make it home before midnight. Guilt and disappointment roll over me and weave into a knot under my ribcage, trapping air in my lungs. I stab the on button of my phone, but the black screen doesn't wake up. I push and shake the device. My hands and heart tremble in agreement. Double shit.

# Twenty-One

# NICK

Tired of pacing the floor, I sink into the couch and adjust the silly sheet I'm using as a toga to complete my Paris of Troy costume. Måneskin's *Beggin* blasts from the party in the apartment below, taunting me, and the muscles in my neck feel like they are going to snap.

Where is she?

I check my phone again. A string of messages from Ryan and Siobhan says they haven't heard from her either. Karina is MIA as well. Were they kidnapped? Did Sarah's car break down again? Are they out at a bar drunk? Have they been in an accident and are lying in a hospital bed? The last thought cripples me, and I put my head between my legs not to pass out.

Sarah has to be okay.

Should I start calling hospitals? The blood that was already rushing in my veins plummets like a waterfall. I don't have a car to drive around in and look for her. Or should I stay put in case she comes back to the apartment? I feel so helpless. My vision swims. This is Mike and the night he got beat up all over again.

A key scrapes in the lock. Tension seizes my calf muscles. I jump off the couch as the door opens, and she's here. Alive.

"Nick, my ph—"

I suffocate her words with my chest as I wrap myself around her. "You're safe." I squeeze her tighter, letting the heat, the realness of her, sink into my skin. I implore it to push out the cold fear I've been fighting for the last three hours.

"Mmmick." She nudges me away. I relent and release her. "I'm so sorry." The ghost of her missing still clings. I caress her arm to prove she's here. There's nothing to worry about anymore. "My battery died."

It was her car. "We just replaced the battery in Betty. What can be draining it?"

She tilts her head and watches me like I'm speaking Greek like my grandparents. "No, Betty's fine. I meant my phone battery. They took my phone away, and I forgot to put it on the charger last night. I need to buy one for the car so I don't have to go through this again."

The worry fog parts, and my brain picks up on the key words in her explanation. "Sorry. Back up. If Betty didn't die, then where have you been all this time?"

Her eyes fall to the toga knot on my side. "I still can't believe it myself. One moment I was cleaning up coffee cups, and the next I was shaking Kyle Bardo's hand. He's not as tall in real life as you'd expect." She's doing that thing where she talks a mile a minute to cover for something else. "I thought about getting his autograph for you but—"

I hold up my hand. "Let me get this straight. You didn't have car trouble?" She nods. A burning sensation ignites at the base of my spine. "Where were you?"

Her hand traces the folds of the silly sheet crossing my stomach, and I can tell by her tender touch I'm not going to like this. She gives it a tug, our signal for me to bend over so she can kiss me. I don't. I put my hand over hers. "Sarah. Where?"

"I drove as fast as I could to get here."

That's not what I'm asking. I push her hand away and step back. Betrayal spreads like wildfire across my skin.

"They were having problems with a scene, and I had to go to the set out in Burbank. When I got there, they took away our phones, and it was too late to call you."

Another brush-off. Her excuse incinerates my heart.

"Let me get this straight. You've been on a TV set, hanging out with actors and directors, while I was sitting here thinking you were hurt in an accident or worse?"

"What?" Her gaze flies to mine, but I can't decipher the look. Can't tell if it's concern or pity in the eyes I love to stare into for hours. "No, Nick. It wasn't like that. I didn't think it'd take so long. I—"

"Really. You didn't think. I'm starting to get that message loud and clear." I turn away and bunch my hands into fists.

"What is that supposed to mean?" she says.

I don't like the tone in her voice. Like I'm the one in the wrong here.

"You heard what I said. Did you even stop to think about texting me?"

"I told you, they took away our phones."

"And there wasn't any opportunity." My voice is too loud, but I don't care. "No union breaks where you could step out and let your supposed boyfriend know where you were? Or, I don't know, alive? Never mind going to be late for the party where all our friends are waiting for us?"

"There wasn't—"

"Don't. I work in the business too. I know how it is on set." The toga singes my skin. I rip the bedsheet off and crumple it. "I might not have your fancy TV writer's job, but I know there are moments when you, if you wanted to, if you'd given a damn, thought about me, you could've given me a heads up."

Sarah puts her hands on her hips. "Whoa. I don't understand where this is coming from. I do give a damn about you. Maybe too much."

What the fuck? I clench my jaw. She did not just say that.

Sarah strides into the path I'm wearing out on the floor. "I blew the last of my savings on your birthday and left work early to set up the hotel room, putting me behind on a shit-ton of research I had to do at night when you're asleep."

"Sorry my birth is such an inconvenience to you."

"And I was already in trouble from the night"—she continues like she didn't even hear me—"I gave up on karaoke to be with you. Do you know what that cost me? They wrote a key scene in-between songs, and I wasn't a part of the brainstorming. I'm still getting flack for not being present. It took me days to catch up. Today, I finally got their attention back."

"Well, excuse me. I didn't know spending time with your boyfriend is such an imposition. Perhaps I should step out of your way, not be a bother anymore." My feet are on autopilot, striding down the hall until I end up in our bedroom. I slam the door, shutting her out.

How could she do this? I smash my fist against the wall. For weeks now I've felt this distance growing between us. The pain from my fingers radiates into my heart. I thought it was simply the busyness of our lives. I wince. We never have enough time together.

I look around the room. Our room. Well, her room really. Ryan has mine. Practically everything here is hers. The closet full of her clothes, my few belongings crammed into the corner. Her makeup, her notebook, her photos. I'm a visitor, an afterthought. Just like today.

The roaring in my ears matches the pounding in my head as I chuck the stupid sheet across the room and cast off the Dollar Store sandals—her costume idea. I wanted to go as Shawn Mendez and Camila Cabello. We're both the right height and the costumes would be easy. But at the mention of putting on a brunette wig, she dismissed the idea. Of course, we went with hers—Paris and Helen of Troy. At the time, Sarah dressing as the most beautiful woman in the world made perfect sense. Today, I wish she'd listened to me.

The unfairness of this situation tarnishes the room. Her costume, her apartment, her car. What only hours ago was a vibrant inner sanctuary for me, a place I felt safe, has been ripped away. I stuff my legs into jeans, toss on a white T-shirt, and jam my feet into my sneakers.

My Best Director award on the dresser is the one thing in this room that's mine. But I can't even have that one thing. Beside it sits the fake one Ryan made for her. The burning sensation prickles across my skin again. I can't be here. I take my jacket out of the closet, put my wallet, phone, and keys in my pocket, and swing open the door. Sarah's there leaning against the wall.

"Nick."

Without even looking at her, I brush by, heading out. Away from all of this.

"Nick." Her shout slashes at me.

My hand twists the doorknob. The smoke from the pyre of our trust suffocates me. My lungs collapse and I barrel down the stairwell, away from the wreckage.

Sarah calls down after me. "Where are you going?"

"For a walk. Need some fresh air."

A car honks when I jaywalk across the street. A group of people in superhero costumes parts as I plow through them. The sound of their jeers punches and stabs at me. A small portion of my brain argues there's no way they could be laughing at me, but my mind swallows the logic.

I blink and I'm standing in front of Mateo's frat house. Orange lights trim the eves and misshapen jack-o'-lanterns line the steps to the door, the tealights inside throwing ominous shadows as I climb past them. Inside, the party is still in full swing, although the makeshift stage is empty, with no Wil or El in sight. My feet hum from all the walking. It takes me a minute to spot my friend through the crowd.

"You made it at last." Mateo surveys me from head to toe and back again. "I don't get the costume. Are you Danny from Grease or Shawn Mendez?"

"No." The thoughts in my head churn. My fists clench. Fuck. I must stop the whirring before I punch someone. The table Mateo's standing beside is littered with a rainbow of cups filled with multicolored liquids. I squeeze the back of my neck. "I need a drink."

Mateo swipes a hand over the air above the glasses. "Pick your poison."

"Beer. I need a beer."

Mateo offers me a red cup. "Red is beer. The blue ones have wine coolers, some fruity stuff." He takes a sip from a pumpkin-colored cup. "Orange and black are non-alcoholic. Juice and Coke."

I snatch the beer from his hand and take a huge gulp. The alcohol tastes sour in my mouth. I want to spit it out but force myself to take another gulp. My phone buzzes.

Sarah: When are you coming home?

Home. The word makes me laugh. My home is in Chicago. Or it was. I don't fit in there anymore. I moved from Mom's home to Dad's couch to Sarah's bedroom. If Sarah isn't my home, what is? I don't fit in anywhere.

Me: Not.

A girl in a sexy white uniform eyes me. "Looks like you could use a little time with the nurse."

Not unless she can mend a broken heart. The soft plastic of the cup crunches in my hand. I loosen my hold and offer my best Blend customer service smile. "Thanks, but not tonight."

I back away from the girl, avoid the dance floor hopping with revelers, and push my way into the hall. The music mutes. Each breath grows shallower. The shreds of my LA dreams drag me down. Numb and defeated, I collapse by a pile of jackets. The world dims. I place the mostly full cup on the carpet. My eyelids close. I don't want the drink.

I don't know what I want.

# Twenty-Two

Sarah

Thursday's writing huddle starts the same way: me first in the conference room, setting it up. My usual seat by Karina has a cup in front of it. Is someone sitting in my spot? Or did they forget to clean up last night while I was on set?

"That's for you." Rod walks through the door with a box of donuts and nods at the drink. "Welcome to the team, Connor." He sets the treats on the credenza. "Get ready to see your name in tiny print in the rolling credits."

"What?" Spots dance in front of my eyes.

"You're hired. If we get picked up next season, you're on the team. Kyle's been raving about you to the bosses, and now I'm sure in the future you'll tell me what you really think. Step up. We don't need wilting wallflowers in this room."

"I'm . . ."

"No need to thank me." He takes a chocolate donut with pink glaze and coconut sprinkles. "Enjoy your coffee, but don't get used to it. I still expect you to know my order."

The rest of the team rolls in, see my solitary cup and the donuts, and somehow, they know. I get a couple of thumbs-up, a pat on the back, and a heartfelt hug from Karina. The sugary feel of her embrace coats me. "I knew you'd fit right in."

I should be happy. This is my dream come true. I'm part of the team. I will have an actual writing credit to my name, listed on IMDb. This is proof I can do my job, even though part of it will still consist of coffees and typing up conversations.

The win feels hollow with the chasm splitting me in two. All I can think of is Nick. He's the one I want to tell. He's the person who fully gets how important this is for me. He knows how much being a screenwriter, making it in this town means. Has known since the moment we met. It's what we connected over. I try to swallow the rising sob, but my mouth is too dry. I look up. I'm alone in a room full of people, part of the team, but I might've lost the person who I want to share my heart with. I bring the cup of coffee to my mouth with both hands. The hot liquid burns my tongue, but I keep drinking, accepting the pain. I need to glue the two halves of my world together. I dig my elbows into the edge of the table. I want to be Team Nick. And I need him to be Team Sarah again.

Two sleepless nights without Nick. One dreary day. Thirty-two endless hours. Hours full of transcribing notes, researching for Rod, editing the pages of the screenplay Karina wants to show Ms. Hansley. Even with incessant work, I check my phone every five minutes. I rush home in case he's there and hold back tears when the apartment is empty. I tug on my hair. My scalp smarts but can't distract me from the Nick-shaped void. He hasn't responded to any of my texts since his one-word answer to my first request to come home.

The uncertainty tears me apart. Is this how Nick felt all summer? Pain jabs between my shoulder blades. I hate that I put him through that. Is this payback?

I curse myself for even considering such a notion. Nick would never punish me. He's too kind, his heart too big.

A heart I crushed.

Without even noticing.

Saturday morning, I don't even bother getting out of bed. What's the point? My head is heavy and pounding. I could drive over to his father's place. I'm pretty sure he's staying there. That or at the frat house with Mateo and Wil. Should I though? Or is it best to let him cool off? Do I give him time, or do I fight for him? The dull throb in my temples intensifies. I don't want to push too much in case I send him running.

I crush my face into his pillow and inhale his scent. Tears prickle at my eyes, and I shut them. I won't cry. I can fix this.

My phone buzzes, and my heart rate doubles. I leap for the device, but my excitement dies when I see Wil's face on the screen. Maybe something happened at Blend.

"Sarah, I need your help."

"Is it Nick?"

"Nick? No. He's fine. It's for El."

Nick's fine. He's fine while I'm withering inside. I dig my nail into the tender spot over my collarbone. "What about El?"

"I want to surprise her with a video shoot for her song. It's a long story, but I owe her this favor. And she'd never ask." Wil's accent is thicker when he's unsure of himself. Today I can tell he's unsettled. "I'll send you the song. Can you help organize the video? It needs a story, a script that matches her lyrics. We have to do it tonight."

"Tonight, as in this evening?"

"Yes. It's our last performance at The Devil's Martini."

I look at the ceiling. I could use the distraction, nothing else to do today but obsess about Nick.

Wil rustles on the other end. "Nick and Mateo are already in."

"Nick will be there?" My heart sputters.

"Of course. He's our director."

I'm not forcing him to see me if Wil arranged it. "Does he know you're asking me to help?"

"Of course."

"I'll be there." I pick up a blank index card and write down Wil's request. He doesn't leave me much time to organize my thoughts, but I'll do my best. I missed their HalloRade gig on Halloween, at least I'll hear Wil and El sing.

Wil and Nick walk in the side door of The Devil's Martini, and my fingers curl tighter around the small gift bag in my hand. For a split second our eyes meet, and he channels recognition filled with anguish before his gaze drops. My insides mirror my fingers, tight and knotted with the pain I've caused my boyfriend.

"Is she here yet?" Wil's eyes dart around the room, intent on finding El, the reason we are all gathered here. "She texted an hour ago that she's on her way. She should be here by now."

"At least she texted," Nick grumbles from his corner.

His words stab at the festering wound in my chest. The guilt laced with regret. I face Nick. He continues to stare at the ground as he kicks his heel against the already beat up wall. "Not helping, Nick" is what I want to scream at him, but I can't.

El being late adds fuel to the firestorm between us. I had a valid excuse as well, but Nick barely listened to me. To be fair, I didn't listen to him either. I wasn't looking at things from his perspective, too blinded by what I wanted, needed. Too hyped on the thrill of being on set and assisting Kyle.

The silent way we could read each other across a room is broken. Not permanently, I hope. I can fix this. I know I can. He needs to talk to me.

I lift my shoulders and step in his direction, determined to have the conversation. Now. Even if Wil witnesses it. The side door opens again, and El bursts into the room.

Wil rushes to her. "You're late."

"Hello to you, too." El's big blue eyes sparkle, and I watch Nick observing the other couple. For another brief moment he looks my way, but this time there is no heartache in his expression. It's a face I've seen only once before, at The Diamond Club when my customer insulted me. Anger laces his features. Anger aimed at me.

Goosebumps erupt on my skin, and my back hits the backstage wall. The shock of him looking at me this way scares me. What if I can't fix this? Can't make him understand?

This can't be the end.

We've barely begun.

There's so much more to do, to see, to love.

Nick shoves the tripod into its leather case and swings it over his shoulder. My head aches, probably from lack of sleep, but the shaking of my hands is from the adrenaline of Nick nailing that last shot. His inspiration to tie his phone to a measuring tape, climb a ladder, and drop the camera got a wicked shot of El staring up at the viewer. It gave me chills.

"What's next?" El looks to me. So does Wil. Nick stares at the floor. It hurts that he can't even look at me. I'm done bleeding all over the floor at being unable to touch him, and he's refusing to acknowledge my presence. He talks to me like I'm a robot, instructing me to shoot at The Devil's Martini with the extra camera from the side, ordering me to explain to the frat guys how to carry El on the mattress so it fits with the story, asking me what's in my script. But it's pure business. Emotionless. You'd think we just met each other today. Each request slices my soul.

"Last shot of the night." I watch Nick's face for any reaction. "Griffith Park." I wasn't lying to El when I said it matches the lyrics in her song perfectly, but I was selfish too. I wanted Nick to myself at the first place we kissed. Our spot. My cheeks heat with the memory.

No matter how much he might hate me now, we have to talk. And I need the magic of that place to work again.

# Twenty-Three

# NICK

With the speed she's whipping through the streets, it takes less than half an hour to make the climb into the Hollywood hills. I saw past Wil and El's story that Mateo needed their directions to get here. I've been in Mateo's classic Corvette. The dude has a tricked-out entertainment system that includes a retractable screen with what I'd imagine is military-grade GPS.

Trees whip by and the wind blows Sarah's blond hair around like a halo. My mind quiets at the memory. It's a repeat of the video I recorded on Christmas Eve. The one I obsessed over for months, keeping her alive in my mind. She looked carefree in the original. Now a scowl mars her face.

The tires squeal as she peels into the parking lot of the Griffith Observatory, and I brace my knees against the dashboard as she slams into a spot. She rams on the parking brake. "We need to talk."

"Not now." I scramble out, shove the door closed, and head for the trunk to get the equipment for the final shot. This is not the time. I look over my shoulder, hoping to see the gold of Mateo's car.

Sarah's hand presses against my forearm. "Yes, now."

"Of course. You want to talk, so we talk. Who cares about what I want?" I stuff my hands into my pockets and try to shuffle around her, but she blocks my way. I veer the other way, but she matches my direction and blocks me again. How can someone so little be such a huge annoyance?

"Nick. Please."

I freeze. The tension in her voice crawls inside me and fights with the anger flaring in my chest. Unable to look at her, I focus on a blond tendril floating in the wind.

"I'm a shitty girlfriend," she shouts over the wind. I suppress the no that's instinctively trying to force its way out. "It's not an excuse, but can you give me a chance to explain?"

"You'll do what you want anyway." My eyes betray me, and I meet her stare. A boiling pot of emotions swimming in her ocean gaze I've lost myself in over and over.

"Why do you keep saying that?" Her fingers grip my wrist. "I haven't done anything on purpose."

The need to control something bubbles up, and I back out of her grasp. The wind whips between us and I shiver, from the cold or the lack of her touch, I'm not sure. Her foot juts out like she's going to close the gap between us, but it hesitates midway then returns to its partner. "Talk to me."

Another command. I pivot and contemplate the grid pattern of lights that make up downtown LA. Black against white, positive against negative. I kick at the ground and send a pebble flying. I think about the first time we were here. My lie prevented me from sharing everything with her. The easy comfort of being together. The intense desire to kiss her. But I didn't kiss her. She kissed me.

When I came to LA this summer, the only way she'd let me be in her life was if we were friends. She decided when that changed, moved us from friends to more, me following like the puppy people joke about. The gusts of wind needle my neck. These last months, I've done everything on her terms.

"But only if you want to." Sarah's voice is quiet behind me. I almost miss the plea.

Thing is, I want to talk to her. Embers of anger burn my lungs as I suck in air. I may have already damaged what we have, what do I have to lose for speaking up? "Fuck." I spin around. "You expect me to do everything you want, and you never ask what I want." I spit the words that scorch my tongue.

Lines form between her eyebrows. "That's not true, I—"

"Yes, it is." She doesn't get to control this conversation. "You're always in control. Right down to the side of the bed I get to sleep on, even though I hate sleeping on the outside edge. I have nightmares about falling out of the bed."

She winces. "You get up early. I was making it easier for you to get out of bed."

That never occurred to me. "Maybe I don't want you to make it easier. Couldn't you just ask me where I like to sleep?"

"Okay." She crosses her arms. "Where d'you want to sleep?"

With you of course.

"No, you're not listening. It's like you . . . like I'm an accessory." I jab at my T-shirt.

Her head snaps backward. "Sorry?"

"You treat me like I'm some . . ." I pull on my hair, trying to find a way to explain how useless I feel around her. How she controls everything, and I spend half my time waiting around for her. "Like a jacket you put on when you feel like it. Otherwise, I'm left in the closet, ignored."

"I don't—"

Lava singes my gut. She's not listening to me. "You moved me into your room."

Sarah's hands fall to her sides. "You don't want to live with me?" Her voice is barely a whisper.

"You're not listening." The lava sputters into my throat, and my feet can't keep still. I need to move, stomp out the heat wave building inside. "Of course, I wanted to move in with you."

"Wanted?"

"I wanted to move furniture around, maybe buy new sheets." I halt in front of her. "The point is, you didn't wait for me. I came home, and you'd stuffed my clothes into a little corner of your closet."

She rolls her eyes. "You're always so busy with school, your job, the documentary, stressed about working for your dad. I didn't want you to have to deal with the burden."

"Fuck. Merging *our*"—I wave between us—"lives is not a burden, Sarah. It's supposed to be fun. Something we do together. I didn't know where my socks were for three days."

"I thought I was making it easier for you."

"Easier for me. Or for you?" The wind picks up and fans her golden hair, light against the dark night. I welcome the cold air against my burning skin. "We do what you want: go to restaurants I can't afford, clubs I can't get into, drive around in your car, drink ginger ale even though I prefer Coke."

"I thought you liked ginger ale." Her lips press into a thin line.

"*You* like ginger ale. I drink it because *you* buy it."

"Well, no one is forcing you to drink ginger ale." Her hands are fluttering like she's trying to take flight. "If you want to drink shitty Coke, drink the stupid stuff."

"Maybe I will. No more ginger ale for me." I wave my hand in the air. "Or sushi." I'm done.

Her mouth forms a little O. "Now you don't like sushi?"

"No. Actually, I do like it." I wave away her attempt to interrupt me. "But do we have to eat the stuff so often? If we're going to splurge, can't we have a burger now and again?"

Sarah takes a step toward me. "I can do that. Redecorate my . . . our room. No more ginger ale. Less sushi. Anything else?"

"Yeah." It's easier to breathe now. The fire inside is down to a smolder. She's listening to me, not running away. I haven't lost her. Yet. I straighten my shoulders and prepare for the worst part. "You don't include me in your life."

There, I said it. It's out in the world.

I study her reaction. At first her face freezes. I shouldn't have pushed this. Should've taken the win on the bed and the burgers and ignored the rest. It's not like it's all bad. There's good. So much good. It far outweighs the bad. I stiffen.

She's going to leave me now.

I'm sure of it.

But she doesn't step away. She stays rooted to the spot. Her bottom lip trembles, and my heart seizes at the little quiver. This is worse. I've hurt her. My arms scream to hold her, make everything better.

She reaches out and hooks her pinkie around mine. "Explain." Her touch is gentle, like her voice.

The muscles in my neck relax. She wants to understand. I hunt for the right words. "You didn't tell me about your job."

She stares at me. "What are you talking about?"

"You knew for a day about the offer, and I didn't find out until you arrived home that Sunday. I had no idea you were even coming back early." I stare at the spot where our fingers are linked. "Siobhan did though. She knew before me. I was an afterthought."

"Oh, Nick. I'm so sorry." Sarah's fingers wrap around mine. "I promise, you were . . . *are* not an afterthought."

"Could've fooled me."

"No. I've been the fool." She raises her other hand to her cheek. "I didn't realize I was making you miserable. I've been so busy trying to make everything perfect for you, and I failed."

"I don't need perfection." I meet her eyes, dark and glossy in the parking lot lights. I lean in. "I'm not a classic cocktail."

"Mr. Old Fashioned." There's a smile on her lips, but it doesn't reach her eyes and quickly fades. "I hate that you felt like this for one moment, never mind weeks. Why didn't you say anything?"

I've come this far. What's one more embarrassing confession? "Guess I was afraid you wouldn't choose to be with me if I didn't . . ."

"Do what I wanted?" She reaches for my other hand, and I tuck it into mine. "I understand now. Thank you for telling me."

A different kind of heat flushes through me. A warmth of comprehension, relief, compassion. I spoke up, and she's still here. Choosing me.

Sarah licks her lips. "I haven't been upfront with you either."

Cold dread slithers down my spine. Is there someone else? Was she really with them on Halloween? Is she breaking up with me?

Her grip tightens on my hands, like I might fly away in the wind like a balloon. "Things have not been going well at work."

"More assholes at The Diamond Club?"

"Always. But not that work. With the show."

I thought she loved the job, lucky to get the junior writing position, and always seemed happy when she talked about the place. "I don't understand. You love it there."

"It was not what I expected." She looks up at the sky. "It's bullshit, actually. I mean, I knew I'd have to start at the bottom, put in my time. I'm not afraid of hard work. But no one was taking me seriously. The room full of experienced people who assumed I was this little blonde who doesn't have a brain and has nothing to offer but take their lunch and coffee orders. It was worse than my bartending job."

"Was? Did you quit?" Why didn't she tell me anything? Because that's what she does. She doesn't share with me. I groan through my teeth. Not like I do with her. I cried in her arms after I read Dad's letter. Doesn't she know she can share anything with me?

"No, after Halloween it changed. I know it was the worst for you, but my helping Kyle on set impressed Rod and the producers. They offered me the full-time position if the show gets picked up for a second season."

"You did it." Happiness sparks inside me. "I knew you would." I grip her tighter.

Her eyes fall to our joined hands. "I did. But for weeks I felt like a nobody."

"You are not a nobody. You are a screenwriter."

A tiny smile, the first genuine one I've seen today, peaks out. "You're just saying that because you are my. . ." The smile fades into the night.

"Boyfriend," I remind her.

"Does that mean you're not breaking up with me?"

I glare at her. How could she think that?

"When you left on Halloween and wouldn't answer my texts I . . . I thought . . . I'd ruined everything," she says.

I let go of her fingers, and she blinks rapidly, like she's holding back tears. I cup her face to relay my support. "We can work through it."

"I hurt you." Her voice cracks. "And I hate myself for it." Her knuckles dig into my shirt. "I hate that you think I don't"— she swallows—"I'd not want to share my life with you. I was so excited about going to the party with you, showing off our couple's costume, being a part of your world."

I bite the inside of my cheek. "There'll be other parties." I pull Sarah into my arms. "Just talk to me. About your work. Your screenplay. Your parents. Anything. I'm not a bystander."

"I'm so sorry, Nick. I'm a shitty person. I can't make it all work, make everyone happy. My job, the club, even writing with Karina . . . I never have enough time. You're the only solid good thing I have. When we are together, I don't want to waste our precious moments and drag you down by complaining about my problems."

I kiss the top of her head and inhale the familiar fruity scent of Sarah. "Listening to you is not a waste. That's what couples do. Share. The good and the bad." She burrows into my chest, and her shoulders shake. My girl is crying, breaking down. She's so strong, but everyone has a breaking point. I should've known.

She can only carry so much weight on her tiny shoulders. My fingers stroke her hair.

We are going to share the load. "You are not alone," I whisper in her ear. Her trembles subside. "You don't have to do everything by yourself. I'm here. I'm in this with you. We're a team." Her hands press against my back. "But you have to let me in."

She releases her grip on me, rubs her nose, and my Thumbelina looks up at me.

"Let me help, Sarah." I beg her for understanding and a commitment to what I'm offering. "Let me be part of your life, not just in it. Let me be your partner."

Lights flash in my eyes and a horn beeps. The crew is here. The video shoot for El. The reason we're at Griffith Park. She doesn't answer, trains her gaze at Mateo's car, and pushes me away. I don't know how else to beg. My heart sinks. I reluctantly let go of Sarah.

# Twenty-Four

# NICK

I STEP QUIETLY OVER the threshold of Dad's apartment. I see
his home differently now. The hallway with just a shoe rack
doesn't scream cheap anymore. It's tidy and purposeful. Like
Dad. The foldout couch that doubles as the guest bedroom—a
thoughtful choice to let me have a place to stay. How long did
he have to save to afford this? I drag my nails through three days
of stubble and stifle a yawn. The sparsely filled bookshelves have
mostly library books and a couple of Dad's favorite screenplays
that I read while living with him. He's constantly reading, but
the books he chooses to spend money on are the ones he re-reads
multiple times.

It's after one in the morning and I expect Dad to be in bed,
but the light in the galley kitchen is on. He's at the small café
table for two—the only table he could squeeze into the apart-

ment—with an empty glass, a can of Coke, and a book opened almost to the last page.

"I was hoping I wouldn't see you today." Dad takes off his reading glasses.

I strip off my jacket. It smells too much of Sarah. "The shoot ran longer than we expected."

"Any good footage?" He's interested in what I have to say. Or maybe he always was, I just didn't see the signs. Like with Sarah. I had no idea she was struggling at work.

"We'll see Monday when I start editing, but I think I got everything we need for the video."

Dad spins my way and watches me switch on the kettle. "Did you talk to Sarah?"

Talked and made her cry. I did that. It hurts to breathe. I should've told her how Mom and Mike decided what was and wasn't a good idea. They stifled me with their love. LA was supposed to give me the freedom to make my own choices. Frequently stupid. And even more frequently ones I'll be learning from. But mine.

"Is it that bad?" he asks.

Do I tell him the whole sordid fight? Gloss over the highlights reel? Or brush him off?

"It's a long conversation." I give Dad the opportunity to bail and claim he has to go to bed or find whatever excuse he needs not to endure the story of my romantic woes.

"I have all night. We're not meeting Colleen until ten a.m. tomorrow." He puts a bookmark in and dithers before closing the book. "Wanna make me a cup of tea too?"

Dad doesn't drink tea, but he knows I love it. Coke. Tea. Coffee. I'll take any way I can to pump caffeine into my veins. "Sarah and I had a fight."

"I gathered that much. You crashing here for two nights with a wallet and no toothbrush or change of clothes was a dead giveaway."

"We had another fight. Tonight." I pull on my ear. "Or at least I think it was a fight." I place two mugs on the kitchen counter.

Dad leans against the back of his chair. "What did you do?"

"Why do you assume I did something?"

"Men in our family tend to run hot. We don't make the best decisions when under pressure."

"I think we both screwed up." I rub my face as if I can peel off the layers of exhaustion. "She doesn't treat me like an equal partner, and I don't tell her when things bother me. It's like we speak two different languages. Whatever silent understanding we had when we met, it's not working anymore. We need words, conversations. And she barely tells me anything."

"Doesn't vocalize her feelings. Hmmm, sounds familiar," says Dad. I meet his gaze. What is he driving at? "She's a writer, son. Not many of us are good with conversation. We tend to be better with the written word."

The texts she sends me, even from the other room like on my birthday. I squeeze the mug. The written word has meaning to her.

"Yeah, now that you say it." I stare at the kettle that refuses to boil. This was Dad and my issue too. Lack of communication. Until I asked Dad about his days after prison, he didn't share. The veil between us could easily have been punctured had we talked. Talking is the key. It helped with Sarah tonight but didn't fix our problems. Longing swirls in my stomach. She didn't say, "Come home with me."

If asked to go back to our apartment, I would've said yes. "What do I do now?"

"What does your heart tell you?"

My heart? Never in my life did I think I'd be having a discussion with my dad about my heart. "It . . . well." I have to say it. "It loves her."

The smile Dad gives me is the widest and most genuine I've seen on him. "That's good news. Have you told her?"

"No."

"Why not?"

"Don't you think it's too soon? We barely know each other. Maybe moving in together so quickly was a mistake. Should we have kept it more casual? Kept separate spaces?"

Dad hands me the tea bags. "Do you want space from her?"

"No." My voice is too loud. The idea too outlandish. I take a breath. "I want to be with her always. With how busy we both are, if we live in different places, we'd see each other once a week. And I want to see her every day when I wake up."

"Sounds like you've made your decision."

I sigh. "But is it the right one? Me wanting to be with her every minute of every day doesn't mean I should. Doesn't mean it's healthy for our relationship. If I step back, maybe then we'll learn to communicate better and no longer assume the other person knows."

"Never assume." He puts a hand on my shoulder. It's solid and comforting. "Tell her. Fighting over things that are important to you is better than silently stewing and resenting each other."

"I hate fighting. Can't we just share things?" Saying it out loud solidifies the need. "That's what I want. An equal partnership. Making decisions together. Making mistakes together. Sharing the responsibility for the good and the bad." I hunch over my tea.

"Tell her that." He picks up his mug and takes a sip, meeting my eyes. "And the sooner the better. Don't waste your time. We have a lot less of it than we think."

Ms. Hansley hits pause on her laptop, the image of Nazhir and his sister locked in an embrace frozen on the screen. I hold my breath. It feels like I've been holding it since we walked into

Blend this morning. Her approval of the scenes I've captured, cut, and compiled will determine if I wasted my time with this project or if we have a winner.

She turns away from the screen and finds Dad's gaze, then mine. Her mouth curls upward. "It's good."

Beside me, Dad exhales. I release my grip on the edge of my chair. "Really?"

"Yep. Nazhir here"—she points to the frozen video—"pulls at the heartstrings. Exactly what I was hoping to capture on film."

Dad breaks off a piece of his muffin. "It was Nick's idea to film him in front of the exit sign."

I can't help but smile at the pride in Dad's voice.

"It works well." Ms. Hansley glances at the screen and back to me. "I want to change a few things. Maybe reorder the sequence of interviews. Chris makes a harder punch for the beginning. He's got swagger and we want to capture the audience's attention." Her words sound familiar. Something Sarah said when we were working on *Indigo*. Something about grabbing the viewer by the throat and never letting go. I wanted Sarah to see this first, give me her storytelling expertise but . . .

Ms. Hansley taps her nails against the side of her coffee cup. "Chris gets out next week?"

"If they don't release him early." I sigh.

"I'll talk to the warden." Dad pulls out his phone. "See if he can give us more of a heads-up if anything changes."

"I'll need this done by the end of November." Ms. Hansley closes her laptop and claps her hands together. Her eyes shine. "The first draft you sent me caught the attention of some producers. They have a major purchasing meeting in December and have asked me to pitch. If this goes the way I think, we might have a more substantial project. And a much bigger budget to work with."

"Will do." I give her a thumbs-up. More money should've sounded fantastic, but I'm too upset to fully enjoy the prospect. While Sarah remains silent, even the possibility of success doesn't dull the pain.

# Twenty-Five

## Sarah

HEADACHE IS MY CONSTANT companion. I don't think I'll be able to sleep well until Nick's back in our room. In our bed. Without him sleeping by my side, I thrash around the too-large bed. It never used to be too big. Everything has changed because of him.

I punch Nick's pillow on his unrumpled side of the mattress. The backs of my eyes burn. He can sleep by the wall. I don't mind him climbing over me when he gets out of bed. I make him wake me up most mornings before he leaves so I can get my first kiss of the day. After all the words I said last night, I thought he'd forgive me and come back. My heart cramps. I can't keep going like this.

I push myself out of bed and amble down the hall into the kitchen. My mouth is parched. I've cried so much again I might've depleted my tear reserves. I need water.

Ryan sits at the table and looks past me down the empty hall. "He didn't come home last night?"

The verbal reminder stabs the base of my throat. Breathing is hard. Standing is harder. Not thinking about Nick is the hardest. I wobble and catch myself on the wall. Nick made the excuse that he and Mr. Parker had to meet with Ms. Hansley early this morning, so instead of begging him to come home, I dropped him off at Theo's place. But doing it felt wrong. A thousand pins prick my scalp at the memory. Does he not want to live with me?

Ryan abandons his chair and wraps me in his arms. The dull ache in my chest doesn't disappear. His hug is comforting, but his are the wrong arms. "Nick's a fool."

"No, I'm the fool."

"I doubt that." He draws slow circles on my back.

The tears threaten again, and I grind my teeth to stem them. "Nick said things last night that I just . . . I don't know why I never thought of them."

"What did he say?"

I replay the whole fight for Ryan, tell him about Nick's frustration, all the instances he brought up. "He basically accused me of . . . not noticing him."

Ryan's hand stills.

I pull away and look my friend in the eye. "What?"

"I don't want to get into the middle of your relationship again. It didn't work out so well for me last time."

His words grate against my nerves. I push away from him and stomp over to the fridge. "So basically, no one wants to tell me anything. I have to guess at everything."

Ryan holds up his hands. "Whoa, whoa. It's just that I don't want to cause more trouble. I don't want to be the reason you and Nick don't get past this."

My gut cramps at his words. I must make this right.

"I also wanna keep my friends. That's you *and* Nick."

"Help me. Please." I do the thing I never do. I ask for help.

"Of course." Ryan pulls up a chair at the table and points to the one across from him. I plop onto the cold pleather. Chills run up my legs. I gather Nick's hoodie around me. I swear the scent of him is fading already. My skin misses his skin. I'm losing him by the minute.

Ryan puts his hands on the wooden surface between us, palms up. He wiggles his fingers, and I let go of the jersey and take his hands. "You and Nick are great together. You have this bond, this link that I don't see very often. I've certainly never been lucky enough to experience it."

This is what I thought we had. These silent communications on the same wavelength. Maybe I had it all wrong. I try to yank my fingers out of Ryan's, but he doesn't let me. "Then why is he so miserable?"

"Because you formed a commensalism instead of a mutualism."

I stare at Ryan. I have no idea what he's talking about.

"Commensalism is a version of biological interaction between two organisms or species. There are other forms, but this is the relationship you and Nick now have."

"Ryan, I don't—" I shake my head.

"At its core, it's a relationship in which members of one species gain benefits while those of the other species neither benefits nor are harmed."

"Are you saying I'm a leech, living off Nick?"

"No, no. I'm not explaining this correctly." He closes his eyes like he's scanning his brain for the right vocabulary. One with fewer scientific terms and more examples I can understand. "I've been living with you for a couple weeks now. I've observed your behavior." He opens his eyes and pins me with his gaze. Why do I suddenly feel like a lab rat in Ryan's grand experiment? "I've seen him sacrifice his own desires to make you happy."

"And I don't make him happy?" I roll my eyes.

"The dude is deliriously happy with you. I guess that's why he never asked for anything he wants or doesn't ever contradict you." Ryan tilts his head. "You go around this apartment arranging everything for him."

I sigh in frustration. I repeat what I said to Nick last night. "I'm just trying to make things better for him. Easier."

"Sure. I see that. You have everything under control. Buttoned-down. Ironed out. What I don't see is you ever asking Nick what he wants. Listening to his clues."

"I . . ." Is Ryan right? I do like to control things. Have I been controlling Nick? Or at least our lives? Keeping things in order lets me deal with everything on my plate. If I don't organize it, who will? My pounding head reminds me I can't control everything.

"Okay." I bite my cheek. The pain distracts from the pain in my heart. Another control thing? "What do I do?"

"What you want is mutualism."

"Mutual sounds good, right?"

"It is good. It's a relationship where both parties mutually benefit. A true partnership."

The word clicks in my brain, like when I find the perfect word for a sentence, the one that encompasses the exact feeling I'm trying to express. The dissonance in my brain changes into a clear picture. "That." I sit up straight. "I want that. How do I get that?"

"Well, ultimately, it's up to you and Nick. I think a good place to start is asking him what he wants. Stop assuming you know what he wants or what's best for him. You have to ask. You have to share what's inside your head. You have to open yourself up to him."

Nick's last words to me before Mateo interrupted us. His plea to let him in. The torrent of Nick's demands bombarded my senses. Stilted my ability to speak. The only way to finish the shoot was to step away from him, to maintain my composure. It was either that or loose it in front of our friends.

"You can't control everything, Sarah. You have to let other people help." Ryan holds my gaze. "Start by letting one person in. Really in. Don't hold back like you did with me."

"I didn't—"

"Our time together was great, but it was like"—he looks at the ceiling—"Swiss cheese."

"First, I'm a leech, now I'm cheese?" I'm upset, but a smile creeps onto my lips. Ryan's analogies never disappoint.

"No, listen. We had a blast while it lasted. Both of us gave what we could to each other. I got the fun, sexy Sarah who made everyone laugh and took me on adventures I never would've found myself. But I never got the real Sarah. There were holes, gaps in the version of Sarah you let me see. Like Swiss cheese. See?"

I nod then shrug. "You had holes too."

Ryan's eyes soften. "I know. I . . . well, this isn't about me." A shy smile graces his lips, and I'm excited to learn about the real Ryan. Is this what Nick wants? The concept settles on me like a blanket. "But let's fix the Nick situation first."

"Please." I pull our joined hands together to make a solid finger sandwich.

"He wants to know the whole Sarah."

"No more Swiss cheese," I say.

"I knew you'd get it. Ask Nick what he expects from your relationship. Tell him when you need help. Like you just did with me. That wasn't so hard, was it?"

I cross my arms. "Not really."

"Show Nick you want you two to work, that you are ready to be in a mutually beneficial relationship. Make room for him in your life." Ryan's words swirl in the air between us.

I don't want to be Swiss cheese to Nick. He deserves more. I deserve more. The whole wheel of sturdy Parmesan. I'm losing track of Ryan's analogy, but I know the type of relationship I want with Nick. If I open up, there is no one I'd rather open up to. He knows me like no one else. That scares the shit out of me but excites me at the same time.

I want Nick to come home. Our home.

An idea pops into my head. "I know what to do, but I'm gonna need your help."

"You've got it." Ryan winks. "Always."

# Twenty-Six

# NICK

Sarah: Could you come over to our place?

The text pops over the screen with Sarah's name and a green call button. Another minute and I would've dialed her but she beat me to it. My fingers tremble.

Sarah: Some time today?

Me: Yes. Be there in an hour.

Dad drops me off outside the apartment complex. I speed up the four flights of stairs to our place. That's what she called it in her text. Our place. Those words give me hope. And I need it. A flutter taps against my ribs. I use my keys to open the front door and do a double take.

Is this our place? The normally neat and orderly open-concept kitchen and living room is cluttered with boxes, piles of clothes, and bedroom furniture I recognize from Sarah's room. A small pile of my stuff sits on the kitchen table, separated from the other items. The beating in my chest takes off. Is she kicking me out?

"Nick." Sarah steps out of the hallway. Her hair is gathered in a messy ponytail, and she's wearing the clothes she only puts on when it's her day to clean the bathroom. We hesitate, like two magnets that are used to being attracted to each other and are pushed apart instead. "Thanks for coming."

It's weird to be thanked for coming home. If this is still my home. "You're welcome."

This is awkward.

"Do you want something to drink?"

"Sure," I say. Is this Sarah the server I'm dealing with? The air in the apartment is different. Something has changed.

She doesn't address her messy state and the furniture she has to dodge. In the kitchen, she opens the fridge and points at the top shelf that's filled to the brim with red cans. There must be two cases of Coke in there. My mind is reeling with questions. I shiver, and the cool air of the fridge has nothing to do with it.

"Ryan and Siobhan are out, but once we text them, they'll be back with burgers. If you want." She passes me a can. "They'll stay away until we tell them to come back."

Coke. Burgers. Why is she plying me with food? What's going on here? Tingles wind down my legs, and I can't name the emotions the sight of Sarah holding the Coke wakes in me.

"Come." Sarah stops her walk back into the living room. "Would you please join me?" She's not mocking me. Her choice of words is purposeful, genuine. Maybe an attempt at not sounding like she's commanding me? "Or not." She pulls on the hem of her tank top and doesn't meet my gaze.

"Sure." I leave the can on the counter and follow her, brushing past her dresser that blocks the couch and squish past her mattress that's leaning against the wall of the hallway leading to her bedroom. She opens the door, and her room is empty. Bare. The beats of my pulse climb into my throat. I take a step back. The pounding in my ears creates a soundtrack for this moment. Every stick of furniture, every item she owns is gone. My head buzzes with giddiness. The parquet gleams and daylight streams through the window. I gulp.

"Spring cleaning?" I don't know why I joke. This is serious. Huge. It's a gesture. The Coke and the burgers and Sarah's furniture in the living room make sense now. Goosebumps explode over every inch of my skin. Hope. That's the emotion I couldn't name earlier. I find her eyes, full of anticipation. Like mine must be. "A fresh start?"

"Our fresh start." She picks up an envelope from the windowsill. "If you'll still have me after you read this." She hands me the white rectangle.

I hesitate taking it from her. My mouth goes dry. "What is this?"

"Open it. Please." She waits for me to pry the triangle flap open. It's thicker than a card.

Index cards. Five green index cards like the ones I've seen her use to plot her screenplays lie in my hand. I instantly recognize the meaning of them. The drum of my pulse slams against my ribcage. The five interview questions Dad and I use in our documentary. The same five questions Dad answered as his birthday present to me. Sarah wrote her answers.

She's sharing herself with me.

The hope that was trickling into my veins since seeing the clutter in the living room courses full-force through me. The stream of it is so powerful, the goosebumps change into light trembles. The trembles grow as hope expands and fills me to the brim.

My fingers shake like they did when I realized what Dad gave me. I close the distance between us, take her hand, and press the cards into it. "Read them to me." It's not a request. Not a test either, but I want to hear her words in her voice.

Her eyes are glossy but I don't think it's from alcohol. They're also swimming with the determination I love seeing there. My heart skips a beat, because I know, I feel that this determination is about me. For me. For us.

"I'm not hiding anything from you anymore." She clears her throat and reads from the first card.

"What do you regret? I could say I regret not being with my family last Christmas. Mémère's last Christmas. But I can't. If I went there, I wouldn't have met you. And I will never regret meeting you. But I do have regrets. I regret every moment I made you wait for me this summer, every time I didn't hold your hand or talk to you. I'm so thankful you stayed. Thankful you were amazing enough to believe in us." Her eyes flicker to me and then back to the card. "But most of all I regret taking you for granted. Not paying attention. Not listening to you. I promise you from this day forward I will do my best to listen, to understand. And if you want to talk, I'll talk until you get tired of me. If you'll have me."

The vise that's been crushing my heart since I last walked out of this room eases. Her words acting like the handle, unwinding the hurt. She lets go of me to flip to the next index card, and I miss the warmth of her hand. I step closer, inhaling her strawberry scent.

"Where will you live? I'd like to live with you. Anywhere. Here in our room. In our own place someday. Anywhere, as long as it's with you. If you'll have me."

I smile.

"What are your family's expectations for you? To be happy. For me that means staying here in LA with you. If it means sometimes we eat ramen for dinner until our next paycheck then I'll gladly live like that. I promise, though, some of the dinners will be burgers." A bubble of laughter bursts from my mouth. "However, I hope there will still be sushi sometimes. Because you don't hate sushi. And I love it. I want to be happy with you. If you'll have me."

She doesn't take her eyes off the cards as she moves to the next one. "What will you do for the next six months? Wake up next to you in our bed and watch you get undressed in the evening to crawl into our bed. I want to live in your arms and under the kind, hot, magical gaze of yours." Her voice lowers. "I want to hear about your day and tell you about mine. Share hopes, desires, secrets, and anything else you want to tell me. Or I want to tell you. I want to be with you. In a mutually beneficial relationship." She looks into my eyes. "I want to be your partner."

Partner. The word flashes in the air between us like a neon sign. I want that more than anything. It's the confirmation I was searching for. The hole in my heart stitches back together, and the ache of being separated from Sarah quiets.

"If you'll have me," she whispers.

There is no one else I'd want to have. And to hold. I was hers the moment she asked me if I liked the ridiculous Old Fashioned cocktail she made me on Christmas Eve. The memory unties my tongue. I open my mouth to tell her, but she holds up her finger asking me to wait.

Her gaze drops to the last card. "Where do you see yourself in five years? With you. No matter what happens. But I have a dream. Us making more movies. My screenplays. You as director. Learning from our mistakes, making new ones, fixing them. Together. Perhaps an apartment or house of our own. You and me. No roommates. No parents. One giant bed to share." Her hand reaches out for me. "If you'll have me."

She's giving me the choice. Asking me what I want. The anticipation is gone from her eyes, replaced by something I don't know. But I want to know. And I have the confidence that if I ask, speak up, she'll tell me. Tell me the truth. My newly mended heart expands and contracts with the certainty. The hope that fills me doesn't burst. It settles into my bones and makes the world I imagine become a reality.

Like the last time she read from index cards, I fall. I fall in love with Sarah all over again. As I do every morning I wake up with her in my arms. What she's offering is more to love. All of her. Not just the sunny, happy girl who colors my life with her energy, not only the smart writer that weaves words like it's the easiest thing to do, not simply a friend who's there to lend a helping hand, but the whole package. I can't wait to open the gift she's giving me. Discover the mysteries of Sarah.

Will I have her? It's the easiest choice I'll ever make. I choose her every time. I wrap my fingers around hers. She presses the green cards against her collar bone and inhales sharply. I pry the paper out of her hand and reread the last one. At the bottom there's a portion she didn't read.

P.S. Maybe a pet. Have you considered a dog? Or are you a cat person? I can't believe we've never talked about it. We need to talk a lot more.

Her words, her humor brushes away the last shreds of the curtain that hung between us. She had a future vision of us when she wrote these words. "I like dogs and cats. Maybe we can have both in our home."

Her smile is immediate. The sun bursting through dark clouds to illuminate the world again. "So, it's a yes? Will you have me, warts and all?"

"It's a yes. It's always been a yes." I pull her close. "The moment I saw you at your bar, it was a yes." I kiss her forehead.

"The moment you kissed me in Griffith Park, it was a yes." I kiss her cheek. "The moment you came looking for me in Chicago." I kiss her jaw. "The moment you gave me the hat and the hockey tickets, it was a yes." I kiss her nose. "Every day is a yes." I hesitate, my lips a breath away from hers. "I'll have you, if you'll have me."

"There's nothing I want more." I wait for her to close the gap between our mouths like she always does. She doesn't move. Sarah is waiting for me. Letting me take the lead. The sensation is heady. It's the night in the hotel room again. Her trusting me with her heart. Another gift.

I don't make her wait long, brushing her lips with mine, thanking her for trusting me. The cards fall to the floor as I crush her against me, savoring the feel of her body against mine, back where it belongs. Her moan sends tingles from my mouth to my heart, and I reacquaint myself with the girl I almost lost because we were both too stubborn to express our needs and our feelings.

"Wait." Sarah's ragged exhale punctuates the word. "We don't have a bed in here."

"Fuck." I'll have her anywhere, but a bed would be a lot nicer. Or a mattress. My abs tighten. I separate myself from her and grab the mattress from the hallway. I try to move it, but the other end flops to the side and slides against the wall.

"Hold on." Sarah walks around me and under the mattress. She takes the opposite side. She's as tall as the mattress on its side, and I don't expect much of a difference in its behavior. But with her help the weight moves, and we drag it into the middle of the room. The power of a partner.

"Where do you want it?" I ask her.

"Where do you want it?"

This is cute, but this game of answering my questions with questions will get boring soon. "I liked it by the wall before."

"Maybe we move to that wall instead." She points to the one by the window. "Put it on the other wall, so it's easier for you to climb out when you sleep by the wall and I sleep on the edge side?"

Fireworks burst in me. I love this woman. "I love the idea. It's"—what did she call it?—"mutually beneficial."

Her smile heats my blood.

We drop the mattress onto the floor and look at the living room where the rest of the furniture and our stuff waits for us. "Should I call Sio and Ryan to come back with the burgers and help us move back in?" she asks.

"I have a better idea." I take Sarah into my arms and drop us onto the mattress. I can't wait to have her. "Maybe we pretend we are in an apartment of our own without roommates on a brand-new mattress and do what anyone does when they move in."

She snuggles closer to me. "What is that?" Her leg sneaks in between mine, and her hand traces my jawline. In a cartoon, sparks would fly where she touches me. In real life, my real life, her body wakes my body up.

"Christen as many surfaces as we can, starting with the mattress." I slip my hand under her shirt, caressing the skin I've missed for too many nights, reveling in the ability to touch her again. "We call Ryan and Siobhan later." I suck on the tender spot beneath her ear and am rewarded with another moan. "Much later."

"I like this idea." Sarah presses her yes into my lips, and we start a new adventure together.

# TWENTY-SEVEN

## Sarah

Maybe it's because I was the oldest in the family and had to help with the bakery, watching over my brothers, pitching in at the café. Maybe it's because I abandoned the cozy life in Toronto my family built. Maybe it's the stubborn streak Mémère insisted we share, but I never expected anyone to do things for me.

Accepting help is harder for me than staying up all night and finishing the task by myself. Sharing my troubles, sharing my disappointments, even splitting the chores is not something I've ever considered. I can handle it. That I get from Mom.

But it's different now. I'm opening up. Letting others in. Well, one person at least. *The* person.

I understand what it was that first night we met that drew me to him. Nick's a great listener, yes, but he's someone I could be genuine around. Somehow with the competition and him moving in, instead of letting him see the bits inside me I'm not proud of, the proverbial warts, I decided letting him be in my space was close enough. I'd never let anyone else get even that close. Burdening him with my feelings seemed a step too far. I didn't want to suffocate him with my drama. Never wanted him to see I'm not always the sunny girl he tells me I am.

The thing is, although the sun shines a lot in LA, there are still hours of darkness. Everything has balance. Mutualism, as the brainiac version of Ryan calls it. I was holding back a part of me, not letting Nick see the ugly underbelly. Not letting him take some of the load. Not trusting him. The light he sees in me, I need to see it too. That's what makes some of my harder days not so crappy. Seeing my reflection in his eyes, I feel more powerful.

Things have changed for the better. I'm sunny most of the time, but I have my dark moments. Nick doesn't let me slip away into my head. He asks me what he can do around the apartment, insists I tell him everything that happens in the writing room, and the truth, not the glossy version I've been feeding him for weeks.

I share the dust balls of my soul and the blows to my ego I get every time I finish cleaning up the writer's room, and my reflection in Nick's eyes does not dim. It's as bright as ever. He keeps seeing the best of me, the potential of my career, my stick-to-it-ness, my willingness to fight for what I want. His positivity is the fuel I need to sweep the shards of my shattered expectations of instant success.

We are a team, and we may be in a three-legged race right now, but with Nick by my side, I'm going to get through this.

I'm going to enjoy and laugh and treasure the fact that I now have the entire Starbucks menu memorized, that I ask better questions, that I can listen and take notes in a meeting at the same time and not waste my free time with Nick at home on cleaning them up. I celebrate that the security guard at Clear Productions recognizes me and greets me by my name. Tiny victories. Not giant failures.

I don't ditch Mom's semiweekly calls anymore.

"Have you made a decision?" Mom's face fills the screen of my laptop.

"I have."

Her lips form a thin line. "You're staying in LA, aren't you?"

"I know it's not what you want to hear, but I'm happy here." A sense of calm settles over me because I'm finally at home in LA. With Nick.

"You're wrong. I want you to be happy. I need you to be happy. I was hoping you could be happy in a place I didn't have to take a plane or drive three days to when I wanted to see you. I miss my daughter."

"And I miss you. As soon as I have enough work experience to find something in my field in Toronto, I'll talk to Nick about moving there. Or maybe spending six months here and six months there. I promise."

"Oh, Sarah." She put her hands over the Côté Fraises stitching on her apron. "Don't make promises you can't keep. Live your life without obligations hanging over your head. Be happy. For him and for you."

"I do miss you."

"I miss you too, honey. But you'll be home for our twenty-fifth anniversary and Christmas. We'll have plenty of time together then. You will be home, right?"

And there's my mother. "Yes, Mom." I roll my eyes. "Filming will be finished in a few weeks. Then we're on a break while we wait to see if we get picked up for season two. I'll have most of December off."

"So, you'll be home for your birthday?" Mom's eyes light up.

"Not quite that early. I'm hoping to pick up extra shifts at The Diamond Club. It's the busiest season, and there's still rent due at the end of every month."

"Fine, fine. But I want you here for a solid week at least. And you'll bring Nick for sure this time."

Nick and I haven't figured out the whole holiday schedule yet. He promised to spend time with his family, and I, mine. "That's the plan." I hear the popcorn maker whir. "Gotta go, Mom."

"Okay. I love you."

"I love you too."

I close my laptop and move into the living room.

My handsome boyfriend looks hot as hell cooking in the kitchen. The smell of popcorn and butter flavors the air. I cross my arms to not peel his T-shirt off and eat the popcorn off his skin. And I don't. Because my Mr. Old Fashioned is old-fashioned. I have to remember to let him take the lead now and again. He wanted to cuddle on the couch and watch a movie. I'm so good with cuddling.

"How did your mom take the news?" He assesses my expression.

I tell him the truth. "Best as can be expected. She wants flight times in writing for our arrival."

Nick pours butter on the popcorn. "I'll talk to Mom and Dad about their plans at Thanksgiving."

"Sounds good. I can't wait for turkey and cranberry sauce."

Nick sets a bowl of popcorn on the coffee table. "Remember how we promised each other to tell the truth?"

"I thought you bared your soul to me." I playfully slap him on his thigh. "Now there are secrets?"

"Not a secret. A confession." Nick tries to kiss my nose, but I move my mouth in time to catch his. It's salty and buttery from the popcorn he snuck in the kitchen. I lick the salt off and run my lips against his. I try to capture his full mouth in mine, but as always, I end up the little spoon in our kiss.

He surrounds me, and my teasing peck changes into one of the slow romantic embraces Nick's so fond of. My neck flushes. His hands bracket my face, and I let him set the pace. For now. There are no cameras around us, but every time he presses into me, I file every touch, every move into my memory bank. For future scripts, for daydreaming, for . . . so many reasons to hold on to the sensation of Nick around me.

"Not about the kissing." His voice sounds like it does on the weekends when he rolls over and wakes me by whispering my name. Urgent but lazy, low but audible. Irresistible. "It's no secret that you are perfect at it."

I wriggle out of his hands, straddle his lap, and cage him against the cushion on the couch with my arm.

"What is it, Mr. Old Fashioned? Enlighten me."

"Now you want to know?" Nick's fingers land on my lower back and he crushes me into his hips, eliminating any space there was between our thighs.

"Only to honor our pact of zero secrets between us." I know we're joking around. And whatever he says will be cute and adoring, but a little part of me is worried, because what if this is something serious? Because I'm not perfect. I've been showing him my imperfections more and more. What if I shared too much? What if his gaze will no longer mirror only the best parts of me when I look into his eyes? I run my finger along the bridge of his nose. My heart takes a little dive. Am I ready to see disappointment on Nick's face when he thinks about me?

I take his head into my hands and bend him down so our foreheads touch. I stare into the brown irises I know and love and re-examine the slight pattern of green and yellow and a much darker almost-black circle around them. I only see the reflection of my love staring back at me. Nothing to be scared of. "Spill."

His thumb rubs circles on the small of my back like he knows I'm nervous. Because he does. He knows me. "I don't love your strawberry smell."

I pull away. Heat rises to my cheeks. "What are you talking about?"

He gives me the space I need, placing his hands on my waist. "For the longest time I thought it was your strawberry smell I loved. And when I moved in with you, I saw your strawber-ries-and-cream conditioner."

"Mom sends it from home. It's artisanal, and they don't sell it in the US. But I'm not following."

"The strawberry scent is one of your shields. The sweet Sarah the world gets to know and love." Nick runs his nose against my neck and inhales me, as if I'm the most delicious perfume. Flutters flit from my neck to my belly button, and I discover I can squeeze myself into Nick's lap a little tighter. I don't care about his confession. I don't want to discuss anything.

My hands sink into his hair as I angle his mouth in the right direction. "And you're saying I'm not sweet?"

"You are." He stashes his lips behind my hair, where my jaw ends. "Sweet. But on your own. Without the conditioner. Without anything added." His fingers slip under the edge of my T-shirt and echo the tantalizing lightness of the kisses he decorates my ear and temple with.

"How is my using a fancy strawberry conditioner related to your confession?" My patience where Nick's touch is concerned is nonexistent. The small movement of his lips and palms stoke the fire inside me faster than any aggressive push-me-against the wall maneuver ever did. I've always thought I liked brawnier guys for the way their brute force made me feel. Nick's tall frame is a lot more dangerous. He drags me against him. He makes my skin sensitive to his touch, and I want to forgo the foreplay and dive into the action.

Not Nick.

He takes his time. Both with his touch and his answer.

His nails scratch a trail up my stomach to stoke the fire in my core. I push against his hand as it finds my bra. The blood in my veins sizzles. I forget what we were talking about.

"You see," he finally says. "I might understand vampires now."

I bite his earlobe. "How did we go from strawberries to vampires?"

"Wait." He unclasps my bra. "I'll tell you."

I lean into him and rest my temple against his, battling the desire to rip off my shirt and his.

"Thing is, there's this constant craving. No matter if you're sleeping next to me in bed. If you are at work on the opposite end of town. If we are sitting on a park bench, or if I'm taking an order at Blend." His fingers fan across my skin, dragging the lace down. His palm cups me. I ache from his touch. He drags his teeth over the pulse below my ear. "I have this endless insatiable desire for you." Combined with his words, it's torture. Glorious torture. Nick's hot breath fans across my jaw. "I thought it was the damn strawberry scent at first." His hand leaves my back and pulls away my fingers that are trying to unbutton his shirt. "But it's not that."

Nick places my hands behind my back, holding them there, rendering them useless.

"Should I change my conditioner?" I whisper and bite his earlobe again. If I don't have my hands, I can find other ways to touch him. I grind against his growing hardness.

"Won't matter." His hips meet mine. "Because that's not what I crave." Nick's teeth graze my collarbone. I jerk from the charge that runs from my clavicle to my pelvic bone. He presses me into him. "What I want to say." His nose nudges my neck. "What my confession is." His lips caress my jaw. "It's not the strawberry scent that I love." His mouth brushes over mine. "It's you, Sarah." His breath teases me. "I love you."

Chills cover me head to toe. The portion of my heart that holds my love for him overflows. I kiss the sweetest words I've ever heard him say, surrender to the moment, and savor him taking the lead.

**There's one more holiday left in the year
of Sarah and Nick's romance: New Year's Eve.
Turn the page for a sneak peek of
Distance, Love, & Us.
OUT NOW**

WILLA DREW
AND US SERIES: BOOK 3
DISTANCE, LOVE & Us

# NICK

It's official. Sarah and I are a couple. I might've thought that was true the day she invited me to be one of her roommates. Or when she moved me into her bedroom without asking. Or when we spent two days rearranging furniture and making her room our room. But it's today. Because today I get to meet her parents. My hand is shaking as I clutch Sarah's. Or at least I think it is my hand. Is it me or is it her?

Sarah's lips tremble, and her eyes are wide and full of unease. Her dread creeps through our connected hands on the armrest between our seats. The cabin of the Airbus shrinks to the two of us. The red-eye flight was my idea. A way to attend my Thursday classes and maximize our long weekend in Canada. Sarah was fine with the plan, and she's been on plenty of planes before.

"What's going on?" I ask.

She's not worried about me meeting her parents and brothers; she made that clear.

"Nothing." She grabs my hand tighter and looks away from the flight attendant demonstrating the proper way to put on a life vest in case of an emergency.

"You can tell me anything," I whisper into her ear.

"The emergency landing in Chicago, on Valentine's Day"—she clamps her eyes shut—"I think it was the same flight attendant. That can't be, right?"

"It's an LA to Toronto flight. And you were on Toronto to LA. Quite possible. You want me to ask her?"

"No." Sarah tugs my hand, as if I'd stand and interrupt the rehearsed spiel. "Unlikely it's her. But I'm having a flashback. Or a premonition. Like something bad is about to happen. My stomach is revolting. I shouldn't have had that second cup of coffee."

"This is an easy flight." I try to infuse confidence into my tone. "Just enough time to finish the pages you promised Karina, so she can work on them while we're celebrating with your parents." I wiggle my fingers in her grip. "A short nap, and we'll be there."

No nap for me. I'm behind already. I pound the space bar with my free hand. This weekend away is bad timing. I need to outline my essay, edit the last prisoner interview for the documentary, and, if there is time, do the research for my Econ 101 project due on Monday.

Sarah nods. "Karina's right. We need to finish the screenplay before *Vampire Club* starts again. If it gets picked up. She'll have new pages for me by the end of this weekend, and I'll have nothing if I don't do it now."

Sarah fiddles with her seatbelt. "This'll sound weird, but . . ."

Between the talk after our Halloween reconciliation, and the times she has cried out in pleasure because of my body parts exploring hers, there cannot possibly be anything she doesn't feel comfortable telling me.

"The only weird thing is that you think there might be a weird thing between us. What is it?"

"Could you give me your driver's license?"

Not an embarrassing request, but a bizarre one. No one needs a driver's license on a plane.

"Sure." I struggle to unearth my wallet one-handed. "Care to explain why?"

"Last time"—her gaze flies to the flight attendant then back to me as I pull out the plastic card—"as we were making the emergency landing in Chicago, I found your fake ID in the pocket of your jacket." She takes my real ID and pushes the corners into the pads of her fingers. "Looking at your photo made me calmer. Maybe I can recreate the feeling." She peers at my flat rectangular image on the card.

I cup her cheek with my palm and turn her to face me. The sunshine she brings into my life spreads through my brain synapses, sparking the love that grows every day. Every second. "You don't need my driver's license." I kiss her nose. Her light flows through my veins. "Because you have the real thing." I kiss the knuckles of her hand and slip the ID out of it. Our gazes meet and I jump into the ocean of her eyes. "And if you need me to stab you with something pointy, I have a better idea." I can't get enough of how easy being next to her is. How fun. All sorts of fun. I poke my finger into the ticklish place in her side. It's one of the sensitive spots I've discovered during my favorite activity: exploring Sarah's body.

Her lips quiver, but not because she's on the verge of tears anymore. She squirms in her seat to escape my sneak attack. "Stop it." She playfully slaps my hand. "There're people."

"So what?" My pulse in my throat, I bite my lip and drop my gaze to her mouth. Sarah's trapped between the window of the airplane, the seatbelt, and my hand that's no longer tickling but is making steady progress up her ribcage.

She giggles. "Nick." She throws a glance at the woman sitting on the other side of me, who's intently *not* looking at us. I'm sure she's very aware of what's happening next to her.

"I'll behave." I steady my breath and reluctantly return my fingers to the waist of her jeans under her sweater. In case I need to poke her again.

Sarah wraps her arm around mine and tugs on my shirt for me to bend closer. Our sign that she's in as much as I am, even if she's not ready to say the words. The air between us crackles when we kiss. Her lips linger much longer than airplane PDA police might find appropriate. We're setting the cabin on fire, but I'm not gonna complain. I'll never complain about her kisses.

"You are better than the card." She nuzzles her face against the cotton of my long-sleeved polo. "And warmer." She pokes my bicep with her finger. "And just as hard."

"You know it." I grin at her glare and the pink hue of her face. I reach lower into her waistband. Desire flickers in my stomach.

"You promised you'd behave," she breathes into my chest. I'm not sure she means it. Her hips lift to allow my downward progress. Her little whimper spurs me on, assuring me she's enjoying this as much as I am. We don't care about the lady to my left or the people behind us that must have quite an eyeful through the gap. I kiss her, and it's not the lips-on-lips thank-you she gave me, it's a let-me-taste-you-because-I can't-wait-till-we're-alone-again maneuver. The heat in my body spikes.

"Are both of your seatbelts fastened?" The flight attendant's voice interrupts before we leave PG-13 territory.

I jerk my hand out of Sarah's pants and tug on her seatbelt. "Yes, ma'am."

Sarah clears her throat. "Of course."

We giggle as the attendant moves to check the rest of the passengers. Sarah tugs on my seatbelt. I still her wrist before it repeats the maneuver. I might not be a teenager any longer, but controlling myself around her is not getting easier, no matter how many times she's touched me. I want her now. Always. I resist the temptation, kiss the soft heel of her palm, and return her hand to her lap. I use the remains of my willpower to calm my raging blood and not ask Sarah to join the mile-high club.

If we were in first class, or on a private jet, I'd have that option. One day that dream will come true. I have Sarah, and with her, life is one shining possibility after another. My heart swells. She's my shield of invincibility. My love for Sarah brightens every second of every day. "Love you," I whisper into her hair.

She sits up, stretches her neck, and seals my declaration of love with her lips. The plane takes off, and I'm soaring.

Being tall has its privileges, I won't argue that, but when you're six-four and stuck in the middle seat of economy class, you'd wish you were Sarah's size.

Her knees aren't bumping against the tray like mine are. I scrub the palm of my left hand over my eyes and yawn. Sarah's head rests on my shoulder. A contraption I've never seen before encircles her neck. She put up a good fight but two hours into the flight, with the cabin lights low and the gentle buzz of the engines, even the extra cup of coffee wasn't enough to keep her awake.

The numbers on my screen blur and I try to stifle another jaw-breaking yawn. If I don't finish at least one of these deliverables, I'll need to stay awake all night at the Connors' place to plow through my homework. I want to be fully present this weekend to make a good first impression.

The module we're covering in Econ is about the GDP of world countries, and I'm supposed to compare the population pyramids of three countries and explain how they reflect on the socioeconomic position of them in the world. I chose Greece, because of my Greek heritage, Canada, because of Sarah, and Japan, because it's on my to-visit list. Today I'll check Canada off it. I am inputting the numbers for Canada into the spreadsheet to build the final pyramid when the lights in the cabin lights come on.

Sarah stirs. "What time is it?"

"My watch says two-thirty."

"Guess we're landing soon. We're supposed to land in Toronto at six." Her yawn rivals mine.

With the time change we lose three hours. Makes sense. Good thing I stayed up. "Need a coffee?"

"I can wait until Tim's. You know that'll be our first stop." She's been talking about the donut shop as if it's the best place on earth. I don't want to ruin her nostalgic glee about the place, but I suspect it can't compare to the proper espresso machine at Blend that I can now operate in my sleep.

"Tim Horton's first. Got it. Then your dad drops our luggage off at their place and straight to Côté Fraise for a proper breakfast. I'm counting on the best butter tarts in the world and homemade croissants."

Sarah's eyes sparkle at the mention of her grandmother's bakery. "Mom'll make enough food for a family of twenty. Even with you, Grayson, and Taylor competing to see who can eat the most, you'll never eat more than Mom prepares."

"I'm up for the challenge." I've never met a plate of food I couldn't demolish.

The plane lands without a hitch, and Sarah's smile is carefree.

"Guess you were right. Having the real Nick by my side is the good luck charm I needed." She stands, leans over, and kisses me while I'm still shorter than her. Her peck wakes the hunger I've suppressed by pouring over my class notes. Not sure we can continue the PDA in front of her parents, I raise my chin and recapture her lips with mine as if it's been months and not hours since I've tasted them. One kiss morphs into two or three and then I lose count, cramming every extra kiss in now.

We go through separate customs lines, but she waits for me on the other side of the security kiosks. We weave through the corridor into the open space packed with eyes scanning the people around us, looking for the ones they are here to pick up. I've seen pictures of Ian, Sarah's dad, but I'm unable to locate him in this sea of faces.

Sarah grabs my arm. Her expression is back to the panic she started the flight with. "What's wrong?"

She shifts away from me, but I tug her close.

"Grayson is here." Her voice cracks.

There are several guys waiting at the arrival gate, and although Sarah and I video chat with him often, I only find him when I follow the direction of Sarah's gaze. Her brother's lips form a thin line as he spots Sarah.

My shoulders tighten. "Did you have a fight?"

"No. Dad was supposed to pick us up. He's not here." Sarah checks her phone. Her palm presses into mine. "No texts from either of them." She looks up at me. The dread from the airplane that I tickled out of her is back. Stronger. "Something's wrong."

# Sarah

"Mom fell." Grayson speeds up the ramp in his vintage Dodge Challenger.

I stretch the collar of my shirt away from my throat, aching for air.

Mom fell.

It sounds so innocent. But adults aren't supposed to fall. Toddlers fall. Leaves fall. My spry lively mom doesn't fall.

"When? Where? Who found her? How did this happen?" The words tumble out to the accelerating beat of my pulse. "Why didn't anyone text me? Did she break something?" I grip my brother's bicep.

"She was moving a bag of flour and tripped on"—he clears his throat— "the corner of a loose tile I tried to fix." Grayson extricates himself from my grasp. "Apparently, superglue isn't that super."

Who fixes a tile with superglue? I want to scream. But I don't. Handyman is not on his resumé.

My brother parks and winds Nick and me through the endless corridors of Toronto General. The last time I was here, Grayson had fractured his foot trying a new trick at his dressage lesson, and we spent the night in the emergency room laughing and crying as he flirted with the nurse stuck on duty.

Today there is no laughing.

We step into an elevator and Grayson jabs the button for the fourth floor, palms his back pocket, and huffs at the ceiling. "Can I borrow your phone again?"

He didn't text me at the airport because his was dead. Again. He's been complaining about his "antique" phone and its useless battery for months. The thing better last a few more weeks, because we've all chipped in to buy him the latest model for Christmas.

"What's the code again?" Grayson lifts one brow.

I roll my eyes. "Mémère's birthday."

"Right." And he's lost to the world of technology.

My brother splits his days between sitting in front of a computer in a lecture hall and volunteering at the stables for extra credit. Assuming he's attending his university classes. He much prefers the company of horses.

My muscles turn into ribbons of steel as the elevator takes forever to climb four measly floors. Nick's pinkie caresses mine. I nestle my hand in his, force myself to relax my jaw, and offer him an "I'm okay" smile.

He tilts his head in what I assume is a silent "How can you be?" Nick brushes his chin against my temple, and I sink into the warmth of him. The prickles of worry dull as I lay my head on his chest. The steady beats of his heart drown out the electric hum of the fluorescent lights and grinding gears of the elevator's motor. The big bad 'what if' isn't as scary with Nick by my side.

"Finally," my brother mutters as the metal doors drag open. His grumble reminds me that he's stressed too.

Being the big sister, I want to tell him it'll be fine, protect him from the pain like I always do for my baby brothers. But I can't. I don't have control over this situation. Air leaves my lungs. My fingers shake. I clutch Nick's shirt like he's a raft and we are lost at sea. I have no idea what we're about to walk into.

Our mother is a pillar of strength, always the first up, the one we turn to in a crisis, the cornerstone of our family. The fact that she's not infallible chips away at the illusion we've lived under.

The nurse's station is empty as we pass by, and the halls are eerily quiet this early in the morning. Visiting hours started ten minutes ago, but Dad stayed with Mom in the ER and is in her room waiting for us.

"Looks like 425 is this way." Grayson gestures to a sign covered in numbers and arrows.

Nick's sneakers squeak on the freshly mopped linoleum as we quietly continue down the corridor. We round a corner, and I spot Taylor leaning against the wall.

"Hey." His hug is tighter than usual.

"How is she?"

My youngest brother's mouth twists. "Cranky."

The word eases the knots in my stomach. "Sounds about right."

Grayson pushes open the extra-wide door and I follow him but Nick tugs on my elbow. "I'm gonna stay out here."

My pulse flies into overdrive. "No, I—"

"You need some time with your mom. I'll be right here." He kisses my forehead. "Go with your brothers."

My lips tremble at Nick's recognition that now is not the time to introduce him to my parents. I need to see Mom, process this on my own. Yet I don't want to leave the comfort of Nick's arms, don't want to shove the role of girlfriend to the background and put on the hat of big sister or oldest child. I bury my nose is his shirt to inhale him one more time.

This whole day was supposed to be different. I groan and grind my teeth. He should be officially meeting my family in the warmth of Côté Fraise, munching on freshly baked strawberry shortcake, not wasting the day in the impersonal hospital hallway.

Nick gently nudges me through the doorway before I have a chance to protest.

Grayson and Taylor stand at the foot of the bed by the window. The room smells of antiseptic. Dad rises from Mom's side. On the planes of his face, deep lines etch the mask of an overstressed spouse. The muddied gray of his skin tells the tale of a sleepless night. I whimper. Dad wraps his arms around me, and I can't hold back my tears any longer.

I stifle a sob in Dad's chest as he strokes my hair. He whispers into my ear like he used to in the movie theater after the main character lands in danger. "She's fine." Dad brushes moisture from my cheek. "Just a little bump is all."

A bump? Why don't I believe him? The tightness in my chest rises to my throat, choking me. My vision blurs. I need to see her. I steady my knees and move around Dad to find Mom lying unconscious on the bed. My stomach drops, and the world falls silent except for the whir in my ears at the sight of the cast wrapped around her right wrist. Her pale skin is almost as white as the bandage covering half her forehead.

"Is she—"

"Alive?" My mother's lashes flutter. Watery blue eyes meet mine, and the sounds of the hospital stream back in. Mom is awake. The vice of dread that's been crushing my heart since I stepped through the gates at the airport releases, and my chest doesn't hurt as much.

"Hey, Mom." I move to the side of the bed, avoiding the arm in the cast and taking her other hand. "How are you feeling?"

She sighs. "Like a silly old woman."

"What?" I muster a smile. "This wasn't your fault."

"I was rushing. Should have waited for Julio to move the flour sack, but the Andersons' wedding party was on my mind." She raises her bandaged hand. "Going to be fun making four hundred cupcakes one-handed."

I suppress the urge to roll my eyes. "Don't fret about that. I'm sure Julio or Sandy can help."

Mom frowns. "We planned on closing the bakery for our anniversary, so I gave them both the weekend off. I was supposed to have the cupcakes baked and delivered before our party tomorrow night." Mom's gaze fly to Dad's. "We need to call our guests, cancel the venue." Her gaze moves to the ceiling. "We won't get our money back."

Dad finds Mom's fingers sticking out from her cast and gives them a pat. "I don't care about the money."

"And you don't worry about the cupcakes." I turn to my brothers, who are both staring at my phone as if waiting in line at Tim Horton's for coffee. Am I the only one worried? I clasp the S of my necklace. The thin gold fails to calm the whirlpool of anxiety in my chest. I glance at the closed hospital room door, wishing for Nick's strength around me, for the surety of him. "Nick and I can make the cupcakes."

"Oh, Sarah." Mom's voice turns sweeter than the sugary glaze she puts on her snowflake cookies. "This is your holiday. You didn't come here to run the bakery for your injured mother."

"No, but I can, and I want to do it. It'll give me a chance to show off Mémère's kitchen to Nick. I've been talking about it for months, and he'll get the immersive experience."

Mom pulls at the covers. "If they let me go now, I can still make them."

Dad and I jump at the same time. We put a hand on one of her shoulders and lower her to the mattress.

"You're not going anywhere," he says.

"Well, I'm not staying here." There's the stubborn streak Mom and I share.

"I'm not sure you have any choice." Dad loosens his grip. "The doctors want to keep you another night to observe that bump. Make sure you don't have a concussion."

"I'm fine." Mom wriggles under our grasp.

"Mom. Nick and I will go and make the cupcakes right now." I step away. "Let us do this." I look at Dad. "Don't cancel. It's your anniversary, and we are celebrating. Connor style."

"Yeah, Sarah's right." Grayson hands my phone to me. "You deserve a party."

I turn to Mom. "You stay here and rest. We'll take care of everything."

Her face crumples like she's about to cry, but she nods. "Okay, honey. If you're sure you can do this."

"Absolutely." The knots in my stomach strain. I have no freaking idea if I can make four hundred cupcakes in a day, but I'm not letting her worry.

"I'll give you a ride." Grayson jangles the van's keys.

"I'll go with you. I can lick the icing bowl." Taylor grins. He has quite the sweet tooth. Must be from growing up in the bakery.

Nick's scowling at the screen of his phone when we emerge from the hospital room.

His brown eyes dart to mine, and I can't quite read the expression but my gut screams more bad news. "What's up?"

He shoves his phone in his pocket and gets out of the chair.

"Just some school stuff." He waves a hand between us like he's batting the idea away. "How's your mom?"

# NICK

Today decided to destroy whatever expectations I had for this mini vacation. Instead of coffee, food, and lounging on the couch looking at Sarah's delighted face, I jam myself into a stiff chair in a hospital waiting room. So far, my impression of Canada consists of colorless airport corridors and gray hospital hallways. This is not how I imagined my introduction to Sarah's parents would go, but at least I'm here to lend a helping hand, shoulder, ear—whatever she needs.

The wooden armrests dig into my elbows, but if I close my eyes, I will doze off. This is not the time nor the place. I unearth my phone and check for messages. It's barely past five in LA, and I don't expect anyone to be awake on the West Coast, but my personal account pings with an email. I rub my eyebrow. A before-dawn message could only be from Ms. Hansley.

"Blaire release is confirmed for Monday at ten a.m. The first cut of the documentary is due to the editor Wednesday night. Plan to be at my office all day Wednesday. Any time after six a.m. works. The earlier we start, the more likely we are to get some sleep."

Finding a sub for my shift on Wednesday will be hard, but I can sweeten the deal by switching for a Friday night closing. Missing my Econ final on Wednesday isn't an option. If I drive Betty from Ms. Hansley's office to campus, take the two-hour exam, and come straight back, I'll be away for at least four hours. My knee bounces so high it bumps the phone out of my hand. I catch it mid-air, cross my feet at the ankles to keep still, and flip to my calendar app. My un-caffeinated, sleep-deprived brain refuses to put the pieces of the puzzle together, unable to see how the combination of events that need to happen on Wednesday is possible.

Sarah, Taylor, and Grayson emerge from the hospital room. Sarah's eyes are pools of sadness. Deep shadows under them and a line between her brows replace the excitement of being with her parents to celebrate their twenty-fifth anniversary.

"What's up?" she asks.

"Just some school stuff." I don't keep things from her anymore, but none of my woes matter right now. Her mom's in the hospital, and that's centerstage. "How's your mom?"

"Mom will stay for observation." Sarah blots her cheek with her sleeve. "Besides the broken wrist, she hit her head hard enough for the doctors to think it might be a concussion."

"Scary." Mike had a concussion after one of his MMA fights last year. He was wonky for a week. "Is she awake?"

Sarah rolls her eyes. "And ready to bake four hundred cupcakes that are due to be delivered tomorrow."

"Sucks. I'm sure her customers will understand."

That look of determination I know so well crosses her face. "We are not letting anyone down."

I love when she says we, but how are we and cupcakes related? "We?"

"The four of us should be able to do what Mom was planning to accomplish by herself."

Behind Sarah, Grayson and Taylor give each other a look I can only interpret as, "We're in trouble."

"I'll drive." Grayson tosses the keys up.

Sarah snatches them mid-air "I'll drive. You need to call Sandy and find out what kind of cupcakes the Andersons ordered."

Grayson waves his hands in a series of large X's. "Sandy will bite my head off."

"Better yours than any of ours. She has a sweet spot for you." Sarah ruffles his hair, even though he's a foot taller than her.

We storm out the hospital sliding door like baking Avengers on a mission to save the universe one cupcake at a time. I'd make the joke out loud if it were not for the grim expressions of the Connor clan. I press my lips together to suppress a giggle. Everything has the potential to be funny at this stage of my twenty-six-hour marathon day.

Sarah leads the way, and the three of us race to keep up. I'd love to wrap my arms around her and dampen the negative energy she's buzzing with, but I'm not sure she'd agree to pause her mission.

I add another gray blur—this time of highways—to my vision of Toronto. The road in the residential area is bumpy. Red streetcars glide on rails that crisscross the streets.

The neighborhood is lined with two- and three-story buildings stuck together block after block, shops and businesses at street level and living quarters above. Occasional bulky apartment buildings break up the patchy matrix. I capture some of the storefronts on my camera as Sarah silently drives.

She rounds a corner and turns into a back alley where the concrete road gives way to a rougher gravel parking spot. She parks near a peeling brick wall painted charcoal gray. We pile out of the car. A cinderblock addition in front of us has one door with the logo of Côté Fraise stenciled in white on the glass.

Sarah slides a metal silver key into the round handle of the glass door, and stands to the side to let me in. "Welcome to Côté Fraise."

The smell of baked goods hits me, and my stomach demands food. A corner of her mouth twitches and I expect a grin, but she tucks the snippet of that smile away and is back to the tight-lipped face I saw her use so much during the Starlight competition—her don't-mess-with-me face.

"Bathroom is to the left. Meet me in the kitchen." Her hands flash right and left before she careens into the hallway. Grayson and Taylor follow and throw save-us-please glances my way. I'm not sure there is anyone who can stop Sarah when she is in control mode.

The bathroom is white with strawberries of every possible size and shade on the tile, the cabinets, even the soap dispenser. The small mat under the toilet and cover on the lid of the toilet is a green shag with strawberries on it. The smell I love on Sarah packs a punch in the small space. It's strawberry on steroids, and the fact that the sink is closer to my knees than my waist isn't the most surprising part.

I leave my hands under the running water and admire the commitment to the theme. Even the toilet paper holder is a thick dark-emerald stalk with two red strawberries on each side of the roll. The only reminder that this is a place of work is a commercial-looking paper towel dispenser with a sign in English and French instructing employees to wash their hands before returning to work.

The hallway leads to a large open kitchen space. Sarah stands in the middle of a quiet room with a collection of pages in her hands. I hang my coat and hat on a hook next to several aprons.

"The theme is Autumn." She twirls a strand of hair between her fingers. "Sandy says they wanted pumpkin spice, red velvet, and lemon cupcakes with fondant leaves on top of white icing. That's a piece of cake."

"Four pieces of cupcakes, you mean." Taylor's eyes crinkle with mischief. His brother accompanies with a low he-he-he. Sarah glares at them, and the noise stops.

"Keep your humor for when the task is done. You are on fondant leaves duty." She gives Grayson one sheet of paper. "Remember, this is not for a child's birthday party. Think wedding, elegance, romance."

"Romance." Taylor resumes his chuckles, only to bite his lips shut when Sarah narrows her eyes. "Got it."

"Taylor—you are on liner duty. We'll use the brown parchment ones. Get the tins and start lining them."

"Nick." She swivels her head to the large stainless double-door fridge next to me. "See if you can find three boxes of cream cheese in the fridge."

The kitchen comes alive with four of us measuring, mixing, and not talking about what happened to their mom.

Sarah pins the recipes to the wall, crosses her arms, and stares at them. I haven't baked a cupcake in my life, but growing up in the bakery, she must've done this a million times.

She re-reads the text and presses her hands into her face. I hear a whimper. Her back curves, her body sags, and her shoulders quiver. The stern shell cracks, and the girl who's worried for her mom caves under the stress of the morning.

"Hey." I brush her arm.

Her hands grasp the counter, a sure sign she's attempting to hide her feelings. My heart feels her heart. I hate that she's in pain, and I'd do anything to bring back the sunny Sarah.

"We are on the same team. A partnership." I pry her hands away from the steel surface. "Talk to me. I'm here. I'm really here for you."

She turns her tear-stained face to me. "I can't."

Catch Sarah and Nick's the happily ever after in

**Distance, Love, & Us**

OUT NOW

Wil & El have their own romance series.
Turn the page for a sneak peek of
WE Blend

the first book in the Falling for the Rockstar's Daughter Series.

Without him, there are no words.
Without her, there is no music.

Fame follows me everywhere.

Not today. This morning I'm invisible. Everything is going according to plan and twelve hours crammed upright in an airplane seat were a small price to pay for my freedom. London commuters rush by on their way to work as I stroll back to my hotel sipping my average cup of Joe. No bodyguard in sight.

A smattering of paparazzi in front of the marble staircase sends my heart beating faster. No. They can't know I'm here. Can they? I tug the brim of my baseball cap. I look nothing like myself. Maybe I should've picked a smaller hotel, but the Four Seasons is where Dad always stays. Lots of celebrities choose it.

I rush past the cameras and try not to groan at how long the doorman takes to open the wrought iron doors. Inside the hotel, it's quiet and calm. Made it.

"Melodie." I hear my name ring across the gleaming two-story lobby.

A shiver shoots up my spine. "Dad?"

I look over to the plush maroon couches arranged in a semi-circle, and sure enough, there's Bill Rockerby. Stepdad to me. Rocker to the world. That's who the press is here for. He's not even hiding his rockstar status, decked out in black leather like he just walked off the stage after one of his concerts. Except he's walking toward me, his mouth pressed into a thin line, the look of disappointment I dread souring the handsome face lots of women, and men, drool over.

"What are you doing here?" I stumble over my words.

"The better question is, what are you doing here?" His voice is low and tense.

"I—" I don't have a comeback. Truth: I'm supposed to be in New York on a shopping spree, chaperoned by my mother-approved cousins, not in this swanky hotel in London.

His hand is on my arm. "Not here." Amber eyes dart left and right and back again. "People are listening." Dad's always paranoid about the press, especially in Europe. He corrals me toward the elevator, presses the call button, and we stand in awkward silence as we wait.

My mind races between two thoughts. Was it Bailey or Zoe who spilled the beans? 'Cause they were supposed to cover for me and not fold less than twenty-four hours into my escape. We have a pact: provide alibis for each other when we need to escape the parental cages, but their end of the bargain is harder to uphold. And I've never left the country by myself before. Zoe asked me five times if I was sure about the ruse.

More important: How do I get out of this?

There's a soft ding, probably a D-flat but the pitch is off a hair, and the gold doors slide open. I jump in first, hit the button for my floor; Dad follows close behind. More silence, like the pause between songs on a playlist. The doors close, and the elevator jumps to life.

"Your mother is sick with worry."

Slash. His words are tiny shavings of metal cutting at me. He knows my weak spot. Making Mom anxious, given what she's going through, is one of the worst things I could do. I squeeze my teeth together and don't reply because I've never learned to lie. My parents' publicist keeps trying to coach me, but the closest I can get is to omit the truth. Ask me a direct question, and I'll blabber, but I can't tell Dad about why I'm here.

"You can't silence your way out of this mess. Is it Dillon? I called him as soon as your mother got the alert on her credit card about the hotel charge." The elevator is playing a Muzak version of Justin's *Holy*, and my ears want to bleed. "He pretended he hadn't heard from you—better at lying than your cousins."

*Mom's card.* The receptionist said they had to have one in case I have other charges but promised they won't use it as long as I pay cash. Months of saved allowance was just enough for a ticket, three nights at the hotel, food, and paying for recording my music video. I'm not staying at this chain anymore. All the talk about keeping their clients' confidentiality, and they sell me out to my parents within hours.

"Talk to me." His voice softens a bit, and he angles his body toward me. "I might be forty-two, but I remember what being young and in love was like. I thought you were over him. With him back in England, you stopped pining for the asshole, pardon my French."

Dillon. Right. If I agree I'm here for Dillon, Dad might not dig deeper. My plan might still have a chance. "I thought I loved Dillon." It's true. I did think that. I don't anymore, but I let Dad draw his own conclusions. I keep squeezing my teeth. I can do it. Don't say anything, don't say anything, don't say anything.

"And what was your thought process? Fly across the ocean, profess your love for him, and hope, what? That he'll ditch his new job and come back to the States for you?"

New job? Is that why he left? He didn't offer me an explanation when he sent me his "I'm sorry, I can't do this" text.

I don't trust myself to speak, so I shrug instead.

"It's been six months."

The elevator doors open, and I trudge to my room, push the heavy door, and sink onto the king-size bed, leaving the chair by the desk for Dad to sit in. The calm gray-blue hues of the room cool the emotions circulating between us.

"You know you don't have to lie."

I want to scream "I do. You won't let me do anything otherwise."

"You know we love you."

"I know." This one's no lie. If anything, they love me too much. So much, there's no room for anything else.

"And that we do these things to protect your privacy. To keep you safe from another paparazzi-triggered breakdown. Can you blame your mother for wanting a semblance of normalcy for you?"

"Nope." After what happened to Papa and me, I can never blame her for wanting to keep me safe. But I don't have to like it. The bubble-wrapped life is smothering me. Sometimes I feel like I can't breathe between the rules, the bodyguards, and the ever-narrowing circle of things to do or people to do them with. Probably not a good time to bring up my complaints. Today, I need all suspicion away from the true reason I'm in London. And it isn't Dillon.

"I'll call your mom while you pack, tell her you're safe. The pilot's getting the jet ready for us."

"But . . ." If I don't show up to my meeting with Mr. Astor tomorrow, I'll lose the fifty percent down payment I transferred. "Can I at least go talk to Dillon?" I run my hand through my hair, find the familiar strands that always feel different, out of place, and pull, causing just enough pain to distract me from spilling the truth. The pain merges with the cloud of cutting metal of Dad's words.

"Why do you want to go down that road?" Dad puts his Doc Martin on his knee and shakes his foot. "No. You're not leaving this room until I escort you to the plane. It's nonnegotiable."

"But, Dad—"

"Melodie." He touches my hand, and I stop with the hair.

I focus on my tennis shoes and not on the buzzing shrapnel in my chest.

"Look at me."

I do as he says, because I'm a good girl.

"Leave it be."

Damn. There is no getting out of this. I'll have to message Lenard Astor and figure out a way, another time we can find two days in his schedule. Even if I do lose part of the money, I'll make it up with several months' of my allowance, if I buy nothing at all.

"Oh, and since you insist on being treated like an adult, it's time you took on some adult responsibilities. How about getting a job?"

"This again. I don't even have a high school diploma. How would it look if your stepdaughter asks 'do you want fries with that' for a living?"

"I wouldn't mind as long as you're happy."

He always says stuff like this. Cares almost too much. Unlike Mom who loves me but uses the tough-love parenting style. Nice or not, my music is my priority. "How can I be happy doing that when what I'd make at such a place is pennies compared to my allowance."

"Your mother wants to cut off your allowance as well."

"She can't. I have expenses." The metal ball of doom swings on a chain, and I cling to it, not wanting to wreck my plans.

"Really?" His bushy eyebrow performs that sky high thing it does when he's being sarcastic. "We pay for everything."

"I need clothes."

"You have two walk-in closets."

"I was going to buy a new keyboard."

"What's wrong with the one in the studio?"

"That's yours."

"I have a solution. Why don't you come and work for me at Rocker, Inc. Nadine needs help in the back office. It'll give you some work experience and you can help discover the next *it* artist."

I don't want to discover them, I want to *be* them. But I need the money to start again, and working for my stepfather isn't the worst thing in the world. "What's the starting salary?"

He smiles for the first time. "You make it sound like you're doing me a favor here and not the reverse. I'll pay you the same as I'd pay anyone I'd hire to do the job. And no special treatment. You'll be like any of my other employees."

It's not as if I have a lot of choice here. "Fine."

I grab the suitcase Mom gave me for my eighteenth birthday and fling the lid open. I stuff the ten outfits I brought for my stay into it and hide my sheet music under the top dress. My independence day's gone. Guess it's back to the US for the Fourth of July.

"This is ridiculous." The bright yellow Louis Vuitton with my initials monogrammed in blue, MVR for Melodie Vella Rockerby, mocks my ruined dreams with its bright cheer.

"You running away is what's ridiculous." His phone dings an F-sharp, and he answers.

"Yes. I'm with her. Yes. Safe." I can feel his eyes on my back as I snap my suitcase shut. "I told her the terms. Love you too."

He puts the phone down and gets up. "I have to go make an excuse to the press. They spotted me at Southend when I landed. Wait for me here. Hotel security has someone by your door. Don't even try talking to them."

The lead ball drops from my chest into my stomach at the sight of the security guard when Dad leaves my room. I grab onto the doorframe and take a moment to survey the hallway, looking for possible escape routes.

"Get inside and stay there." Patience is no longer in Dad's voice, and I want to scream. Instead, I slam the door.

The heavy metal doesn't connect but bounces off the fingers on my left hand, still clutching the white casing. I jerk them toward me and watch the indentations on the index and middle finger bloom pink. At the sight, the numbness disappears, replaced by blinding pain. The scream I've wished for erupts from my lungs. I suck air and glare at the places where the edge of the door tore through the skin. It doesn't look that bad. That's when the throbbing begins, and I can barely hear Dad barking orders at the guard to get the hotel doctor.

This is not how I imagined my first jail break would go.

I HAVEN'T BEEN IN LA for more than five minutes, and he walks right by me. So close, I can almost smell his designer cologne. A few steps, and I could slap him on the back, assuming I could get past the security detail.

My father. The rockstar.

Bill Rockerby strolls through the airport, his entourage carrying bright yellow luggage like little ducks in a row, while I stand here at baggage claim waiting for mine like a normal person.

Is that his stepdaughter in the back? She sure lucked out when her mother remarried, getting a rockstar as her new father. Some tossers get all the breaks. She doesn't look happy about being home. One hand sports a splint binding her fingers together. Did Daddy's little girl's vacation get ruined? Poor her. Not.

The sunglasses that hold up her red hair surely cost more than my entire wardrobe. Her signature streak falls on the left side of her face. If not for that shock of white, from this close she looks more like a girl next door than the glossy spoiled brat in the pages of the magazines Mum used to bring home from the clinic. Without the makeup and the posh clothes, her beauty shines. Not my type, but plenty of people would love to have someone like her as their arm candy.

Whispers start around me, and phones turn in their direction. Some brave souls take a few steps to get closer, others shout about getting a selfie. Rocker and Melodie keep walking. We're nothing but an annoyance to them. They could've smiled, waved, but no, not rock-n-roll's elite. They press on with sour faces and disappear from view.

"I almost touched him," a bloke in denim overall shorts and flip-flops gushes to the girl next to him. American fashion is not something I'll ever understand.

I unzip the inside pocket of my GOODBOIS messenger bag, the one nice thing I own, and get out the small notebook covered in black faux leather. With a pop, the pencil snaps out of the elastic holder, and I jot down:

*Annoyance on the clean face or a perfect*
*smile on a glossy page*

*sound of flip-flops on a linoleum floor*

*Almost. Always almost.*

Notebook safely tucked away, I roll up the sleeves of my dark green shirt. Mum's been supplying me with the pocket notebooks ever since I started writing up the ideas that pop into my head on my hands and arms. There's a drawer full of them at home and two more in my pack that, with any luck, is not lost. I shift the beat-up guitar case from my feet and onto my shoulder and walk closer to the conveyor belt.

Time to let Mum know I've arrived. I connect my phone to the free airport Wi-Fi, pull up WhatsApp, and type "I'm here." She'll relay the message to Opa, who doesn't get the whole text-message thing. I can hear my grandfather grumbling, "Why can't you just pick up the phone?" Even though it's midnight in Bremen, I get a barrage of messages back. Mum should be sleeping, she needs it, but I type back some deets.

The LAX Airport Shuttle bus goes to the Transit Center, where I catch the Number 3 Big Blue Bus, which gets me to Westwood for fifty cents. My kind of price. I get off and make sure my backpack doesn't hit anyone when I turn—the top part is higher than my head, and I'm taller than most men around me. A short walk, and I arrive at the UCLA campus. It has people, but it's quiet, unlike the one I just left. Had to bail on the rest of the semester for this, but I'll be back in time for the October session.

There are a few people around, and I catch the eye of two beauties lying on a blanket on the grass. They both smile at me, and I make sure to return the gesture. I may be here for serious business, but that doesn't mean a fella can't have fun in the process.

Part of me can't believe my luck in getting into the program. I applied to the Starlight Future Filmmakers Foundation's annual film competition as a laugh. I never thought I'd get a call for the audition. The committee gave me the option to fly in or do it over Zoom. Yeah, 'cause I have the dough to drop on a trip to LA for a bloody interview. Harder to turn on my charm over the internet, but I made it work, and here I am—an almost-all-expenses-paid trip to the U.S. of A.

Checking in to the dorms is the simplest thing I've done today. Let the free ride begin. After the airfare, the credit card I usually only use for emergencies is almost at its limit. Finding a job will be one of the first things on my list. I stick my key into the door but before I turn it, the pale wood slat opens, and a bloke with a buzz cut smiles at me.

"Welcome, bienvenidos, bienvenue—all the languages I know."

"Willkommen," I say.

"Ah, isn't that what they say in Germany?"

"Yup. Born and bred there, so I can vouch for that."

"More of us internationals." He scratches his head. "What's with the British accent?"

"That's ten years learning English at school in Bremen plus summers with family in Sussex."

"Willkommen then, Mr. German."

"It's Wil Peters actually."

"I'm Mateo. Mateo Gallardo." He opens his arms and steps away, so I can enter. The common room isn't a fancy resort, but the light is good, and we're far away from the stairwell. In the middle there's a pair of brown leather couches separated by a low glass table, dominated by a flat screen TV hanging on the wall. Pushed up against the window is a wooden table with six matching chairs. Home sweet home.

"You're the last to arrive, so the only bed left is in my room." He points to the second door on the left. "Me and the other dudes were about to head out and grab some grub. Wanna join?"

I want to drop my stuff and take a shower, but some food wouldn't be bad either. "Sure. Any idea where I can get a SIM card around campus?"

"I'm your man. I scouted all the things we're going to need in this country."

"Including a grocery store? The website said there's a kitchen I can use on this floor." I've learned over the last year living on campus how much Mum did for me. First time I did laundry, I washed my clothes in one load. I still have the shirt that used to be white and is now a combination of gray and splotches of blue. Cooking is another thing I had to figure out.

"You're ambitious. It's just for three months. One thing my mami never let me do is cooking. I already miss her empanadas."

Mateo shrugs as he follows me into the room we are to share. Why do the people who design dorms lack imagination? They're all the same. Two single beds pushed against opposite walls, one night table, and what I presume is a closet the size of a coffin.

I drop my backpack on the bed and prop my guitar in the small space against the wall.

"You here to make a movie too?" Mateo sits down on his bed.

"Yeah, I'm the sound person."

"Way cool." He taps his chest. "Set designer. I'm on the green team."

"Green?"

"Each team has a color. Don't worry." Why would I worry? "You'll get one at the orientation session tomorrow. We can go together in the morning. Already checked out the building."

Seems my luck is holding. Mateo is doing the heavy lifting.

I hang up a classic white long-sleeve shirt Mum snuck in that raises the number of clothing items I brought to eleven. My side of the room looks spartan compared to Mateo's, who on his twelve-hour drive from Mexico brought twice the stuff I had in my old dorm room at uni. I'm particularly impressed with the precise placement of the array of multicolored pens and pencils he's using to draw something in a large notepad. He catches me eyeing them.

"Tools of the trade. I always sketch by hand first."

Day one in the States rushes by in a blur of dropping more money on my credit card. I thought the giant Coke I drank with my first American burger would keep me up but incessant yawning reminds me I've been awake for twenty-four hours.

When I get back from the shower, the bedroom is empty and quiet but for the laughter filtering from the living room where my new flatmates are gearing up to play a video game. I set my alarm for five a.m. so I can fit in a quick workout before orientation. The gym on campus even has rowing machines, so I can keep up with my crew in Berlin. They'll be rowing on the river daily. Can't get out of shape.

Exhaustion seeps out of me into the mattress, and I stare at the curtains filtering thin pinpoints of light through the top. I'm here. If Opa's right, I'll figure out a way to meet Rocker. I've come the farthest I've ever been from home to talk to the man. And for Mum, I'd go around the world in a rowing boat to improve her health.

The rockstar can spare the money, go without another car or a house in Fiji. It's not like he had to pay child support for eighteen years. What I need is a fraction of what that would've cost him. I'm not looking for a father. Opa filled those shoes for me, but Rocker should help. Mum's done everything for me, her only son. Even if I am just the product of a one-night stand, I'm the only blood offspring that wanker has in this world, and I'm ready to use that fact.

I'm not going home empty-handed.

# El

THE DANG SPLINT PROTECTING my injured fingers gets stuck in the sleeve of my turquoise dress shirt, and I have to rethink my outfit. No sleeves. I move the hangers in the silver section around until I spot the vintage Paco Rabanne metal chain halter I kept after the *Rock Squad Magazine* photoshoot for Dad's kids charity fundraiser. The cold links were my armor against the photographer's words telling me where I should stand and what my face should look like. I hang it back up. That is Melodie Rockerby's outfit, not El Vella's.

What will El wear? My stage name is my nod to Papa. Technically, it's still my name, the Rockerby added when Mom married Bill Rockerby. He sat me down and asked if I was okay with him adopting me, explained he never had any kids of his own, would never replace Papa, but he wanted us to be a family. It's not like I could say no. True to his word, Bill, Dad, has always treated me like his, and I do love him. I know I'm lucky, but Rockerby is too famous, too recognizable. No one outside of the opera world will know the last name Vella, which is perfect. I need them to see *me*.

I tuck my hair behind my ear. What would I wear if I didn't have to think about the tabloids and eventual comments on social media? Something comfortable, because tonight's gonna be tough enough without having to worry about my clothes; something I can keep my cool in, because I'll be sweating all over; something I can sit down in without worrying about showing my underwear.

My last vacation in Malta with Papa's family, I went shopping at the local market and got the most comfortable moss-green palazzo pants that sorta looked like a long skirt, along with a simple white tank top. My arms glide through the holes and my heartrate slows a bit. Memories of the sun and the simple conversations envelop me, offering support. There's something about clothes that sets my mood, and I've found the right ones for El Vella's first stage appearance.

"Are you ready?" Sven asks from behind the closed door. "We have to leave in five." My friend is less than pleased with me since Dad reassigned him from lead bodyguard duty to my personal babysitter. I lucked out, though. If Dad only knew the messes Sven cleaned up for me. There's no one I'd rather have by my side day and night.

Am I really doing it? Stepping on a stage, however small, and not fainting from the greedy eyes trained on me, ready to judge my every wrong word, false pitch, awkward movement? My hands shake when I open the door and follow Sven down the stairs, panting a little too hard. Not good signs, but I have to ignore them. We sneak past the theater room where Mom and Dad are binge watching some historical drama about a queen.

"And where are you going?" Mom's voice stops me in my tracks. I'll need a better route next time.

"Ice cream with Zoe." I've already texted my cousin to cover if my parents get nosey.

"And Sven?" Mom turns around and sees my human shield looming behind me. "Be home by midnight."

I hurry down the hallway before she changes her mind.

Sven opens the back door of the light blue electric Rolls Royce Dad got for my required bodyguard to chauffeur me around, and I slip in. The door clicks shut, surrounding me in silence. Almost. My ears are ringing. My personal Superman jumps in and starts driving us to downtown LA.

Outside the tinted windows, the sky deepens into a purple haze as day morphs into night. Time for my transformation as well. I pull out my phone and follow the instructions on the YouTube video I've watched a hundred times. I finagle my shoulder-length auburn hair into flat twists and cover them with a wig. The platinum locks are longer than my real hair and feel odd falling over my shoulders and down my back to my waist. A little shine on my lips completes the look.

"You are not allowed to go into the actual bar." Sven repeats the instructions he gave me twice before, ignoring my new look. "All the performers under twenty-one have to stay backstage."

"I know."

"I've checked out the place, and I'll be in the back, the left corner closest to the hallway that leads backstage. It'll take me maybe thirty seconds to get to you if you are recognized."

"Left back corner. I got it."

"And you're not talking to anyone but me and Pauline, the manager. You're there to get that job, not have fun at a bar."

"Aye, aye, captain."

"Not funny, Melodie. You don't have to do this. We can turn around and go home." He stops at the red light and looks over his shoulder at me. "There are other ways to get money. Let me help you for once. I'll get a loan and give you the cash, and you'll pay me back once Mr. and Mrs. Rockerby reinstate your allowance."

"Which, according to Mom, is never."

"They're still angry. Give them time."

"I'm angry too."

Sven does his silent listening routine.

"If I'm doing it, and dammit, I am doing it, I'm doing it on my own. I'm not the useless, spoiled baby they think I am. I might not have a formal education"—I air quote the words—"but I had the world's best tutors. Taking the GED seemed more trouble than it was worth. Not like university has ever been in the picture." I sit up straighter, raise my chin, and meet Sven's eyes in the rearview mirror. "But I know a lot about music, and I can earn my own money, live my own life, and be my own person. I don't need them as much as they think I do."

Even though I booked Mr. Astor's last available session in November, my down payment is gone, and the salary at Rocker, Inc. is a start but it's not going to get me the amount I need to cover the cost. Zoe felt bad about the London debacle and offered to make up the difference. After I refused to accept her money, she pulled some strings and snagged me a spot in tonight's open mic competition. The winner gets paid to perform at the Devil's Martini's coveted Saturday night showcase.

This gig alone won't cover the whole sum, but it'll make a big dent. If my plan is to become a singer, why not start now? I've spent enough hours practicing in my room and Dad's home studio to stand a chance. If I win, I prove to everyone I can earn a living with my music.

We enter through a side door of the Devil's Martini, and a preppy young woman in glasses, who looks more like a librarian than someone who'd work at a bar, shoves a clipboard my way.

"Write your name here. You're number five." She hands me a sticker with the number hand-written in red marker. "Are you performing too? Or just the boyfriend?" Her eyes survey Sven's solid body from head to foot, and I swear the top of her cheeks pink up.

"Friend. Audience." Sven gives his standard just-the-facts reply.

"Oh, straight through there, then." Her cheeks are definitely pink when she shows my fair-haired "friend" the way. "And you go left." She switches to me. "You get one song. Hang around till the end, Pauline'll talk to you about the gig if you win. And don't try to butter me up, I'm not one of the judges. Break a leg."

The door slams behind me. She glances at Sven one more time and aims her smile at the next person. We head past her, and I take the door to the left that says, "STAGE. STAFF ONLY," and Sven gives me a thumbs up as he heads up the long hallway and into the bar. I wipe my sweaty palms on the sleek silk crepe of my pants.

The stage is my friend. The stage is my friend.

I'll get on it even if I have to ask someone to push me out. Recording a video for my EP won't happen if I can't perform in front of a crowd. Doubt this dinky bar will even have more than twenty people here, but as long as it's more than zero, it won't be easy.

I knew this day was coming. I just didn't expect it to be this soon. I thought I'd have time. Shoot the video, send it to some producers, make a whole album before I had to perform in front of real live people.

Twenty minutes later, the open mic competition begins, and Jeremiah is not here. My feverish texts go unanswered, and although they have an extra keyboard and a couple of guitars I could use, my broken fingers will take at least five more weeks before I can start using them again. This is what Jeremiah is for:

study the music for my songs, bring a guitar, and accompany me. Now what do I do?

I walk up the hallway to the bar area, peek from the door into the room, and scan the place. Jeremiah is steps away, beer in hand, sitting at a dark wooden bar talking with some guy. That jerk. He shouldn't be drinking before we perform. He should be backstage rehearsing, or at least have the decency to answer his phone. I'm not letting him screw this up for me. Google informed me both Dasher and Carlee Waters had their break after winning the open mic competition here. Maybe El Vella can be next.

"Jeremiah," I shout across the room. "Jeremiah, over here."

Jeremiah looks up and meets my eye. My breath hitches. He can barely focus on me. How much has this dufus had to drink? I look at my phone. Our slot is in ten minutes. How can I sober him up? I look for Sven, but he's far off, the librarian's hand on his impressive bicep and his attention on her blazing cheeks and not the bar I'm not even supposed to be in. I don't need him to show up, scare Jeremiah, and end this night before I even get a chance. One eye on Sven, I slink over the black floor to Jeremiah's barstool.

"Jeremiah?" The way his body sways when he moves his head kills any hope of him being my hands today.

"Elllllllll." The happy drunk sings my name. I could kill him. He's no use to me in this state. I side-eye his companion who's drinking . . . water? Odd.

"Meet my new friend. He'sss from Germany. How cooool is that?"

I don't have time to meet people. I need Jeremiah to sober up. I don't have a choice.

"Hey, I'm Wil." I turn to him because my parents taught me manners. His one-sided grin is certain to score, but it's not going to work on me. I'm here on a mission, and it's not a random hook-up with a hot stranger. This is the one time I wish Sven were by my side, so I could get him to remove this playboy. I flick my gaze to Sven to reassure myself he's there and if I scream his name, he'll run over and rescue me.

"Hey. Um, can I talk to Jeremiah? In private."

Light brown, almost golden eyes examine my outfit, the ends of my hair sweeping my hip bones, the exposed skin at my neck, and finishes the round with my face. If I weren't already hot from nerves, that stare would've gotten me there. He's cute, jet-black hair flopping all over the place in that boy-band-wannabe way. He reminds me of someone, but I can't quite put my finger on whom. I shake my head. I have bigger problems.

"Could you please give us some space?" I take one step closer, as if I can intimidate him into vacating his spot.

"Not sure it's smart for you to be next to him before your turn on stage." Wil nods at the number five sticker on my shoulder. His accent is decidedly British. Didn't Jeremiah say this dude was from Germany? Or is Jeremiah too drunk to know the difference between the two countries? "He might just chuck up all over your pretty clothes and ruin your performance before you begin. How about I keep an eye on your boyfriend, and you can talk it out after you're done?"

"No."

"No?" His thick dark eyebrow climbs up, and a smile returns to his face. Maybe it is working on me. Would've worked if I didn't have a drunk Jeremiah and my dreams riding on the line.

"No. He's not my boyfriend. Who has time for that?" Why am I telling him I'm single? Need to focus. "I hired him to play the guitar for me." I raise my splinted fingers and shove them in front of Wil's face. "See?"

"Well, that clears that."

If I expected sympathy from this dude, I didn't get it.

"I don't do the girlfriend thing either. Not planning on starting it now." He licks his lips like I might be his next meal. "Jeremiah might have difficulty standing up, so playing an instrument is bloody unlikely."

"Dammit." I know the guy is right.

We both turn to regard the hoodie-clad Jeremiah, currently staring into his half-empty beer glass as if the golden liquid has the answers to every mystery in life.

"What did you say your name was?" Wil's molten stare focuses on my eyes then my mouth, as if he were ready to catch whatever tumbles out next. And I wish I were here for fun. Hot, kiss-worthy fun.

"El. El Vella." My voice sounds raspier than normal.

His eyes flash back to mine. Something switches in them. He re-surveys me, and his demeanor changes. The relaxed flirty vibe drops as fast as the last note of Dad's latest hit. He loses his smile, the fire in his eyes gone, and for reasons I can't understand, I miss it already.

Wil leans in like he's going to kiss me, his fiery breath tickling my ear instead. Is this his signature move? Is he going to ask me out? Would I say yes? Goosebumps run down my arms, and my heart rises to my throat.

"I know who you are."

Read the complete

Falling for the Rockstar's Daughter series.


WE Blend

WE Breathe

WE Balance

Siobhan has her own romance series.
Turn the page for a sneak peek of
Star Struck

Tonight on *Extra*.

**Maria Fernandez:** Maria Fernandez here covering the prestigious Starlight Foundation Gala. On the red carpet with me is Asher Menken, star of romantic comedies like *Legally Hot* and the now-classic heartwarming historical tale *Tomorrow's Love*. Such a pleasure. It's been a couple of years since anyone on this side of the pond interviewed you. Where have you been?

**Asher Menken:** Thank you for the glowing introduction. Glad to be back in LA. I've enjoyed what the stages of Dublin and London have to offer, but I sure missed the California sunshine.

**Maria Fernandez:** We're glad to have you back. Hopefully, for good?

**Asher Menken:** For a while. My project—a collaboration with the winners of this year's Starlight competition—is the first movie my production company will take on. And I have my own reasons to stick around for the next nine months.

# Siobhan

A CARDBOARD TUBE WITH a shred of toilet paper mocks me. Of course, I end up in the bathroom stall that's missing the key element. My parents ran out of Irish luck when they had me: I'm the only member of the Casey clan born on US soil.

"Can't open the flippin' holder." My best friend isn't her usual happy-go-lucky self. She's nervous for a reason. Months of hard work, and the possibility of writing for a big Hollywood movie comes down to tonight.

"Don't break your new nails. Just shove a bunch under the divider."

The coveted wad of white toilet paper and Sarah's undamaged red nails appear beside the spike of my stiletto.

"Got it." My voice sounds strangled, because I'm holding the bottom of my floor-length sequined dress between my chin and my chest.

"Good. Now hurry. We don't want to miss the opening number," says Sarah. "I hope we'll be celebrating more than just your birthday tonight."

The best birthday present would be hearing, "And the Starlight award goes to Sarah Connor." Ever since I met her two years ago when she moved to LA, Sarah's been the one with a plan: become a screenwriter. May have hit a few bumps (okay, craters) on the road, but my girl is making her dreams come true.

The shapewear I have on at the insistence of Mrs. Marino, my boss who lent me this elaborate golden gown worth a year of my salary, doesn't want to go back up. How do people spend all night in these things?

"We were so sorry to hear about you and Leyla," the interviewer says on the TV in the lounge part of the restroom.

My ears perk up. I'm not sorry at all. I've been obsessing over my favorite romantic star's newfound freedom for weeks now.

"Well," Asher Menken's deep baritone loses its smoothness, "all I can say is—"

"Ladies and Gentlemen"—the TV switches from the pre-recorded interview to the real-time coverage of the awards ceremony—"welcome to the Fifth Annual Starlight Foundation Gala."

For feck's sake. The world is dying to know Asher's take on his ex. Okay, I'm dying to know. Even if I get a chance to see him, it's not like I could ask him myself.

"How much longer?" Sarah can't hide her impatience. "I don't want to miss anything."

"Just go." I wave my free hand at the closed door as if Sarah can see me. "I'll be in as soon as I can wrangle this tiny torture device back onto my crotch."

"You sure?"

"Aye, go already. Nick's waiting." Probably cursing me. Boyo is also nervous tonight, and we don't get along at the best of times. "Enjoy yourself. You've worked so hard for tonight."

A few clicks of her high heels plus the sound of the door closing, and I'm left alone with my tight beige nemesis.

I tuck the bottom of the dress into my décolleté. This is bollocks. I peel the undergarment off my thighs and balance on one, then the other silver strappy sandal as I struggle to free myself. Dress righted, I take my first deep breath of the night, ball up the offending material, toss it into the bin, give it the finger, and exit the stall.

A quick check of my stomach in the mirror shows it's as flat as it was with the awful contraption. I wash my hands and ensure my hair survived the battle of the bulge. The aquamarine dye I've been using this summer is starting to bore me. Might be time for a change.

The blue corner of the tattoo on the inside of my wrist is showing. I tug the long sleeves of the dress down, causing the neckline to plunge even more. Gotta make sure I cover up my body art tonight. While highly unlikely, Mum and Da might see pictures. They don't exactly know about this version of my artwork. My tastes run more towards black ink than gold sequins, but I do rock this dress. I blow myself a kiss in the mirror. Time to get this show on the road.

I reach for the door handle when the painted wood panel flies open and smashes into my shoulder. For a moment I teeter on my heels, sure I can save myself, but this battle I don't win. I land hard on the solid tiles of the bathroom floor.

"Bloody hell," I yelp.

The door slams shut, then opens again, and a tuxedo-clad figure enters the room. "Damn it, sorry, I didn't mean to . . . didn't know . . . are you hurt?" The crisp black silk of men's trousers crinkles as the offender crouches down and stretches his hand my way.

I blink. Then blink again. Wide pools the color of whiskey I've drooled over during movie nights with the girls peer at me.

"Are you okay?" An expression worthy of an Oscar nomination graces Asher Menken's face as he scans my body for broken bits.

I wiggle my toes, rub my shoulder, and swivel my head around. "All in one piece, no thanks to you." I've wanted to approach him since I first saw Ash on the red carpet a couple of feet ahead of us, but he was in the middle of an interview, probably the one I'd just been listening to. He and my big brother Owen are still best friends, but over a decade has passed since the superstar and I have been in the same room together.

"What can I do?" There is no spark of recognition in his eyes despite the fact that other than the long hair, I'm a mini copy of my brother. I wait to see if anything clicks, but his focus is not on my face. Rather, he gawks at my naked leg, exposed in all its glory thanks to the thigh-high slit in this fancy dress. His gaze travels up my leg and I follow, until we get to where the lace of my aquamarine thong is visible, no longer shielded by the Spanx. He looks at my hair, then my thong, and swallows.

"I still like matching things," I say.

"Sorry?"

"My hair matches my thong. Like my hair bows used to match my clothes, remember?"

His eyes narrow, and he tilts his head. "I think you might've hit your head."

"I'm Siobhan." I lift the sleeve off my left wrist and show him the tiny star, my very first tattoo. I got the memento as soon as I moved here seven years ago: my design, based on the one I drew for Ash a lifetime ago. "Réiltín?"

Another sweep of his eyes takes in more of my face as he scans me up and down, or left to right, or however the horizontal plane is looked at. "Owen's little sister?" His eyebrow rises.

"Aye."

"Unbelievable." He reaches inside his jacket, pulls out his wallet, and takes out a piece of paper. Ash sits next to me on the icy floor as I tug at the dress in a too-late attempt to cover up. He gives the paper to me. "My good luck charm."

I stare. In my hand is a faded copy of what I now have on my wrist. The original little star I drew for him when I was nine.

"You . . . kept this?"

Asher casts his eyes to the floor, and my pulse takes off. I mean, I've seen the expression before, both on and off the screen, yet up close and personal like this he's . . . gorgeous. Yes, the teeth are perfect, the chin is chiseled, and the hair—oh, how I want to run my hands through his hair to test if those strands are as tuggable as they appear. But this is more than the good looks. He's lit up from within.

I hand the piece of paper from the past back to him and will my heart to slow.

"Owen did say you lived here." Ash tucks the drawing carefully back in his wallet and puts it away. "Of all places to run into you." He smiles, and there's the "I'm sorry" smile that got him out of a trip to the police when he bumped into a car in front of us. The lady who owned the Peugeot let him go with, "What's one more scratch on this old heap of metal?" She would've berated any of my brothers for doing the same thing.

"I promised my friends not to get starstruck, but I didn't think they meant literally." I smile back. "Howeyeh, Ash? Can I still call you that?"

He nods, giving me the once over again. "Can't call you Little Star anymore. You're no longer . . . little."

My turn to swallow. The way he said *little* sends a shiver through me that I can't blame on the chill of the tile floor. My name is a puzzle for most people in LA. At work I heard a million attempts at my name until I came up with "she-Vaughn." Sarah shortens it to just Sio, "she." Back in Ireland my family calls me Shiv, and Mum insists on Baby Girl. But Asher's nickname for me, Réiltín, which means Little Star, might be my favorite. "I don't mind." He can call me anything.

"Réiltín it is, then." He runs his hand through the thick light brown strands he inherited from his movie star mother and rests his fingers on the nape of his neck. "We should probably get off this floor." He jumps to his feet, wraps his fingers around my wrist, and lifts me up. I wince in pain.

"Did I hurt you?"

"The shoulder is a bit tender." I lower the neckline and see a red line across my skin. Ash's thumb traces the mark from the door. His touch doesn't make the pain go away, but I'm both nervous and more secure with his skin on mine. His presence has always had this effect on me. The thrill and the comfort at the same time.

The first time I met him, my nine-year-old self didn't know what to think about Ash. He wasn't a famous Hollywood star then, just the nineteen-year-old friend my brother brought home for Christmas break because Ash had no family in Ireland to spend the holiday with. A breath of fresh air all the way from California to light up our middle-of-nowhere in County Kerry.

I fix my dress. "We should get going. My friend Sarah must be wondering where I am."

"Sure you're okay?"

"I'm tougher than I seem."

"You look"—he pauses—"great in this dress. All grown-up." His eyes stray to my cleavage.

"Yup." I straighten and push my chest forward. "Got me big girl boobs and everything."

"I didn't mean to . . ." His "I'm sorry" smile is back. "This isn't what I—"

"Just having a laugh." I tap him on the arm, like we're old pals. "Great way to start my next quarter century."

"Today?"

"'Tis."

"Well, happy birthday to you." He purses his lips, and his eyes brighten. "We could have a drink after the gala? Celebrate? Catch up?"

"Bang on." I don't jump up and down like I used to when I got to spend time with him, but I flash him my "thank you for a great tip" smile. Asher Menken wants to have drinks with me. I ain't saying no.

"Great. But"—he rubs the wrinkles between his eyebrows—"a favor? Could you check if there is a guy in a red velvet tuxedo hanging around by any chance? If he is, I'll stay here a while longer."

"Aye." I peek out of the door and see empty hallways. "The coast is clear."

Reporter 1: Did you see Asher on the red carpet tonight? No Leyla by his side.

Reporter 2: My heart broke when I heard about the demise of #AshLa.

Reporter 1: But he did look fine. Like, rebound fine. Any bets who the next lucky girl will be?

Reporter 2: One-night stand with Asher Menken? Sign me up.

SIOBHAN CASEY.

I can't believe Owen's baby sister scared my bathroom stalker off with foul language worthy of an R-rated movie. The creep thought he was clever hiding around the corner, ready to accost Siobhan and me on our way to the ceremony. Her vocabulary, among other things, has grown. In fact, there isn't much left of the little girl with a short bob, matching hair accessories, and hand-me-down outfits from her brothers. Although the eyes, those sometimes green, sometimes blue, sometimes gray eyes of hers, and Owen's, and their Ma's. I should've recognized those eyes.

When my publicist Jackson asked me to be part of tonight's ceremony, I almost said no. I hate these types of affairs. The fakeness. The shallowness. The constant vying for attention. I never dreamed my night would be like this.

I glance out into the sea of creativity, and the rush of youthful exuberance hits me like a tidal wave. My partnership with the Starlight Foundation was the right decision. This is the perfect project to kickstart my new production company. I already got the green light for two TV shows, and this movie, with the proper amount of press, will give me the cachet to do more.

Still, the best part is the opportunity to give back, do something worthwhile with the fame I've been lucky enough to achieve. And when the tall kid accepts his Best Director award, he's genuinely ecstatic. I can't help grinning like a fool along with him.

"That's Nick." Siobhan sits down after she finishes clapping her hands raw. An empty seat next to me had been an open invitation for the opportunists looking to pitch, but now I'm glad the organizers assumed I would bring a date. "He's been in LA less than six months, and look at him. I'm here seven years and keep slinging drinks."

"You want to be in the movie business?"

"God, no. Owen is the one with the acting bug in our family."

"Why LA then?" Owen refused to tell me the full story.

"Farthest place I could escape to with my American passport that met my criteria."

"Which were?"

"Far from Ireland, fun, sunny, and not an island." She winks at me. Good to see she hasn't lost her spunky attitude. "Had a string of jobs. Let's see, I was the Belgian waffle girl at Disneyland first. Girl's gotta start somewhere. Graduated to waitressing at a fifties themed diner. Gawd, that was horrible. They put that yellow American plastic they call cheese on everything. Who puts cheese on pie?"

Siobhan has the right to judge. Her family's cheese is the best I've ever tasted. Of course, I've had the privilege of stealing the stuff fresh from the cheese fridge when no one was looking. As a teenager I preferred to ask for forgiveness rather than permission. The bonus of performing in Dublin was that in three hours I could be at the Casey farm indulging in unlimited quantities of first-rate cheese. Well, and pretending I'm part of their large warm family. Owen is so lucky.

"Anyhow, now I work at a swanky resort bartending with my girl Sarah over there"—she swings her champagne glass in the direction of a group of young people, of which Sarah could be any one of three girls—"but the hours give me time to play artist."

"Well, lucky me. You saved me from being cornered by overeager fans and wannabe writers." And she saved me before. The first Christmas I spent at her family's farm, she saw me struggle to memorize my part for *The Little Prince*. I was ready to throw in the towel. Maybe the acting gene skipped a generation, maybe the tabloids were right and my good looks and family connections were the only reasons Trinity's theatre program accepted me.

Siobhan didn't let me give up. She ran lines with me, jumped up and down every time I got one right, and even drew me a picture of a little star, a réiltín, for good luck. The folded piece of paper with her design was in my pocket when I first went on stage and has been with me ever since, calming me when I'm nervous. And being back in the States has me super nervous tonight.

"He deserved the tongue-lashing. Shoving his script at you in the middle of the event is the worst way to get your attention."

"Hollywood is hard, I get it. But he was going to stuff the flash drive inside my jacket if you didn't interfere. I should've just shoved him off, but that'd end up in the papers with me as the unreasonable superstar, too stuck-up to talk to his fans." I take another sip from the flute the server keeps refilling. "The guy's face matched his red suit after you told him off. You're more effective than my bodyguards."

She laughs. Not the polite tut-tut of reporters reacting to my lame jokes or the light tinkle that warmed my heart when I managed to get Leyla to break character. No, this is a roaring, full-bodied, full-of-life laugh.

And I'm laughing along with her, feeling lighter than I've felt in months. No, years.

My real smile hasn't graced my face in forever. The world thinks Leyla and I broke up a few weeks ago. In reality, we've been apart for over a year. Our publicists timed the news for maximum impact, every step calculated to advance our careers. Well, her career. It's always been about her career. Every fight, a tug of war between her need to shoot for the stars and mine to settle down. In the end, our marriage came down to one thing: I can't wait to have kids, and she didn't want any.

"Gotta stand up for myself and those I care about," Siobhan says. "You know my older brothers; add waitressing in LA, and there's no better verbal self-defense school." She curls her arm and almost spills champagne onto herself. I catch the glass in time. "I know how to punch, too, if it comes to it. Owen made sure to teach me. And I always keep my thumb out."

She puts her glass down and demonstrates the proper fist technique. "Brothers." Her eyes widen. "Oh." She holds out her hand. "Give me your phone. Let's send Owen a selfie. It'll freak him out."

I like nothing more than pulling pranks on my best friend. My phone in hand, Siobhan leans in, her shoulder brushing against mine, and I inhale a mixture of honey and something spicy. "Smile," she instructs.

Easily done.

She plucks my cell from my fingers, her thumbs fly over the screen, and in a second, she flashes our smiling faces at me. "Check out who I bumped into," is written underneath our picture.

"Bumped into, huh." I chuckle at her play on how we met in the bathroom. She sends the text.

Siobhan opens my jacket, the gesture she berated the guy in the red suit for. "Done."

My body shrunk away from the rando's touch, but with my grown-up réiltín, I savor the contact. She puts my phone in the inside pocket and adjusts my sky-blue tie. Her eyes narrow, and she runs her fingers against the dots on the smooth silk.

"This tie, doesn't it remind you of the *Infinity* exhibit Yayoi Kusama did with the mirrors at The Broad a few years ago?"

I nod. "Like being inside a kaleidoscope." I took Leyla on a private tour of the immersive art installation at The Broad Modern Art Museum. We spent the evening lost in the multi-reflective rooms.

"Exactly." She smooths my tie one more time. The touch of her hand on my chest does things to me it should not. "Wasn't it deadly? Blows you only got five minutes in each room."

She's deadly. Real and beautiful. And alluring.

Gone is the little girl who doodled on anything she could get her hands on. Before me sits this vivacious, gorgeous woman. Her green—or are they blue—eyes twinkle in the low light of the reception hall.

"Did you study art?"

"I take classes when I can, but nothing official. I love to explore—oils, watercolors, sculpture, loom, pottery, print—tried them all. I even thought about costume design. But I think skin is my favorite canvas." She looks down at the star on her wrist.

This woman is a bright star in the dark night that has been my life lately. I can't look away; I won't, not when there's so much to see.

Even her dress teases by covering up practically everything yet accentuating her body in a way no garment should be allowed to. But I've glimpsed the secrets the fabric hides. Thinking about her long leg and how I'd run my hand up the curves to . . . I feel a twitch I haven't felt in a long time.

What am I doing? How can I be thinking like this? What would Owen say if he saw me ogling his sister?

*Hey, boyo, don't even think about touching her.*

Which is exactly what I'm doing. Thinking. And that's where I'll be stopping.

"So, you've traveled the world?" Siobhan reaches for another glass from the server walking by and our hands brush.

There it is again, the little electric shock like when I touched her in the bathroom. What is she doing to me? Am I having any effect on her? It's so hard for me to tell these days, reality and fiction always blurring. Is a woman truly interested in me, or is she just caught up in my fame and fortune?

It was easy when I met Leyla. We were both unknowns at the time, just starting out in the business. When our movie hit number one at the box office everything changed overnight. I was used to my parents' fame and seeing my face on the cover of tabloids wasn't new, but with my own fame, the frenzy reached a whole different level. Leyla and I relied on each other, bonded in the fire of chaos.

Siobhan is different. She knows me and doesn't have the starstruck expression my fans get. Talking to her brings the instant comfort I associate with my visits to her family farm. She taps her glass to mine, and I enjoy another brush of our fingers.

Her skin is cool. No, comfort isn't the right word. Connection? There's something here. We're on our third glass and I should be feeling the haziness of the alcohol, but instead, everything is crystal clear. For the first time in a long time, I'm alert and aware.

Four delicate fingers brush over the back of my hand, as if she's painting me with invisible watercolors. Her pupils dilate, and I'm sure mine do too. A slender index finger wraps around my thumb and slides up, down, and up again. If I'm reading her right, my year of celibacy is ending tonight.

She touches a sensitive part at the base of my thumb. "Wanna get out of here?" Siobhan's eyes confirm her invitation.

"Yes" escapes my lips before I even think about consequences.

"Give me a minute."

As she walks away, I text my security detail to let them know I'm ready to leave and there's going to be a plus one. Hopefully, we can slip out the back door and not get noticed.

Across the room, Siobhan's talking to a short blonde in an even shorter silver dress. They hug, and my little star's walking back toward me. Her slender hips swing with the movement, glittering gold. My body reacts with more than a twitch this time.

"Where to, sir?" asks the limo driver.

"The hotel," says Siobhan.

"How'd you—"

"Know? Figured you'd be staying with your parents since you just got back. Their house is in Malibu, right? A tad too far for tonight."

She's too smart for me.

The hotel is only a short ride from the venue, and in no time we're in the underground garage. I hop out of the car hoping to open the door for Siobhan, but she's too quick for me too. Leyla would've waited, expecting a grand gesture from me in case there were any cameras around. Always a show with that woman.

This girl—woman—however, pinches my security guard's arm. "Oh, you're a tough one." The guard sticks out his chest and eyes Siobhan up and down. "Spend every day at the gym, do we?"

I feel a pang in my chest. Jealousy? I jut out my arm. "Shall we?" Siobhan slinks hers through and leans into me. My temperature rises with the contact of her warm body as we make our way to the private elevator.

The metal doors slide together and once again we're alone.

"What is it about elevators?" she asks, a hand running down my arm.

"What d'you mean?"

"They're just so damn sexy."

"You think?"

She reaches up and tugs on my tie, giving me a low, breathy, "Yes."

I'm done for. Reason, propriety, and resistance are out the window. My lips collide with hers, one hand circling her waist to pull her closer, the other finally getting to touch the soft skin of the long lean leg she's hooked over my hip. My palm travels up her thigh and cups her butt.

The sequins of her dress scratch against my thin shirt as if they are clawing to get at me. She's amazing, and so alive. Her taste, her scent, her heat invade me, send currents through my body, and light me up like no other. The twitch is now a throb.

I don't have enough hands. I need to touch more of her, but there's no way I'm letting go of this luscious ass. I tear my mouth from hers and explore her chin, her neck. I pause, pressing my lips against her pulsing artery, the thump matching my own racing heartbeat.

The soft ding of the elevator indicates we've hit my floor, but I don't want to leave our little cocoon. Siobhan has other ideas and starts backing out of the elevator, my tie still clutched in her hand. I'm happy to follow, as long as I get to keep kissing those amazing lips.

We move down the hall, and I reluctantly break the kiss. "Wait."

"What? Bored already?"

"Not in the slightest." More like alive for the first time. "My room is this way." I clutch her arm and haul her down the hallway in the opposite direction, searching for my hotel room key with my free hand. I jam the card into the reader, the light goes green, and we burst into my suite.

Before the door closes, her fingers are undoing my belt.

"Careful of the gown. It's not mine."

The first time I roll a condom on, she doesn't even take her dress off.

Guess who ordered two burgers, not one?

Burger with Fries . . . $36.95

Burger with Fries . . . $36.95

Chocolate Cake . . . $22.95

# Siobhan

For years I went to bed ogling the poster of Asher in my bedroom in Ireland. Now I'm in America lying in bed with the real thing. I stare at his sleeping form, my fingers itching to trace the outline of his jaw, those plump lips.

"See something you like?" He peers at me through one half-closed eye.

"Lots. I—"

Ash's lips crash against mine, and my words are lost. Unnecessary. I open my mouth and grant him access like it's the most natural thing in the world. My lungs are screaming for air by the time he pulls away.

He doesn't go far. As if he can't stay away, he presses his forehead against mine. "I'm starved. Wanna order room service?"

Wasn't expecting that. The appetizers at the Starlight Foundation Gala were enough to sop up some of the champagne in my system, not replace a dinner. "I could eat."

Ash stretches across my body and slides the remote off the bedside table. My skin alights from the brush of his arm against my ribs, and I want his mouth back on me, charting a path along my side. I bite my lip instead. On the way back, Ash kisses my shoulder, the base of my neck . . . My brain argues with other parts of me. We are not going to get any sustenance if I don't stop this. "I thought you wanted something to eat."

"I do." His words are muffled as he savors my ear lobe. With a sigh, he pushes himself up into a sitting position and turns on the TV. "Let's see what they have."

The heat of his body leaves mine. I mimic his posture and pull up the sheet, so it covers our almost-touching knees.

While he rolls through the menu, his other hand settles on my leg. His thumb grazes my thigh, and I order my brain to concentrate on the food items scrolling on the TV instead of following my urge to grab Ash's hand and put it somewhere that thumb could be of better use. Cheese pizza, ravioli, pesto risotto . . .

"How about a burger and fries. France has decadent food, but they can't do a burger like here."

The only French food I've had is quiche lorraine at the bakery Sarah buys her butter tarts from. Must be nice to have had so much French food you crave a burger. How long has Ash been in Europe? At least two years. He followed his wife. No, ex-wife. Shit, am I his rebound?

That movie star smile flashes my way, and my heart skips a beat. So, what if I am. I don't care. I'll file away my time with him, from his hand helping me off the floor in the bathroom to what we did in this bed. Everything about this night, tucked away and treasured alongside the memories of him at our farmhouse before he was famous.

"Add some chocolate cake and you got yourself a deal." I give him my most dazzling smile, because two can play that game. He stares at my lips, menu forgotten. I bring my mouth to his. "Burgers, fries, chocolate cake, and then I'm all yours," I whisper, with our noses millimeters apart. The desire in his eyes says he wants a bite of me much more than the food, but he leans back and completes the order.

The meal arrives blazingly fast. We sit cross-legged on the bed, the tray of food between us. Ash inhales the fries like there's no tomorrow, and I have to fight him for the last one. For a man who looks like he works out every day—scratch that, several times a day—watching him wolf down a burger before I start on mine brings back the teenage Ash I knew in Ireland years ago.

"I see your eating habits haven't changed much." He used to scarf Mom's meals and ask for seconds before any of my brothers finished theirs.

"I can pretend to be more civilized when I'm on display in public, but with family this is what you get." He winks and I forget to chew. "Dad enrolled me in etiquette classes when I was in middle school because he could not stand my table manners. Now imagine me, a short pimply teenager with braces in a room where I'm the only boy, surrounded by white tablecloths and a million forks and glasses, learning how to debone fish while looking cool as a cucumber.”

“The latter part I can imagine, but you as a pimply youth? Impossible.”

“Just wait until my mother sits you down with a stack of photo albums. You’ll get to see more of my naked ass, and the array of pimples that plagued me for a couple of years in middle school.” Ash runs his finger across my cheekbone, and I forget about the fries. I want his fingers to touch my salty lips, but he takes his hand away before he can get there. “I don’t remember you having those. Any time I saw you, you looked like an angel.”

“Angel? Mum would disagree. She thinks I was harder to raise then the boys.” I lift my chin and show off my skin that Sarah thinks is flawless. “You missed my puberty years, but I’m the lucky one. Never had a problem with bad skin. My smile is a different story. I should’ve had braces, but that was not something we even considered.” I smile wide and reveal my less-than-perfect teeth.

“So no embarrassing teenage photos of you at your Ma’s place?”

“I didn’t say that. Mom still drones on about my attempts at copying the latest makeup trends. I’m sure there are photos where I look like a cartoon character. Like my year 4 portrait. She won’t let that one die.”

“I have to see those.” He laughs, and the sound is not like in his movies. It’s lighter but deeper at the same time. “Next time we’re in Ireland, I’ll ask your Ma.”

"I'm sure she'll do whatever you tell her. I'm surprised you don't know the combination to her safe. Unlike you, I'm my mother's worst nightmare. I moved on from makeup you can wash off to coloring my body with permanent images. Look at me."

He does, and there's that pull again as his eyes travel over my shoulder, under my right breast, and down. "They suit you. Everything I see when I look at you is beautiful."

"You probably say this to all your one-night stands."

He drops his smile. His gaze roams across my exposed skin, this time without the lust I've enjoyed seeing in them this evening. He's way too serious, and my skin prickles in anticipation of what he's going to say.

"I haven't done a one-night stand since I was twenty." His gaze finds mine and holds it. "I mean it when I say you're beautiful. You're so beautiful I have to touch you constantly to remind myself you're not a figment of my horny imagination."

I take his hand and place it on top of the blue cornflower tattoos on my rib. "Definitely not imaginary."

His thumb runs over the petal imprint. "Does it hurt when you get them?"

"Feck yeah."

"Why do it again if it hurts?"

"Because I love them so much. I can take pain if I know it's going to be temporary and lead to better things." After the first one, my little star celebrating my freedom, I swore I'd never get another one. The Celtic knot behind my right ear I got in a moment of weakness, of missing home. That pain was worth not caving in. "Plus, you sort of forget how much it hurts. Mum used to say women have more than one kid because they forget how much it hurts giving birth. If they remembered, we'd all be only children."

"Do you believe it?" Ash runs his finger through the leftover ketchup in little infinity loops.

"Sorta. I think if you want a kid, you'd go through any kind of pain to have one."

His finger freezes. "Do you want to have kids?"

"Absolutely. Maybe not four, like Mum, but a couple." I bop my head and point at my heart. "I'd be a cool hot Mom. The talk of the playground."

One side of his mouth hitches in a smile. "I can picture that."

"But I need to figure shit out first. My life is, well . . ."

"Like that ever happens." He licks the ketchup off his finger.

"It happened for you." I poke him in the shoulder, trying to get that smile back. I get a glimmer. "You're successful. You can have a gaggle."

"Might look that way. But money doesn't equal success. Or happiness." His serious expression returns.

I poke him in the shoulder again. "But it buys excellent chocolate cake."

"Let's hope it does." Ash takes the silver lid off the plate.

A slice of four-layered chocolate cake filled with chocolate ganache and drizzled with so much chocolate it forms a little lake on the plate is not what captures my attention. In the middle of the decadence there's a single unlit candle. A pack of matches with the hotel logo completes the still life.

"You remembered?"

"That it's your birthday? No way I could forget anything about you." He lights the candle, and in a quiet baritone starts whispering, "Happy Birthday to Réiltín." Each note lights a little candle in my chest. The heat builds until my heart is a puddle of tenderness. He ends with a breathy 'you' worthy of Marilyn Monroe and focuses on my lips.

I tear my gaze away and blow out the candle. My wish is for Ash to be my birthday present every year.

He removes the snuffed candle and digs into the top two layers with his fork. "Would you like some?"

I open my mouth to take the gooey chocolatey forkful, but he changes direction and shoves the cake into his instead.

"No way, it's mine." I lunge at the cake and snatch the plate away from him. He stabs in the direction of where the plate was, and I lower my mouth to the crest of the slice and bite the largest chunk I can out of it. I can feel the buttercream on my cheek, but I'm not letting him win.

Ash abandons the fork and brings his face to mine. He bites from the other side, chocolate icing smudging his perfect face. I fake taking another mouthful of cake and lick the goo off his skin instead. The bristles of his stubble rub against my tongue, and the combination of Ash and chocolate might be the favorite thing I've ever tasted.

I scoot closer, and the plate slides out of my hand onto Ash, coating his abs in chocolate ganache. "Oh shite. Sorry."

"The cake is good, but I prefer to eat it, not wear it." Ash pushes off the bed and places the tray on the table. "Be right back." He disappears into the bathroom, the door closing with a soft click.

I climb out of the ginormous bed, my limbs heavy with disappointment. I was hoping this was a refueling for more fun, not a goodbye treat. If I get one night with Asher Menken, I want it to last until dawn. That's hours away. I don't want to leave but I've been through this enough to know the signals. Hell, I'm usually the one doing the "bathroom time to leave" move.

Why would this time be any different? My stomach swirls and I regret the cake, but not the laughter. Nor the genuine warmth of our conversation or the ecstasy of our bodies together. He said he doesn't do one-night stands. Does it mean I'll see him again? Or was that the old Asher? Now that he's divorced, does he only want to play? Wouldn't blame him. Play is all I ever do.

I've managed to pull on my thong and silver sandals when the light from the bathroom falls on me.

"Hey." Ash leans against the doorframe. "Where do you think you're going?"

The way he's looking at me, I have an urge to cover my naked breasts. I straighten my back. "This was fun, but it's getting late."

He crosses the room. "It's not late. Unless you want to go." His fingers brush against my wrist then, circle it. His touch sends tingles to places I shouldn't think about if I want to leave this room. I don't want to leave this room. He traces the tiny tattoo again. "My little star." His whisper is like a benediction.

Ash raises my wrist to his lips and gently caresses it. Whiskey-colored irises scan my face from under long eyelashes, and my heart gallops out of my chest. He leans forward and presses soft kisses on the tattoo on my shoulder, his hands flutter at my hip, and the hotel room begins to sway.

He drops to his knees, those long fingers pulling at the string of my thong, his tongue licking the 'not easy but worth it' line of script on my hip. I place a hand against the wall to steady myself as he strips off my underwear, lifting one foot out of a sandal, then the other. As my toes hit the plush hotel room carpet, his hot lips suck on my inner thigh, and my legs begin to wobble.

I'm floating through the air. Literally. Ash throws me over his shoulder as he stands, and a giggle erupts from me at the swift motion. Then the softest sheets I've ever slept on touch my back as he returns me to our bed. I miss his warmth, his skin on mine for the moment it takes him to climb in with me, but it doesn't last long before his lips find mine. I sink my fingers into the silkiest hair in the world and pull. I'm rewarded with a moan that radiates through his lips into my core.

"Condom." He rolls onto his back, propping himself up on his elbows. "You do it."

Those intense eyes watch my every move as I tear open the foil, release the disk, and find the right side. His body stiffens as I roll it on, and a delicious thought enters my mind. I lean down and kiss his hip. My name escapes his lips in a low moan. My tongue finds his abs, and they taste better than the chocolate cake. His fingers thread through my hair, and I sense his desperation. I feel it too. I find his lips, and he wastes no time as his body covers mine.

We fall out of time and space. Just Ash and I, together, as one.

Unlike our first or second time, everything is slow and sweet. Small movements cause ripples of pleasure I never thought possible. His fingers thread through mine, and the grip is anything but gentle, like he's afraid I might float away. I squeeze back, silently telling him I'm not going anywhere. I don't want to be anywhere but right here.

For once I'm not chasing the next high. Being with Asher is the high I want to ride forever.

END OF SNEAK PEEK

STAR STRUCK

OUT NOW

Acknowledgements

We never intended to write a book with a vampire show as a plot line, but our characters take us where they take us.

We did intend to explore Nick's relationship with his father. Gala has been holding on to the details of Theo's back story for . . . years, because she started writing Nick's brother's story in 2021. (If you want to encourage her to publish that book, send her an email at willadrewauthor@gmail.com with "I Want Mike's Book" in the subject line.)

We did intend to use Canada as a backdrop for the book. After the teaser in Misses, Hearts, & Us we knew Sarah's home would be a location we had to visit. DL's cottage in Muskoka is the inspiration for the Côté cottage. And yes, they really do play hockey on the lake.

We didn't intend to get beta reader feedback on this story, but our Advanced Reading Copy team asked us. We're still gushing over the entertaining comments, emojis, and valuable corrections from Tanya, Danielle, and Ashely. You made this story better. You can also thank them for the extra spice in Chapter 10 after Sarah's shower. That was added based on our beta readers' request. We had so much fun we can't wait to see what they think of the early version of Distance, Love, & Us, book 5 in Falling for the Liar Series.

We did intend to offer the best reading experience. We thank our editors, Julie and Victoria, for helping us remove random body parts behaving badly, run-on sentences, and Canadian spelling.

We did intend to continue with the holiday-themed object cover design, and we adore Books and Moods for creating another beautiful cover.

We did intend to publish all five books of Sarah's and Nick's romance in one year and time them to the holidays each book is about.

We did not intend to burn ourselves out by releasing five books in one year. The pace has been fast, but we're almost to the finish line. One more book in the Falling for the Liar Series to go!

We did intend to grow our community of Willa Drew Readers. Thank you for your encouragement, reviews, and comments. We love chatting with our readers. Discord fan? Join our server. Prefer a newsletter? Sign up for ours at willadrew.com (we send it out twice a month). Don't forget to follow us across our socials at @willadrewauthor

As always, we thank our assistants, Cece and Eliza, for keeping this ship running no matter how troubled the waters; our friends and families for supporting us on our author journey, no matter how winding; and each other, for following our creative passions and not giving up, no matter how bumpy the ride.

We're grateful we get to write the stories our characters tell us.

We intend to write many more.

# SERIES BY WILLA DREW

## SECOND CHANCE BILLIONAIRES

The Second Chance Billionaires series follows five lifelong friends—a grumpy CEO, a charming playboy, a retiring hockey pro, a British aristocrat, and a sci-fi author—from college roommates to billionaire boardrooms as they each get one more shot at love.

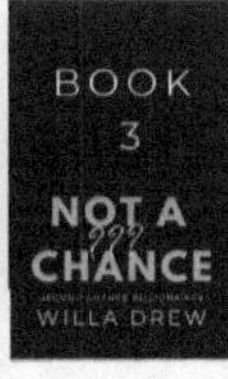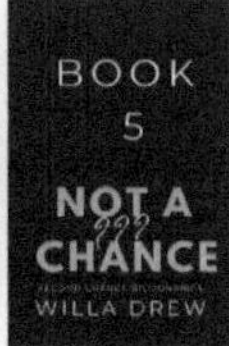

## AND US

Watch movies and real life collide with Sarah and Nick in a right person/wrong time, hidden identity, new adult romance. One year, five parts, six major holidays, many twists.

Kisses, Lies, & Us

Passions, Hopes, & Us

Distance, Love, & Us

or binge the complete series with bonus scenes in
Friendzoned By My Crush

## FALLING FOR THE ROCKSTAR'S DAUGHTER

An upper young adult, friends-to-lovers, slow burn romance
featuring a reluctant collaboration between two musicians.

WE Blend

WE Breathe

WE Balance

## ANDERS INVESTIGATIONS

Meet the men of Anders Investigations, a new contemporary
romance series with a romantic suspense element.

Taming the Grumpy Bodyguard

Loving the Grumpy Bodyguard

# FALLING FOR THE MOVIE STAR

If you like an age gap, brother's best friend romance featuring LA's red-carpet glamor, Irish charm, and a reunion written in the stars,

Siobhan and Asher's story is for you.

Two authors. Two countries. One obsession with love stories.

Willa Drew's contemporary slow-burn romances are full of feels, playful banter, and high-stakes emotions. Their globe-trotting characters fight for love as they discover who they are and where they belong.

Willa, a proud Canadian and devoted Leafs hockey fan, and Drew, a Russian-American with a lifelong love of languages, always search for the perfect words to capture heartbreak and connection.

Their books guarantee swoon-worthy kisses and happily ever afters.

Come hang out with them
@willadrewauthor
willadrew.com